"WHY'D YOU DO IT?" Flack asked. "You're just a garden-variety gay-basher. Why'd you graduate to murder?"

Mulroney shrugged. "Sonofabitch did a take-out slide."

"This was at the ball game?" Flack was taking notes now.

"Yeah." Mulroney looked up at Ursitti. "Some genius thought it'd help 'foster a commonality' between us and the towelheads if we played a nice friendly game of baseball. National pastime and all that shit." He snorted. "I don't even know what 'foster a commonality' *means*."

"So what happened?" Flack asked.

"Yoba gets up."

"Greg Yoba, in for robbery," Ursitti added.

"Right, and he grounds it to Hunt. I run to second, Hunt flips it to me, and I'm all set to turn around and throw to first, when, wham! The sonofabitch picks up his leg as he's sliding into second. My shin *still* hurts."

"That when the fight broke out?" Mac asked.

"Yeah. Bastard shouldn't have done that."

"So you killed him," Flack said.

Mulroney shrugged. "It wasn't right. And the COs broke it up before I could get my own back."

"In the majors," Flack said, "they don't shiv guys who do that."

Smiling, Mulroney said, "Well, maybe they should."

Original novels in the CSI series

CSI: Crime Scene Investigation
Double Dealer
Sin City
Cold Burn
Body of Evidence
Grave Matters
Binding Ties
Serial (graphic novel)
Killing Game
Snake Eyes
In Extremis

CSI: Miami
Florida Getaway
Heat Wave
Cult Following
Riptide
Harm for the Holidays: Misgivings
Harm for the Holidays: Heart Attack
Cut and Run

CSI: NY
Dead of Winter
Blood on the Sun
Deluge

CSI:NY™

FOUR WALLS

a novel

Keith R.A. DeCandido

Based on the hit CBS series
"CSI: NY" produced by CBS Productions, a business
unit of CBS Broadcasting Inc. in association with
Jerry Bruckheimer Television.

Executive Producers: Jerry Bruckheimer,
Anthony E. Zuiker, Ann Donahue, Carol Mendelsohn,
Andrew Lipsitz, Danny Cannon, Pam Veasey,
Peter Lenkov, Jonathan Littman

Series created by: Anthony E. Zuiker,
Ann Donahue, Carol Mendelsohn

POCKET STAR BOOKS
New York   London   Toronto   Sydney

Pocket Star Books
A Division of Simon & Schuster, Inc.
1230 Avenue of the Americas
New York, NY 10020

This book is a work of fiction. Names, characters, places, and incidents either are products of the author's imagination or are used fictitiously. Any resemblance to actual events or locales or persons, living or dead, is entirely coincidental.

First Pocket Star Books paperback edition May 2008

POCKET STAR BOOKS and colophon are registered trademarks of Simon & Schuster, Inc.

For information about special discounts for bulk purchases, please contact Simon & Schuster Special Sales at 1-800-456-6798 or business@simonandschuster.com.

Design by Richard Yoo

Manufactured in the United States of America

10 9 8 7 6 5 4 3 2 1

ISBN-13: 978-1-4165-1343-8
ISBN-10:   1-4165-1343-4

To Phil Rizzuto, 1917–2007.
His voice was an important part of my childhood,
watching Yankee games on channel 11, and I still
miss his "Holy cow" cry from the broadcast booth.
He would've loved the cannoli at Belluso's.
Rest in peace, Scooter . . .

ACKNOWLEDGMENTS

PRIMARY THANKS MUST GO to my wonderful editor, Jennifer Heddle, who gave me the chance to once again write a novel taking place in my hometown, the greatest city in the world.

Secondary thanks to Paul DiGennaro, who has been a corrections officer in the state of New York for many years and whose guidance was invaluable in the descriptions of life in the fictional Richmond Hill Correctional Facility. It's safe to say that I couldn't have written this book—or, at least, the bits that involve the RHCF—without Paul. Thanks also to Linda Foglia of the New York State Department of Corrections and Deputy Superintendent of Programs Edward Adler and Captain William Caldwell of the Arthur Kill Correctional Facility for the tour of the latter site, which was incredibly useful. Any deviations or mistakes in relation to prison life are entirely inventions (a nice way of saying "screwups") of the author and should not reflect on any of these fine people.

Of course, I must also thank Gary Sinise, Melina Kanakaredes, Eddie Cahill, Hill Harper, Carmine Giovinazzo, Anna Belknap, Robert Joy, Claire Forlani, Emmanuelle Vaugier, A. J. Buckley, Mykelti Williamson, and Carmen Argenziano, who all provided face and voice for many of the characters herein, thus giving me material to work with.

Although it was the inspiration for a different TV show on a different network, I have to give props to David Simon's *Homicide: A Year on the Killing Streets*. That's the true-crime book that got me interested in police procedure in the first place.

Huge thanks also to Reddy's Forensic Page (www.forensicpage.com), a fantastic online clearinghouse for forensic info and a researcher's dream site. Fellow *CSI* novelist (and forensic expert in his own right) Ken Goddard helped out with some scientific details as well. Also for sheer cool value, thanks to the good folks at CLPEx.com (Complete Latent Print Examination), who have a PDF of Francis Galton's groundbreaking 1892 book *Finger Prints* on their website.

The usual thanks to GraceAnne Andreassi De-Candido, who again provided an excellent first read.

Finally, thanks to them that live with me, both human and feline, for everything.

HISTORIAN'S NOTE

THIS NOVEL TAKES PLACE between ". . . Comes Around" and "Snow Day," the final two episodes of *CSI: NY*'s third season.

CSI:NY™

FOUR WALLS

1

DETECTIVE DON FLACK STARED at the lone pill that rattled around the bottom of the prescription bottle.

A cup of coffee sat on the Formica table in front of him, steam rising toward the ceiling in the air-conditioned diner. It had certainly taken long enough for the coffee to show up. The waitress—a woman named Doris, according to the nameplate affixed to her bright pink uniform; her face was caked in enough makeup to make her look em-balmed, her breath smelled like an ashtray, and her nasal voice threatened to decalcify Flack's spinal column—had ignored him for quite a while before deigning to take his coffee order.

In theory, he'd wash the pill down with the cof-fee.

Assuming, of course, he could bring himself to dump that last pill out into his hand.

It had been a year. A year since the explosion that nearly killed him. A year since that idiot with the headphones who didn't hear the fire alarm. Flack ran back for him.

Then the world exploded.

When he was recovering in the hospital, after it was all over, Flack sometimes wondered what would have happened if that jackass hadn't been wearing those big, stupid noise-canceling headphones. Said jackass—Flack could no longer recall his name, nor did he particularly wish to—hadn't heard the fire alarm, hadn't heard the screams of panic, hadn't heard two dozen people running for the fire stairs, hadn't heard Flack and Detective Mac Taylor screaming that there was a bomb in the building.

You usually didn't find that level of obliviousness in New Yorkers. Certainly not since 9/11.

If not for that guy, Flack might've been in the stairwell. Or at least back with Mac, farther down the hallway. Mac got out of the explosion with only a few scrapes and bruises.

Flack almost died.

But he didn't. A few months in the hospital, and he was fit for duty. He tried to avoid situations where he'd have to take off his shirt in public, as the crisscross of scars wasn't particularly pretty.

Stella Bonasera and Lindsay Monroe had both ribbed him about using the explosion to flirt with women, and they hadn't been entirely wrong—but Flack hadn't shown anyone the scars.

The pain was near constant.

When it got bad, he was supposed to take the pills. But Flack defined *bad* differently from the docs. He avoided taking the pills. Taking the pills meant admitting to weakness.

But sometimes, Flack was weak.

Now, though, it had been a year, and a prescription bottle that was intended to last him six to eight weeks had finally run out.

When he got up this morning—earlier than usual, since he was meeting a friend for coffee— the pain was agonizing. That happened when the weather changed, sometimes. The last few days it had been unseasonably chilly, but this morning it was already eighty-eight degrees, and it was supposed to go up into the high nineties. Flack felt like someone had taken a hot knife and shoved it through his lower back up into his rib cage. (He'd been hanging around with Mac and his crime lab crew for too long—he could actually picture that happening in gory detail, something he never used to think about before he made detective.)

But there was only one pill left.

If he took the last pill, he'd have to refill the prescription and get more.

Weakness again.

Donald Flack Jr. was the latest in a long line of cops, most recently Donald Flack Sr. Cops didn't admit to weakness. On the street, they can *smell* that. You don't let the assholes know that there's a single chink in your armor, because they will find it and they will nail you to the wall.

So Flack tried to avoid the pills.

"Y'know, Donnie, it's been my experience that the pills work better if you swallow 'em."

Looking up, Flack saw his breakfast companion approach the table. "Hey, Terry."

Terry Sullivan squeezed his massive frame into the vinyl-covered bench opposite Flack. Sweat beaded on his pale forehead. Indicating the pill bottle with his head, he asked, "That's from the bombing, right? What they gotcha on, Percs?"

Flack nodded, pocketing the bottle in his suit jacket.

"What, you ain't gonna take it?"

"Don't need it." Even as he said the words, Flack winced as he moved his arms.

Sullivan shook his head, his shaggy blond hair flopping around. "You're so full of it, those baby blues of yours're turning brown, Donnie. Take it from the human dispensary, they prescribed them things for a damn good reason. You're in pain— take the painkillers."

"I'll be all right."

Like Flack, Terence Sullivan Jr. was dressed for work, though unlike Flack, he wasn't wearing his entire uniform. Not that Flack had a uniform per se, just the expected suit and tie. As for Sullivan, he wore clothes that identified him as a corrections officer of the state of New York—at least, they did to Flack. He wasn't wearing the light-blue shirt that would have completed the outfit, as COs generally didn't wear the full uniform outside of prison walls, but he was wearing the dark blue slacks, black boots, weapon, and belt. Said belt was filled with key clips, pouches, a radio holder (the radio was property of the prison and stayed on-site), and a lot of other stuff that reminded Flack of his days in uniform. There were several reasons why Flack liked being plainclothes, and one of the biggies was not having to carry around half the world on your belt.

The summer weather had darkened the armpits of Sullivan's white T-shirt with sweat. Sullivan's broad shoulders and well-muscled arms filled the T-shirt well, which made up for his pale baby face and shaggy blond hair. From the neck up, he looked like a twelve-year-old. People still called him "Junior" even if they didn't know that Terry, like Flack, was named for his father.

The two Juniors had spent many of their formative years at each others' homes, as both Donald Flack Sr. and Terry Sullivan Sr. were NYPD. They both came on in 1978 (the year both their sons were born), when then–new mayor Ed Koch was trying to increase police recruitment in the wake of fiscal disaster, the "Son of Sam" murders, and the '77 blackout. Flack remembered lots of shared dinners throughout the eighties with the Sullivans and other cop families, their fathers bitching about Howard Beach and Mayor Koch or singing the praises of the new Springsteen album.

Sullivan and Flack were expected to follow in their daddies' footsteps, but only Flack did at first. He remembered young Terry idolizing his father and talking about becoming a cop just like his old man, right up until Sullivan Sr. asked his wife for a divorce in 1992. After that, Sullivan wanted nothing to do with his father. When Flack was a rookie, Sullivan was working as a bouncer at strip clubs.

Eventually, though, Sullivan grew weary of that life and realized that he still wanted to be a cop. He'd told Flack that he "felt stupid" going to the Academy in his late twenties, so he decided to become a corrections officer instead. Currently, he was assigned to the Richmond Hill Correctional Facility on Staten Island. The diner where they were meeting was right by the Manhattan end of the Staten Island Ferry. After the ferry, Sullivan would take the long ride on the S74 bus to RHCF.

Changing the subject, Flack said, "Don't expect

quick service. Took the waitress half an hour to—"

Before he could finish, Doris came over. "Hey, Terry. You know this flatfoot?"

Sullivan grinned. "Yeah, I grew up with this guy."

"Whyn'tcha tell me you were with him?" Doris asked Flack, her voice making his ribs throb more.

"Didn't think I needed to."

Doris shrugged and looked at Terry. "The usual?"

"Yeah, and refill my pal's coffee, will ya?"

"Sure."

After Doris walked off, Flack shook his head and chuckled. "Swear to God, Terry, I been a cop almost ten years, that's the first time I heard anyone use the word *flatfoot* in real life."

"So you gonna take that pill or what, Donnie?"

Flack gritted his teeth. "Or what."

"C'mon, I can tell you're in pain. It's like that time when you cracked a rib during that basketball game and wouldn't tell anybody."

"We had a game to finish." Flack grinned. "I was the only guy on our team who could play worth a damn, so I had to stay in."

Sullivan laughed, resting his arm along the back of the seat, one meaty hand clamped over the end. "Yeah, we sucked pretty hard, didn't we?"

"What's this 'we' crap? I was fine."

"You still play?"

Flack nodded. "I do some work with the YMCA, helpin' out the kids there."

"And if one of them was on some kind of medication, would you let 'em get away with not taking it?"

Rolling his eyes, Flack said, "You ain't letting this go, are you?"

"Hell no. I wanna see you take that pill. And don't try any tricks—I stand over nurses who give out meds every day to people a lot more devious than your ass, and I know every trick in the book."

Flack raised an eyebrow. "Every trick?" He picked up the coffee and lifted it gingerly toward his lips, trying to ignore the pain in his ribs, finishing off the drink in anticipation of Doris's return with a refill.

"Please, it's like these guys think we're morons. I swear to Christ, every single newbie that comes in tries to hide it under their tongue the first time. And they keep tryin' to palm the things, like we ain't gonna look in their hands. Unbelievable." Sullivan shook his head. "Then again, if they had brains, they probably wouldn't be inside."

"Nah," Flack said, "just means their lawyer couldn't do a decent plea."

Sullivan shrugged. "If you say so."

"Trust me, I seen PDs that couldn't do a deal with Howie freakin' Mandel." Flack sighed. "Anyhow, I don't wanna take the pill, okay? Pain's not that bad," he lied.

Doris came back with a plate holding a slice of toast cut into two triangle-shaped slices, which she managed to hold in the same hand as an empty cup and a saucer. In the other hand, she grasped a round glass pot filled with coffee, steam rising through the brown plastic rim along the top of the pot. She put the plate in front of Sullivan—it made a light clink as the porcelain hit the Formica—and then did like- wise with the cup and saucer, pouring Sullivan his coffee, then refilling Flack's. Then she walked off, giving Sullivan a smile and ignoring Flack.

"So," Sullivan said, "I see your boy Taylor got off."

Grateful for the change in subject, Flack said, "Course he got off, he was innocent. Dobson was bad news."

Clay Dobson was an architect who moonlighted as a serial killer. He was caught, arrested, and con- victed—and then released a few years later when his arresting officer, Detective Dean Truby, was imprisoned. Truby was a dirty cop, and Flack knew it—in fact, Flack's notes to that effect had helped put Truby away. Mac Taylor had strong-armed Flack into turning over the notes, and Flack still hadn't completely forgiven Mac for forcing him to give up a member like that.

But that was the least of it. Dobson had money,

which meant he had one of the good lawyers. Truby's incarceration put the detective's entire arrest record into question, and Dobson's lawyer felt that constituted reasonable doubt. A judge agreed, and Dobson was kicked.

Didn't take Dobson long to go back to his old habits. He killed one woman and had taken another, who was able to ID Dobson as her kidnapper. Mac tracked Dobson down, fought with him, cuffed him—and then, according to Mac, Dobson jumped off the roof, claiming he would take Mac down with him.

It almost worked, too. Mac was the subject of a hearing; it was all over the press. Ironically, it was Truby who saved the day—he had some dirt on Deputy Inspector Gerrard, and Mac used that to make sure he was cleared.

"I got a buddy up in Riker's," Sullivan said, "and he told me about Dobson. There's three types inside. There's the innocent guys who got screwed. There's the guilty guys who feel bad about what they did. Then there's the guilty guys who don't give a rat's ass. That's most of them, really."

"Dobson was one of those?" Flack asked.

Sullivan nodded. "Big-time. Your usual asshole, that's one thing, but my buddy told me when he heard what your boy Taylor said, about how he jumped to get back at Taylor? Said he bought it. Your boy couldn't have done anything different."

Flack said nothing.

He supported Mac. Mac was his friend. The first face Flack saw when he woke up in the hospital after the bombing was Mac's. And Flack knew that Sinclair, the chief of detectives, and Inspector Gerrard were trying to score points with the media and cover their own asses in the Dobson case. And Mac had every reason to be pissed off at Dobson, since it was because of Mac's actions that Dobson was sprung, and Mac felt responsible. Flack doubted he would have done anything differently if their positions were reversed.

But Mac also went after Dobson without telling anyone what he was doing, which was strike one. He didn't call for backup, strike two. And then he and Dobson got into a fistfight, which was strike three, and would've been strikes four, five, and six if they went up that high. You brawl with a suspect, and that's a get-out-of-jail-free card for the bad guy, because nothing you do after that will matter to the DA's office or the perp's lawyer. The cop beats the perp, the perp walks.

What Mac did was a step down a dangerous path that led to the likes of Dean Truby.

Still, Flack said none of this to Terry Sullivan, because while Sullivan was his friend, so was Mac Taylor. You didn't rat out your friends. Not even to other friends.

That was weak. Flack didn't do weak.

The pain in his ribs grew tighter. He imagined he could still hear the last Percocet rattling around against the plastic.

Finally he said the only thing he could say, words that were still true regardless of any doubts Flack might have had: "Mac's the best. Department'd be a worse place without him."

Sullivan lifted his coffee cup. "Then here's to him."

Flack didn't lift his cup very high, as it hurt.

Seeing him wince in pain, Sullivan said, "Jesus Christ, Donnie, take the damn pill, would you please?"

"Maybe later. How's Katie doing?"

It never failed. The best way to distract Sullivan had always been to ask him about his daughter. His baby face broke into a huge smile. "She's the best. You know she's in kindergarten now?"

"Really?" Flack couldn't believe it. "Wasn't she just born last week?"

"I know. It's crazy. We can't keep up with her; it's like we have to buy a whole new wardrobe every month. And she's reading, too. Teachers wanted to put her in the first grade, but Shannon didn't wanna. I guess I don't blame her—keep her with kids her own age, y'know?"

They kept talking through two more cups of coffee each, before Sullivan looked at his watch. "I gotta get a move on. Uncle Cal'll be on my ass."

"'Uncle Cal'?" Flack asked. He tried not to grind his teeth as he reached around to get his wallet.

"Calvin Ursitti. He's my shift lieutenant."

"You don't call him that to his face, do you?"

"Do I *look* suicidal?"

Flack chuckled and tossed a five down onto the table. Taking a deep breath, he then got to his feet.

"Will you *please* take the pill, for the love of Christ?"

"I'm fine," Flack said through clenched teeth. "Give Shannon a hug for me, okay?"

"Shannon hates your guts, Donnie."

Flack sighed. "Still?"

"You went out with her sister and dumped her after two dates, Donnie. You think *my* wife's gonna forgive that anytime this millennium?"

"Apparently not." Flack looked around, caught Doris's eye, and gave her a friendly wave. Doris just rolled her eyes and went back to reading the *Post*.

"She's crazy about you," Sullivan deadpanned. "I gotta get the ferry. Be good, Donnie."

They left the diner, Sullivan headed to the ferry terminal, Flack headed to his car. He pulled out his cell phone and turned it back on. He didn't turn it off very often, but he hadn't seen Sullivan in way too long. Just once, he wanted to get through a meal without being interrupted.

Only a cop would consider three cups of coffee a meal.

But then, Flack had been living on coffee lately. He had to do something to swim upstream against the sleepless nights. The pain was worse when he was lying down.

Miraculously, there were no messages on the phone. Somehow, he had made it all the way to seven in the morning without the NYPD requiring his services.

Flack didn't anticipate that state of affairs surviving to his lunch hour.

2

DINA ROSENGAUS HATED THE morning shift.

It wasn't the getting-up-early part. Dina had always been a morning person, both back home in Russia when she was a little girl and since coming to the United States as a teenager. And it wasn't even every morning shift. Wednesdays, Saturdays, and Sundays were fine.

The other four days of the week, though, the morning shift was a nightmare, thanks to some ridiculous concept known as alternate-side-of-the-street parking.

In order to keep the streets clean, the city of New York designated two-and-a-half-hour blocks during the day when one side of the street had to be clear of parked cars so that the street sweepers could come through.

That was the theory, anyhow. Dina couldn't recall ever actually seeing these mythical street sweepers.

Dina worked at Belluso's, an Italian bakery and café in the Riverdale section of the Bronx—in fact, it was located on Riverdale Avenue, right in the neighborhood's primary business district. Riverdale was predominantly Jewish—that was why Dina's family had moved there—and Dina had been surprised to find an Italian bakery there, but the place was popular. They served cookies, cannoli, pastries, coffee, tea, bread, and more. You could come in and grab something to go or sit at one of the round tables for as long as you wanted. Salvatore Belluso, the owner and Dina's boss, always said that he wanted people to feel like they were in a café in Florence and encouraged customers to stay as long as they pleased. He even had a clock upstairs with the hands removed to symbolize that it didn't matter what time it was.

But it did matter to Dina what time it was when her shift started. Parking in the area was hard enough under the best of circumstances, but on weekday mornings, several spots were unavailable between 7:30 and 8:00, and several more were off-limits between 9:30 and 11:00. That made parking nigh impossible. Sure, all the spots were legal when she arrived at a little before seven to open the bakery, but they wouldn't be for long, and Mr.

Belluso didn't like it when you left the counter to do "personal things." Not getting a ticket apparently qualified as personal. One time, she had to park seven blocks away—she might as well have left the car home.

Today, though, she was lucky. Someone was pulling out of a spot on Fieldston Road, a one-way street that ran alongside Riverdale between West 236th and West 238th. (There was no West 237th, at least over here. This made even less sense to Dina than alternate-side-of-the-street parking, but she'd learned to accept it.)

She had begged Mr. Belluso to keep her mornings limited to the weekends—or to Wednesdays. For some reason, there was no alternate-side parking on Wednesdays. But Dina hadn't been there long enough; Maria and Jeanie had Wednesday mornings, and the competition for weekend spots was fierce. Most of the girls who worked there (Mr. Belluso only hired female high school and college students to work the counter) wanted the weekend also, since they didn't have school. To some extent, Dina was a victim of the schedule, as most of her summer-session classes at Manhattan College were in the afternoon.

As she turned the corner onto Riverdale Avenue, a bus pulled up to the stop right in front of the bakery. The back door whooshed open and four people stepped out, one of whom was Jeanie Rodriguez.

Jeanie was an undergraduate student at Lehman College, planning to be a nurse. They made an odd pairing. Jeanie was small and compact, whereas Dina was tall and broad shouldered. Jeanie's hips were modest and sexy; Dina's were wide and ungainly. Back in Russia, she'd have been considered healthy; here in the States, they seemed to want their women to all look like Paris Hilton. Jeanie was better-looking than Paris Hilton, though, in Dina's opinion. She had a bright face; olive skin that looked much better than Dina's pale complexion; and small, long-fingered hands, whereas Dina's were short and stubby.

The only thing that kept Dina from despising this skinny, pretty, perky young woman was the fact that she was also the sweetest, nicest person Dina had ever met. When Dina had started at Belluso's four months earlier, Jeanie had been very patient with Dina, especially since her English still wasn't as good as Dina wanted it to be.

Jeanie was also the most senior of the six girls who worked at Belluso's and had become the unofficial manager of the store. (Making her the official manager would have required that Mr. Belluso pay her more.) That meant she was the one Mr. Belluso trusted with the keys, so Dina was very glad to see her coming off the bus just as Dina arrived. If she hadn't, Dina would've been stuck outside waiting in the heat. It was already unbearably hot this morning, and she knew it was going to get worse as the day went on. The one advantage to being on the morning shift was that she missed what one of the regular customers called the fly-under-the-magnifying-glass effect. Belluso's had a huge picture window that faced west, and in the late afternoon, the sun blared in, raising the temperature in the place higher than the cheap air-conditioning system could handle.

"Hey, Dina, what's up?" Jeanie said in her perky little voice as she stepped off the bus. She was wearing, as usual, all pink: light-pink Hello Kitty shirt, hot-pink shorts that came up to the top of her thighs (she had the legs for it; Dina was embarrassed to show her own thighs in public and wouldn't go out in shorts that short if you put a gun to her head), and pink flip-flops.

"Okay. I just arrived," Dina said. "How are you?"

"Slept through the alarm. Thank God for Goldie."

Dina smiled. Goldie was Jeanie's dog, a golden retriever. "Your backup alarm?"

Jeanie chuckled as she rummaged through her purse. "Yeah. If I'm not up by quarter after six, he's all over my face with his tongue." She shuddered. "Kinda like my ex-boyfriend."

To that, Dina said nothing. The only ex-boyfriend she had was the boy she left behind in

Russia. She still missed Sasha. Of course, she'd been hit on quite a bit since coming here, both in college and at the bakery. The one guy who was there all the time, Jack something, he was an outrageous flirt. Dina had been flattered until she noticed that he flirted with everyone *else*, too, which took a lot of the fun out of it. Still, his compliments certainly seemed genuine.

But nobody had seriously caught her interest. In fact, most of the ones who hit on her here, including Jack, were a lot older. In Dina's experience, older men never treated younger women with respect.

Jeanie finally excavated the key from her purse and inserted it into the lock, turning it to the right.

The key made a thunking noise and stopped before it could go all the way around. "What the hell?" Jeanie said with a frown. She turned the key back around and pulled it out.

Then she pulled on the door, and Dina was shocked to see it open. The door had never been locked the night before.

Dina looked up. The lights were all out, like they were supposed to be—but the door was open? That didn't make sense.

"Who closed last night?" Jeanie asked.

"How should I know?" Dina asked back.

Jeanie shook her head. "Right, you weren't working yesterday." She closed her eyes. Dina imagined she was visualizing the schedule. "It was—right, Maria and Annie."

That surprised Dina. Both Maria Campagna and Annie Wolfowitz were very conscientious. If it had been Karen Paulsen, Dina would have understood—that girl was what Jeanie called a *flake*—but not Maria or Annie.

Dina had never liked Maria all that much. She always kept gloating about how well she was treated by her boyfriend and how he bought her so many nice things, like the eighteen-karat-gold necklace she *always* wore. Sasha couldn't even afford to take Dina out with any regularity, much less buy her presents, expensive or otherwise.

So, perhaps uncharitably, Dina hoped it had been Maria who'd forgotten to lock up.

When they entered the bakery, Dina moved around to the back while Jeanie went to turn on both the lights and the air-conditioning. Dina planned to get the cappuccino maker going, then start taking the cannoli out of the refrigerator in the back.

Flies buzzed all over the place. Dina was looking forward to the AC driving them away.

Oddly, the flies got worse as she came around behind the counter. And something smelled—

She screamed before her conscious mind recognized Maria Campagna lying on the floor, her eyes open, her face pale, flies buzzing around her body.

"What is it?" Jeanie said as she ran around to the other side of the counter. "Dina, what *is* it?"

"It's—it's—it's Maria!"

Dina had no idea how Jeanie reacted, because she couldn't take her eyes off Maria. Dina had never seen a dead body—Jewish tradition kept caskets closed during funerals. For all her uncle's dire warnings about how dead bodies lined the streets in New York, she'd never seen a corpse before, except on those police shows on television.

Maria's body looked different from what she expected. For one thing, she figured someone who was dead would be paler. And there wasn't any blood that she could see.

But she knew that Maria was dead. For one thing, she wasn't moving *at all*. Dina had never realized before just how *still* someone could be.

And she had dead eyes.

Then Dina heard a distant, tinny voice say, "911." Turning, she saw that Jeanie had taken out her cell phone—a razor-thin phone that was the same shade of pink as her shorts.

"I'm at Belluso's Bakery on Riverdale and 236th. There's a dead body here."

3

Officer Tim Ciccone was seriously hungover.

He had only gone to the bar last night intending to unwind after another long day at the Richmond Hill Correctional Facility. He'd spent half the day filling out paperwork and the other half standing out on the baseball diamond while the inmates played a ball game. Skinheads versus Muslims, and what dumbass bureaucrat had thought *that* was a good idea? COs like Ciccone knew that it was the same story in virtually every prison: race stayed with race. A disproportionate number of inmates in RHCF were either white men who hated black people or black men who hated white people.

When Lieutenant Ursitti had told his shift about the ball game, Ciccone had assumed it was a joke. He'd laughed and everything. So, of course, Uncle

Cal had to put him on that detail. At least the weather had been nice—only in the sixties. Perfect baseball weather, unlike today. On the drive over from his place on Van Duzer Street this morning, Ciccone nearly got baked alive. He really needed to get the AC in his Camry fixed.

Ciccone, a lifelong Jersey Devils fan, didn't even *like* baseball. Unlike hockey, which was a *man*'s game, baseball was a pansy sport. Well, except when Muslims and skinheads went at it. Greg Yoba hit a ground ball to Brett Hunt, he flipped it to Jack Mulroney—but Vance Barker did a takeout slide. Naturally, a fight broke out.

After a day that included an outdoor brawl, Ciccone had desperately needed a drink. He'd been born and raised on Staten Island, and he never wanted to live anywhere else. It was far enough away from the rest of the city that it felt like the suburbs, but close enough that he could go into Manhattan and take advantage of all the cool stuff you could do in a big city. Like any good suburb, his neighborhood had a bar where everybody knew everybody else. In this case, it was the Big Boot. It catered to goombahs like him—Italian-Americans who'd lived on Staten Island since the big immigration wave in the late nineteenth and early twentieth centuries—and was right around the corner from his apartment, so it was within stumbling distance of home. Ciccone figured he'd have a few beers at the Boot and call it a night.

That was before Tina DiFillippo walked in. Ciccone hadn't called Tina for weeks, and Tina wanted him to make it up to her. So he did shots with her throughout the night: Jägermeister, Harbor Lights, and some other things that Ciccone could no longer remember.

He didn't remember taking Tina home, either, but there had apparently been sex, based on the used condom he'd found on the floor.

Eventually, Ciccone would regret being too trashed to remember the sex. Right now, he just wanted someone to get the brass band the hell out of his head.

Ciccone had already downed enough coffee to float the ferry, and he still could barely keep his eyes open. But he did his usual routine, hoping to hell that Uncle Cal didn't notice anything.

First up was shaving. Ciccone had always thought allowing the inmates to shave was kind of stupid. Let the assholes grow beards; it wasn't like they needed to look good in here. But a lot of these guys had parole hearings, so they had to look their best, and besides, not letting inmates shave was the kind of stupid thing lawyers liked to sue the state over.

So they went through a routine. The CO was given a box full of razors. He handed them to each con in his group as they went into the bath area, and then when they were done shaving, they handed them back, and the CO would put them in a plastic recycling box. In maximum security, they made the cons put the razors on magnets to prove that there was really a razor in there. Cons were fond of substituting tinfoil for the blade and keeping the razor for themselves as a weapon. It was harder to do that with a safety razor, but cons could get damned ingenious when they decided they wanted a weapon. Why they couldn't put that ingenuity into getting off the charges against them, Ciccone never understood. But he didn't give much of a good goddamn, either, especially today.

Uncle Cal used to work in max security in Sing Sing. He thought the magnets were a good idea, and he somehow talked the bosses into shelling out for one off the books. The COs were supposed to use them every once in a while, keep the cons on their toes. Today, Ciccone was supposed to use it in light of yesterday's brawl, but the goddamn magnet made this *humming* noise that made it feel like someone was drilling right into his left eyeball. No way he was gonna be able to make it through the day with that thing going.

So he didn't bother. He checked some of the safety razors at random, but otherwise, he just wanted to get the whole thing over with. Once this task was done, he had library duty, which meant air-conditioning. The humidity of the bathroom was killing him.

If he could just make it to the library shift, everything would be fine.

Jack Mulroney couldn't believe his good luck. Mostly because he hadn't had very much of that type of luck lately.

It had all started at work. How the hell was Jack supposed to know that Billy, the new supervisor, was a fag? Billy had heard Jack and Freddie making a comment—it was some stupid joke about how you don't drop a coin in front of a Jew or a fag—and Billy went ballistic. Jack got put on probation, got a letter from HR saying that the bank didn't appreciate such commentary, that it was bad for business if the customers heard such talk—never mind that it was in the goddamn break room; he'd never tell jokes in front of the customers, he wasn't *stupid*—and if such comments were heard again, he would be suspended.

So he was a good little boy, did everything the fag told him to do. But that wasn't enough for Billy, oh no. He started leaving flyers in his in-box, brochures and other garbage—all gay-rights crap.

One night, after he got off work, he went out for a walk to blow off steam before hopping the subway home. Eventually, he got tired of walking and had a serious need for a beer, and he went into the first bar he could find—some dive on Thirty-fourth. He got a Bud Light—they had it on tap and everything—and gulped down half the pint right there. Already he was feeling better.

Then two guys sat next to him. Crew cuts, goatees, tight T-shirts, equally tight jeans, black boots, and one of them called the other "*girl*friend."

"Jesus Christ," he said, "can't you fags get your own island or somethin'?"

One of them—the one wearing eyeliner, for God's sake—looked at him like he was peering over his glasses, except this guy wasn't actually wearing glasses, and said, "We *have* our own island. It's called *Manhattan*."

That was when Jack beat the shit out of him.

It had been stupid in lots of ways. For one thing, if you were gonna beat up a fag, you shouldn't do it in public. Public meant witnesses. Goddamn ADA who prosecuted must've brought half the damn city onto the witness stand. And if you *had* to do it in a bar, do it in one where they knew you and might cover for you. A stranger beating up one of the regulars wasn't gonna fly.

So Jack was stuck, especially since the DA had been on a hate-crimes kick as part of his reelection campaign, so they were going full-tilt boogie on Jack's ass.

But at least he showed those fags what for. It was worth it just for that.

After he arrived at RHCF, it didn't take long for Jack to figure out that he needed to pick one of three sides: the Muslims, the skinheads, or the victims. (There were also lots of gangs represented inside, but you had to have been one of them on the outside first.) No chance with the Muslims. Jack never had a problem with black people—hell, the guy he'd told the coin-dropping joke to *was* black, and he'd busted a gut laughing—but Jack was still too pale for them. And no way he was gonna just sit on the sidelines and be one of the fish they all stepped on.

Besides, when they found out he was in for "fag assault," the skinheads welcomed him with open arms.

But it was hard being a white guy in any prison—suddenly, he was the minority, which, as a white male Christian, Jack wasn't really used to. And then at the baseball game yesterday that asshole Barker had to go and do the takeout slide.

You just didn't do that. When Jack was a kid, he used to watch the Yankees' second baseman Willie Randolph jump over guys who tried that. Jack had always liked Randolph—in fact, he started paying attention to baseball again when the Mets hired Randolph to be their manager.

But Jack was no Willie Randolph. Barker's foot slammed right into him, and Jack couldn't leap out of the way fast enough. His shins *still* hurt.

Then they had to go and put him in the goddamn box. He spent the whole night in solitary confinement, with no windows, no light except when they opened the food slot. It was a nightmare. It was *torture*. He could barely sleep, mostly because closing his eyes and opening his eyes were the exact same thing. It was like living with a blanket over his head.

In the morning, they let him out. That was the first piece of good luck, as usually you were in the box for at least twenty-four hours. But Sullivan said something about how everyone thought the ball game was stupid anyhow, so they only gave him and Barker an overnight stay. Jack was grateful, as just the one night had left him exhausted, sweaty, and hyper.

They'd put Barker in the box, too, and he looked just fine coming out of it, like it was a day at the goddamn beach. Sweat plastered Jack's short hair to his scalp, but Barker only had a few dots of sweat on his dark forehead, and his hair was dry. Bastard.

From the moment of the takeout slide, Jack had wanted Barker dead, but it wasn't until the other man came out of the box pretty as a picture while Jack was a total wreck that Jack decided he needed to kill Barker himself.

First thing he did was go to Karl Fischer, as he couldn't retaliate without permission. Jack hated talking to Fischer, though. A *major*-league skinhead, in for murder, Fischer was only in RHCF because he was in the middle of a long appeal.

But nobody white did anything in RHCF without talking to Fischer first. Fischer had pull, and he had people. Most of the few white folks in RHCF banded together under Fischer, giving them strength in numbers, and part of that was protecting each other. Fischer had given Jack his blessing, and Jack knew that Fischer would have his back.

His good luck held: Ciccone was the CO in his block today. He'd pulled the razor out already and was pretty sure he'd be able to sneak it past Ciccone. If it had been Bolton or Sullivan, or that new guy, Andros, Jack would've been worried, but Ciccone didn't know jack *or* shit, so he figured he was clear.

Then Jack saw the magnet and panicked. He'd shoved the razor under his tongue, which was fine as long as he didn't talk.

But the magnet wasn't on. And Ciccone looked like hammered shit in any case. Sure enough, he took the empty safety razor, left the magnet off, and dumped it. He didn't even acknowledge Jack.

Now Jack had a weapon. He'd never killed anyone before. Beat lots of guys up, but that was it.

Barker, though, he'd earned it. He'd shown Jack up, not once, but twice. So now Jack would kill a man for the first time.

He wondered what it would feel like.

4

THE LAST TIME DETECTIVES Stella Bonasera and Lindsay Monroe had investigated a murder in the Riverdale section of the Bronx, the victim was also a teenage girl. Then, Lindsay had bolted from the scene, as seeing a dead teenager brought back all-too-vivid memories of being the only survivor of a massacre in a Bozeman, Montana, diner ten years earlier.

Lindsay had been in the bathroom when Daniel Kadems came into the diner. He had planned on robbing the place after it was closed but before the staff locked up; however, Lindsay and her friends' exuberant gabbing had kept the diner open later than expected. Kadems panicked when he realized his robbery attempt had gone sour and shot all the witnesses.

All but the one in the bathroom. Lindsay's response to the sound of gunfire had been to curl up in a corner until it went away. Afterward, she had felt compelled, for the sake of her best friends, to do *something* to stop people like Kadems from hurting others. But her paralyzed reaction to the shooting meant, in her mind, that becoming a police officer was probably not the right choice for her, so she went into forensic science instead.

Eventually, the memories of her friends and their violent deaths made it too painful to stay in Bozeman, so she moved as far away as she could: to New York, to join the Crime Scene Investigators of the NYPD, under the supervision of Detective Mac Taylor.

Which was fine, as long as she didn't see any dead teenage girls. Unfortunately, one night around Christmas last year, she'd come to Riverdale to find the body of Alison Mitchum, and Lindsay hadn't been able to handle it. Stella had been the one to cover for her with Mac.

Since then, the Bozeman cops had caught up with Daniel Kadems, and he'd been tried and convicted, in part on the strength of Lindsay's own testimony. So when they got the call to join Detective Angell at a new crime scene in Riverdale, Lindsay figured she could handle it *this* time, as that particular demon had finally been laid to rest. At least, that was what she had told Stella.

They drove up in one of the department SUVs. The Bronx was the northernmost of the five boroughs and the only one attached to the U.S. mainland. They were making good time; this early in the morning, most of the traffic was going into Manhattan, not leaving it. The last time, they had gone up the West Side Highway, but this morning Stella chose to take the FDR on the east side. "We got a memo," she explained as they took the exit for the Third Avenue Bridge. "Apparently, the crime lab's spending too much on E-Z Pass, so they want us to avoid tolls wherever possible."

Lindsay shook her head. "All the money we spend on our crime-scene equipment, and they're worried about *tolls*?"

Stella shrugged, her long curls bouncing slightly. The SUV pulled onto the bridge, taking them over the Harlem River. Looking to her right, Lindsay saw Randalls Island and the Manhattan skyline through the haze of this humid morning.

"Apparently," Stella was saying, "we passed our toll allocation for the year by Memorial Day, so some bean counter got pissed. Hold on."

"Why should I—" Lindsay cut herself off when the SUV hit the end of the bridge and got back on regular paving. Or, rather, irregular paving. The road was one long series of massive potholes, and even the SUV's state-of-the-art suspension couldn't keep her from bouncing around in the passenger seat, the seat belt biting into her ribs.

After a few minutes, Stella made the left onto the entrance ramp that would put them on the Major Deegan Expressway. "That was fun," Lindsay muttered, now holding on to the handle over the SUV door for dear life. "You know, we don't even *have* toll bridges in Montana."

"You also can't get a decent cannoli, I bet." Stella grinned.

Lindsay grinned right back. "I wouldn't know, I've never had a cannoli."

After merging the SUV into traffic, Stella stole a shocked look at Lindsay. "You've been in New York how long now, and you've never had one of the finest Italian delicacies?"

"I thought that was pizza."

Stella shook her head. "Pizza's an American invention. Cannoli are *real* Italian food. The best ones I've ever had were at this place down by the courthouse in Little Italy." Stella got a momentary look of rapture on her face. Lindsay had never understood Stella's fascination with food. But then, Lindsay's idea of exotic food growing up was the Olive Garden. She'd made the mistake of saying that to Stella once, which had prompted a look of disgust on Stella's face that Lindsay had previously only seen reserved for serial killers.

Lindsay looked out the window again as they passed Yankee Stadium, with the massive edifice of the Bronx County Courthouse looming behind it. Lindsay had been up here to testify a few times. Each borough in the city was its own county, so each had its own courthouse. While most of the time Lindsay testified in the New York County Courthouse on Centre Street in downtown Manhattan—the one near Little Italy, as Stella had said—she'd been to the ones in Brooklyn, Queens, and the Bronx several times, and even to Staten Island once.

The last time she was up here, Danny Messer had made noises about taking her to a game. She'd also seen the broken ground for the new Yankee Stadium that was scheduled to open in 2009—or, as Danny had called it, "the abomination." That was part of why he wanted to get her to a game; he wanted her to experience the "real" Yankee Stadium before it was gone.

Lindsay hadn't had the heart to tell Danny that she had no interest in baseball—football, yes, but not baseball. He was so cute when he started waxing rhapsodic about Derek Jeter and Mariano Rivera and Reggie Jackson and Don Mattingly and how much he hated the Red Sox, not to mention his own short-lived minor-league career.

Soon they reached West 230th Street, where Stella got off and then navigated her way through some local streets that Lindsay quickly lost track of. Lindsay only did the driving when they stayed in Manhattan, with its grid-pattern streets. Once she got into the outer boroughs, she tended to get hopelessly lost.

They went up a very big, very steep hill, then pulled into an area of the street that was designated as a bus stop but in which two cars were parked— one a departmental sedan, probably Angell's, and a blue-and-white from the Fiftieth Precinct. Stella pulled in behind the blue-and-white.

Detective Jennifer Angell was standing outside the door to Belluso's Bakery, which faced the bus stop. A svelte brunette, she'd originally been temporarily promoted to take on Flack's caseload when he was injured and had been groomed to replace him if he didn't make it back. Flack did come back, but Angell did well enough during her probation that they gave her the full promotion anyhow. She'd put down a lot of good cases in the past year.

She also never got the memo about the dress code. Plainclothes cops who worked homicides were supposed to dress formally. Angell, however, mostly stuck to denim. Lindsay was surprised she hadn't gotten called on it. Today was no different: she wore a plain light-blue T-shirt and faded jeans. Her long brown hair was tied back in a ponytail in deference to the oppressive heat and humidity.

Stella had actually done likewise with her curly locks, and Lindsay was starting to think she should have done the same.

Peering through the large picture window, Lindsay saw two long display cases perpendicular to each other, filled with pastries. There was a staircase in the center of the space going up to a balcony-style second floor. Around the staircase were several small round tables surrounded by three or four wooden chairs each. Two uniforms were inside, along with three young women and one older man.

"Vic's name is Maria Campagna," Angell said without preamble. "She works here part-time. She was one of the ones who closed last night. Two other girls found her when they opened this morning." She smiled. "And now you know everything I do—I only just got here."

One of the uniforms came out through the glass door. Lindsay briefly felt the enticing cool breeze from the air-conditioned interior.

The uniform's collars had "50" pins on them, indicating his home base of the five-oh, which Lindsay knew was the local precinct. He was tall, barrel-chested, crew cut, and was pale except for his nose, which was bright red with sunburn. His name tag read O'MALLEY.

"How you doin', angel face?" he said with a grin.

Angell winced. "Deej, what'd I tell you about calling me that?"

Still grinning, O'Malley said, "That you'd shoot me. But I've seen your range scores, I ain't worried."

Shaking her head, Angell said, "Detective Bonasera, Detective Monroe, this jackass is D. J. O'Malley. We were at the two-four together back in the day. Deej, these two are from the crime lab."

O'Malley nodded. "You guys work with Mac Taylor, right?"

"Yeah," Stella said. "You know him?"

"Nah, just heard about his getting reamed over that scumbucket Dobson. Glad he got off."

"Us, too," Stella said with a nod.

"So," Angell said, "who're the players?"

O'Malley didn't take out his notebook, which surprised Lindsay. "Dina and Jeanie found the bodies. Dina's the big one, Jeanie's the skinny hottie. The old fart's Sal, he owns the place, and the cute blonde's Annie—she closed with Maria last night."

Stella frowned. "These people have last names?"

"Probably." O'Malley shrugged. "Me and Bats come here all the time. I know all these people—including the vic. She was a good kid—always knew how much milk to put in my coffee." He turned to Stella and Lindsay. "Nobody touched anything, so you two're all set."

Lindsay nodded, wondering why O'Malley's partner was nicknamed "Bats."

"Let's get out of the oven," Stella said, moving toward the bakery entrance. O'Malley jumped to grab the door and hold it open for them. Chivalry right after describing the women inside in terms of how good they looked. Lindsay sighed—but she'd been in law enforcement long enough that the contradiction didn't surprise her.

As Lindsay walked through the door O'Malley was holding, she noticed the bakery's hours stencilled on the glass. Sunday to Thursday 7 A.M. to 11 P.M., Friday and Saturday 7 A.M. to midnight.

As soon as they entered the bakery, Lindsay felt goose bumps on her flesh as the air-conditioning evaporated the sweat on her forehead and neck. She closed her eyes and enjoyed the sensation for a second as the door shut behind O'Malley.

When she opened them, O'Malley was pointing at the corner behind where the two display units met. "Body's over there."

Lindsay followed Stella around the counter facing the door. The owner, a large man with a bulbous nose, liver spots all over his skin, and thin white hair, was muttering something in an accented voice—Italian, she assumed. He was standing by the staircase, near the table at which the three young women—Dina, Jeanie, and Annie—were seated. All three had bloodshot eyes, indicating that they'd been crying, and Annie still was. She was the only one of the three not wearing makeup—the other two looked like raccoons thanks to smudged mascara. Standing next to the owner was another uniform from the five-oh with a nametag reading WAYNE, which went some way toward explaining the nickname. Lindsay wondered if his first name was Bruce.

As she passed by the young woman, she heard Annie mutter that it should've been her.

Angell spoke to the owner while Lindsay and Stella went to check the body. They came around the corner and stepped up onto a boardwalk-like set of wooden slats that put the people behind the counter a little higher up than the customers. Lindsay saw the logic: all the employees here seemed to be young women, who tended to be shorter than men, and it didn't do to serve the public when the counter only came up to your chin.

Lindsay stepped up onto the riser and looked down at the body.

Kelly lying on the floor, a stunned look on her blood-covered face . . .

She looked away, forcing the image out of her head.

"You okay?" Stella put a hand on her shoulder.

Nodding quickly, Lindsay said, "Yeah, yeah, I'm fine." She reached into her bag and took out her

Nikon D200 digital camera, flipping the strap over her neck.

Then she looked at the body again.

This time, to her relief, she didn't see Kelly. She saw Maria Campagna, a skinny young woman with short dark hair. She was lying on the riser, legs bent, knees pointing toward the back wall, her back flat on the riser, her head turned in the opposite direction from her knees, her arms splayed on either side of her. She was wearing a white T-shirt with the words SAN FRANCISCO HERE I COME stencilled on the front, hip-hugger blue jeans, brown leather sandals, and no socks. Her fingernails and toenails were both painted purple, the polish chipped here and there, indicating that she'd applied it at least a day or two ago.

After taking a deep breath through her nose and letting it out slowly through her mouth—a method her former psychiatrist had suggested and that had allowed Lindsay to keep it together on more than one occasion—she raised the camera to her face. She set up Maria's—rather, *the victim's*—face in the center of the viewer and started clicking pictures. That was something Mac had told her shortly after she joined his team: that it was easier to work a scene when you thought about *the victim* or *the body*, not a name. There was time enough to think about who they were later, but when you were doing the scene, you focused on what happened, not who it happened to.

She heard Angell say, "Officer Wayne, could you please take everyone except for Mr. Belluso upstairs? I need to talk to each of you in turn, starting with Mr. Belluso."

"Sure," Wayne said. "Ladies?"

Lindsay heard the shuffle of feet up the wooden staircase at the center of the bakery, but she didn't look, focused as she was on photographing the body. She made sure to get images of the body as a whole, then from every angle, then close-ups.

Stella stood behind her, taking in the scene from a distance while Lindsay took her pictures.

After taking a close shot of the victim's eyes, Lindsay said, "Petechial hemorrhaging around the eyes."

Nodding, Stella said, "Probably strangled." She moved in closer and looked down. "Lots of scuff marks on the riser, but that's to be expected. She could've been killed here, or she could've been dragged around back here." Stella got down on her knees. "Just eyeballing it, there's trace up the ying-yang here. Good thing we brought a lot of envelopes."

"Have fun," Lindsay muttered as she continued snapping photographs. Collecting trace at a scene like this—one that had been tramped over and used a great deal—was incredibly frustrating, because ninety-nine percent of what you picked up was stuff that was supposed to be there. The crime lab's job was to find that one percent that didn't belong.

To make their job even tougher, if the killer was Mr. Belluso or anybody who worked there, they'd have left trace evidence all over the place, but none of it would be indicative of guilt in this crime.

But that part was Angell's problem. Lindsay's job right now was to document the body.

Stella had pulled out her tweezers and put on her rubber gloves, and was now bagging and tagging things she picked up off the floor. In a place like this, most of the trace was going to be organic, and Lindsay was now counting the microseconds until Stella asked her for a hand. As it was, she was thrilled that she hadn't simply been asked to do it all in the first place. As the newest member of the team, scut work like that had almost always fallen on her. She still recalled her first case, which involved digging through tiger dung looking for body parts. Took *weeks* to get the smell out of her hair. Lindsay viewed it as a sign of progress that Stella was no longer treating her like a rookie.

Letting the camera rest against her stomach, Lindsay slipped on her own rubber gloves and started taking a closer look at the body. Gently touching the neck and chest, she could feel that the hyoid bone felt out of place, which, along with the hemorrhaging, indicated strangulation. It could have happened right there—the position the victim was in was one she could have easily fallen into if she died standing up behind the counter.

She also saw a stray fiber on the victim's neck. Picking up the camera, Lindsay zoomed in and took a picture of that before pulling out her own set of tweezers and grabbing one of Stella's evidence bags. "It's a black fiber," she said to Stella as she plucked it off the victim's neck. "Doesn't match anything she's wearing."

"Any hand or finger indentations?"

Lindsay shook her head. "It was chilly last night—the killer could've been wearing long sleeves and wrapped his arm around her neck."

Stella nodded as she got down on all fours and pulled something out from under the display unit. Lindsay didn't want to know what it was. "When the ME gets her on the table, we'll have a better idea how it was done. Just keep collecting for now."

"Right." She checked the victim's arms and hands, hoping to find evidence of defensive wounds of some sort.

Sure enough, one of her fingernails was missing. The right forefinger's nail had been half ripped off, possibly while trying to grab at the arm around her neck. To Stella, she said, "If you see a fingernail with purple nail polish on it, let me know."

"Okay."

Lindsay looked more closely at the victim's fingers. There was material of some sort under the fingernails she had left. If she had scratched her attacker, the attacker's DNA might still be under her nails, so Lindsay grabbed another envelope and used one of the tweezer prongs to scrape it all out.

Then she turned the hands over and found abrasions on the victim's knuckles. They were only slightly discolored, and the blood was not completely dry. If she had been killed around closing time last night, eight hours earlier, this bruising was consistent with her putting up a fight.

Lindsay wasn't completely sure, though, so she took several pictures of the bruises. The ME would be able to determine whether Lindsay's suspicions were correct.

Lindsay checked over the rest of the body and found only two other abrasions of any sort: a cut on one arm that was too far along in the healing process to have happened eight hours earlier, and a minor bit of abrasion on the back of the neck that was indicative of something rubbing against the skin. She shot them both in close-up, as they could have been involved in the murder somehow. The cut could have been from some previous incident that had only now escalated into murder, and Lindsay had seen similar neck abrasions before on murder victims who wore necklaces. The abrasion came from the clasp being pushed against the neck. Robberies often went hand in hand with murder, which was why the LAPD, for example, had merged their robbery and homicide divisions into a single unit. The fact that Maria had worn a necklace long enough to form that abrasion but didn't have it on her body now meant that the theft of that necklace might have had something to do with her murder.

If it was a murder. You weren't supposed to jump to conclusions. Until the manner of death was pronounced by the medical examiner, it wasn't officially a homicide. Not that it was easy for someone to strangle herself, but it was within the realm of possibility.

Pursuant to that, Lindsay, having satisfied herself that she'd checked as much of the body as she could at the scene and recorded everything she'd need, started searching near the body for evidence of anything that could've been used for self-strangulation—or, for that matter, as a murder weapon. Of course, even the most brain-dead murderer was unlikely to leave behind the murder weapon, but it didn't hurt to look. Some murderers really *were* that stupid, especially if murder hadn't been the intent. She had seen it before: a fight would get out of hand, one person wound up dead, and when the adrenaline wore off, the perp ran like hell, leaving all kinds of evidence behind.

She didn't find anything, though—nothing except that single black fiber.

"Wanna give me a hand down here in the ick?" Stella asked from the floor.

Lindsay turned and smiled down at her. "Sure, why not?"

"I cannot believe this. You know, they shut us down two weeks ago? I remember, you people came and you did your inspection, and the man, he was very rude to my Maria."

Angell pursed her lips, her patience thinning with each digression Salvatore Belluso made. "Actually, the health inspectors aren't 'my' people, Mr. Belluso. Completely different department."

"Apf," Belluso said with a wave of his hand. "It's all the government. He was rude to my Maria, and she was rude right back to him like he deserves. Ask anybody, he deserved it, but then he shut my store down. Next day a different inspector come, and he says we pass with flying colors. I bet it was that rude man who did it."

Maybe not a digression, then. Angell made notes accordingly, though the health inspectors she knew weren't really the murdering type—unless the ability to bore you to death counted as a lethal weapon. "I'll need a copy of both inspections." He obviously had copies, as there was a photocopy of the thing on the front window, with the relevant parts of the inspection form circled with a Sharpie. Angell had thought that odd at first, but at least now it made sense. And it was a lead, however flimsy.

"When was the last time you saw Ms. Campagna, Mr. Belluso?"

"I was not here yesterday," he said. "I was at the Arthur Avenue store, making sure my girls there are okay. There were some robberies over the weekend, and I wanted to make sure all security was good." He shook his head and started twisting the wedding ring on his left hand. "Is crazy, no? So last time I see my Maria was Saturday when I brought by my wife to check on her and my Jeanie."

Idly, as she took notes, Angell wondered how the young women who worked here felt about being referred to as his all the time. She also wondered about an old man who only hired attractive young women. He had already provided a full list of his employees and, except for the man he hired to clean the place, they were all women between the ages of seventeen and twenty-five.

Belluso waved his hand again. "Apf, it had to be the inspector. He was very very rude to my Maria!"

"Thank you, Mr. Belluso, we'll look into that." She nodded to O'Malley. "Officer O'Malley will take you upstairs now. I may have more questions later. Officer, could you bring Ms. Wolfowitz down?"

Smirking obnoxiously, O'Malley said, "Sure thing, *Detective.*"

Vowing to kill him later, she waited while he followed her instructions. As often happened when she was left alone, her brain started pinballing. *If she mouthed off enough at a health inspector to get them shut down, she must've really sucked at customer service. My range scores are fine, and I can shoot that smirk right off Deej's face. Dealt with four older brothers, I can deal with him. Nothing was stolen, so not a robbery of the store. Gotta ask Stella whether anything was stolen off Campagna. Looks like I'll be doing OT on this one, so no going to the Raccoon Lodge for me tonight. Christ, I hope I can get OT, they're getting all budget-conscious again, and right in time for the heat wave that always means a bump in violent crimes. Wonder why Wolfowitz didn't close with her. I really need to get my bangs trimmed.*

O'Malley brought Wolfowitz down. Her cheeks were puffy and her eyes were still bloodshot. A tear streaked down her face as she sat at the table with Angell. Her blond hair was a rat's nest. When she'd arrived, Wayne had told her that she'd been woken out of a sound sleep by Rodriguez when they'd found the body, and she'd come straight to the bakery. She was wearing a plain white T-shirt, black sweats, and sandals with little red hearts on them.

"Ms. Wolfowitz, I'm Detective Angell. I just need to ask you a few questions, okay?"

"Sure," the young woman said in a very small voice.

"You and Ms. Campagna were both working until eleven last night, right?"

She nodded.

"Then you both closed?"

"She did—she told me to go ahead, and she said she'd take care of it. I was really wrecked, y'know? I had crew, then a whole day of classes, and then work, and I just needed to crash, y'know?"

"Where do you go to school?"

"Mount St. Vincent."

"And you're on crew?"

She nodded again. "I was at Spuyten Duyvil at six this morning. We go around Manhattan, like the Circle Line, y'know? Then I had four classes, then I came here." She sniffled. "I should've stayed."

"What happened at eleven?"

"I actually left at a quarter of. I was just *so* messed up, y'know?" She palmed a tear off her cheek. "Maria said not to worry about it, she'd take care of it."

"What's the usual closing procedure?"

Wolfowitz took a deep breath, then started counting off on her fingers. "We wipe down all the tables and straighten the chairs. We sweep and mop the floors—that's usually done about an hour

before closing, actually. We take all the money out
of the register and put it in the safe. We turn off the
cappuccino maker and the coffeemaker. We turn
out all the lights, and in the summer, we turn off the
AC. And then we close and lock the front door."

From what O'Malley and Wayne had said,
Campagna had done everything except for the last
two—and possibly even that, as Rodriguez and
Rosengaus could've turned the lights and AC on
when they came in before they found the body.
She'd check on that when she talked to them.

"Did anybody come in after you left?"

"One guy, yeah, he came in just as I was walking out. I don't remember his name, but he's a
regular." She gave a quick smile. "He's sweet, he
tips well, and he's always flirting with us. But especially with Maria."

"Do you remember what he looks like?"

"Oh, sure. He's got long brown hair—he had it
tied back in a ponytail. And a beard. And glasses.
He had on a black sweatshirt and jeans, and he was
carrying a gym bag—like usual, really. He goes to
the karate school around the corner, and he usually comes in on his way home from class to get a
bottle of water."

"So it wasn't unusual to see him?"

"*God*, no, he's always here."

Angell asked a few more questions, then asked
Rodriguez to come down. Again, she asked about

the closing-down procedure, and Rodriguez's description matched the one Wolfowitz gave, though Rodriguez felt the need to number the steps as she described them.

"When you got here this morning, was anything else unusual besides the unlocked door?"

Rodriguez shook her head. "The lights and AC were off, the tables were all neat, and the chairs were tidy. She must've just been ready to close up when—" Her voice caught.

"It's okay."

"Oh, one other thing I noticed—I didn't really see it until the two officers got here? But Maria wasn't wearing her necklace."

"She usually wore a necklace?"

Nodding, Rodriguez said, "Yeah, her boyfriend gave it to her. She wore it *all* the time. It was eighteen-karat gold, too."

Angell noted that down, as it constituted motive, although she'd learned quickly in this part of the job that motive was the least important thing in a murder investigation. For one thing, motives were usually mundane and common: jealousy, greed, or some other deadly sin. For another, learning the motive almost never actually led to an arrest. It was always a combination of the detective asking the right questions and the crime lab folks finding the right evidence.

"What's the boyfriend's name?"

"Bobby—Bobby DelVecchio."

"Don't suppose you know where he lives?"

Rodriguez shook her head again. "He came in a few times to see Maria."

She made a few more notes, including a reminder to find DelVecchio. That also added to the list of condolence calls she was going to have to make. It was her least favorite part of the job. According to Belluso, Maria's father had died a year earlier, and she lived with her mother. Historically, the two people who reacted worst to death notices were mothers and boyfriends, so of course that was what she had with this one.

Putting it in the back of her mind for now, she said, "Ms. Wolfowitz said that she saw someone come in with long hair, a beard, glasses, and a gym bag—goes to the karate school?"

"Jack," Rodriguez said without hesitating. "Dunno his last name, but he's in here all the time with his laptop. Always drinks iced coffee in the summer and hot chocolate in the winter, and usually gets a cannoli or two. He's a great guy. He really liked Maria, too."

"Did anybody else really like Maria?"

"Well, sure, lotsa people. I mean, Jack talked to her a lot, and there's this one lady who knows her mother who comes in a lot—oh, and there's Marty. He's a tech from Feldstein's, the vet across the street. He's always hitting on her, too."

She asked Rodriguez more questions, mostly relating to what happened that morning, then called Rosengaus down. She told much the same story as Rodriguez did. What she said was different enough to show that they hadn't rehearsed it, but similar enough to indicate that it was probably the truth.

"Did you notice whether or not Ms. Campagna was wearing her necklace when you found the body?"

"I do not remember," Rosengaus said in her heavily accented voice. "I just saw the dead body and I remember nothing else. I am sorry. I do remember it was very nice necklace."

"It's okay." Angell made a few notes, then asked, "Do you know a regular customer here named Jack?"

"Yes. He is sweet. Sometimes he compliments me. It is nice. He likes all the girls."

"Did you notice that he liked Maria more than the others?"

"Not that I noticed, no. Besides, Maria has boyfriend."

"Bobby DelVecchio? The one who gave her the necklace?"

"Yes. I think he came into store a few times."

"You *think*?"

Rosengaus shrugged. "She never introduced me. We were not very close."

"What about a man named Marty?"

"I know Marty, yes. He works in the vet across the street."

Once she was done with Rosengaus, she turned to see Bonasera and Monroe come out from behind the counter. Monroe looked a bit disheveled, but Bonasera still looked bright and shiny after poking around behind a bakery counter for an hour. It was a skill Angell envied. After just being at a crime scene, Angell wanted nothing more than to shower for a week, but Bonasera—who dug much deeper into a crime scene than she did—always stayed pristine.

Plus, she had that fifty-megawatt smile. Angell had never been able to make her smiles seem like anything but smirks—which was handy when she was being hit on by the less civilized members of humanity, a number that included most of her suspects and her coworkers.

As the two crime scene techs came over, Angell got up and said, "Let's step outside." She didn't particularly want to go out into the heat and humidity, but she also didn't want the foursome upstairs to hear their conversation about the crime scene.

They quickly filled each other in. Palming sweat from her forehead, Angell said, "Last person to see our vic was a guy named Jack something."

Monroe's eyes widened. "Do we know what he was wearing?"

Angell double-checked her notes. "Black sweat-shirt and jeans. Why?"

"We found a black fiber on the vic's neck," Bonasera said. "We need to find this guy."

"Need a last name first. Also, apparently our vic had an eighteen-karat necklace that was missing."

"We found a small abrasion that's consistent with a necklace," Monroe said, "but the necklace is gone. We checked all around the body—plenty of garbage and crumbs and hairs, but no jewelry."

"There's one possible motive," Bonasera said.

Nodding, Angell said, "We also only have Wol-fowitz's word for the fact that she left early—and, for that matter, that this Jack guy came in at all."

Bonasera folded her arms. "We'll get reference samples from everyone upstairs. And we should get ones from everyone else who works here. This way if any of the hairs we found *don't* match someone who's supposed to be there, we've got a lead."

"Want me to do it?" Monroe asked.

Shaking her head, Bonasera said, "Nah, you should get our big pile of trace back to the lab. It'll take ages to process it. Get Adam to help out." She grinned. "Besides, if I stick around, I can have one of those cannoli."

Monroe laughed. "You'll be okay getting back?"

"I'll give you a ride," Angell said.

O'Malley opened the door, holding a piece of

paper. "Hey, angel face, Sal said to give this to you." He held out the sheet.

Taking it, Angell saw a copy of the inspection form, which matched the one hanging in the window, except without anything circled with a Sharpie. "Here's another potential motive. Our vic apparently got into a shouting match with"—she peered at the sheet— "Gomer Wilson from the Health Department."

"His name's really Gomer?" Bonasera asked.

O'Malley shrugged. "Don't look at me, I busted a guy last week whose name is George Washington. People don't think when they name their kids, I'm telling you." Then his face lit up. "Oh, hey, almost forgot, that hippie guy the girls were talking about? I know him."

"Who, Jack?" Bonasera asked.

"Yeah." O'Malley started digging around in his pockets. Finally he found what he was looking for—a pile of business cards and receipts. He liberated one of the former. "Here it is—Jack Morgenstern. He's a web designer. Gave me his card a while back. I'm thinking about making me a website."

"For what?"

"Never mind," O'Malley said quickly.

Angell smirked, making a mental note to find out what kind of plans O'Malley had for a website. She suspected that information would be enough to get him to stop calling her "angel face." "Anyhow, here's his address," O'Malley said. He handed Bonasera the card. "He's freelance, so he's probably home now."

"He's local," Bonasera said. "Lives on Cambridge Avenue and 235th." She looked at Angell and handed her the card.

"Tell you what," Angell said as she snatched the rectangular bit of bond paper from Bonasera's hand, "I need to notify the family. Why don't you do your vampire thing with the people inside while I do that, then we'll meet back here and talk to our suspect, okay?"

Out came Bonasera's fifty-megawatt smile. "Sounds like a plan."

5

Jay Bolton hated his job. That didn't make him unusual. Most people he knew hated their jobs. Jobs weren't there to like, they were there to be tolerated for the sake of a regular paycheck and inadequate health insurance. That was just the way of the world.

But in his experience, there were two types of employees: the ones who were devoted to their job, who were defined by them, and the ones who did their jobs for the money and stability, but really wanted to be doing something else.

Bolton was one of the latter, and it really pissed him off that it hadn't come to anything yet.

For all of his life, Bolton had wanted to be a writer. He always got A's on his essays in school, and he even had some stuff in the high school literary magazine. Of course, the only people who read that magazine were the teachers, but they thought he had potential. So after he graduated, he started sending his short stories out to get published. He wasn't stupid; he knew writers didn't make a lot of money until they got to the Stephen King or Dan Brown level, so he needed to make a living.

His dad, of course, wanted him to be a cop, like him and Uncle Jake and Grandpa. Dad always went on about how Italian-Americans, Irish-Americans, and Polish-Americans in the city had deep-rooted legacies in the NYPD, going back to the early part of the previous century, and he wanted African-Americans to start building their own heritage among the police force as well.

So it broke Dad's heart when Bolton went into corrections instead.

The problem with being a cop was you couldn't just leave it at the office. Dad, Grandpa, and Uncle Jake certainly couldn't. Bolton had figured being a CO would be a good compromise—still in law enforcement, but in a line of work that gave him plenty of time to think about his stories while on the job and wasn't so stressful that he couldn't focus on putting fingers to keyboard while off the job.

Yeah, Dad was unhappy, but once Bolton was a famous writer with book tours and stuff, it wouldn't matter.

Except for one problem. He hadn't sold anything yet.

Not for lack of trying. He'd written a dozen short stories and four novels in the last six years, and all of them came back with form letters with some variation on "We're sorry, but your manuscript does not fit our needs at this time." It was insane. Bolton read all the time—he lived in Chelsea, and his commute included a subway ride, the ferry, and a bus ride, which gave him *plenty* of time to read. He kept up with all the latest books, he knew what publishers were buying, and he wrote just like those folks on the bestseller list.

But still, all he got was "your manuscript does not fit our needs at this time."

Made him crazy.

At least yesterday he got to take out some of his frustration during that brawl between the skinheads and the Muslims on the ball field. It wasn't much—you touched a convict, you had to fill out paperwork for a week—but at least he got to yell at some of the skinheads when they tried to get up in Vance Barker's face. He even brandished his nightstick, though he didn't use it.

It wasn't much, but the yelling really let off some steam.

Today, though, the only steam was coming off the ground. It was hot and humid and disgusting. So of course today was the day Ursitti sent him out to watch the convicts in the yard. The ball field was off-limits after yesterday, but they could still wander around the rest of the yard, jog, sit on the benches and play cards or watch television, or use the weight yard.

The weight yard itself was a fenced-in square in the middle of the yard. Right now, forty-five of the Muslims were using it, and the only reason there weren't more was because that was the maximum capacity for the space. Bolton didn't understand why they thought lifting weights was a good idea today, as there was no shade in there. He was half expecting one of them to collapse from heat exhaustion.

But Hakim el-Jabbar wanted to work out, and where he went, as many Muslims as possible followed.

The fence was locked and would stay locked until their time was up, which would be in another twenty minutes or so. After that Bolton was assigned to one of the classes. He couldn't remember which—it was on the board, he'd check. It didn't matter, as long as he was inside. The classes weren't air-conditioned, but at least they had a big fan in the room. It was better than standing out here with no shade.

He shook his head, wiped the sweat off his forehead, and tried to focus. He hadn't been able to think about his latest novel all that much lately for some reason. Instead, he was spending all his time being pissed off about all the rejections, which wasn't helpful.

Since he couldn't seem to focus on the story, he decided to focus on the work. Ursitti had been bitching at him anyhow, saying he was daydreaming on the job.

So he looked around. He had only twenty minutes left, but Bolton had seen fights break out in mere seconds.

Over there, on the far end of the open grass field on the north side of the weight yard, a bunch of Latinos, all members of the Latin Kings, stood around smoking cigarettes and laughing. Another group of the same number stood near enough to keep an eye on them, but far enough away so that they weren't close—these were members of the Bloods. They'd been pretty quiet lately, being wary of each other, not actually getting into it. With this heat, Bolton figured that cease-fire would end damn quick.

Diagonally across the grass field from the gangbangers were Karl Fischer and his redneck squad. They were sharing a laugh over something. Bolton was concerned about that. People didn't laugh much around here, and they certainly didn't in this heat. Every con Bolton saw had darkened armpits and sweat glistening on his forehead. Surly at the best of times, most of them were downright hostile if they were outside right now.

Except Fischer and his boys.

On the south side of the weight yard were the picnic benches, which were under trees and therefore in blessed shade. A bunch of guys were playing cards—gin rummy, from the looks of it, and a couple of guys on the far end were playing some kind of fantasy card game or other. Some were watching one of the two large TVs that were set up. Bolton couldn't see what was on, nor did he care much. He hated television—didn't even own one.

Then he glanced over toward the weight yard, and *that* got his hackles up. Fischer's boys were slowly moving in the general direction of the weight yard.

After yesterday, no *way* that was good. Hell, even without the brawl, you didn't want skinheads and Muslims anywhere near each other, even if they were separated by a chain-link fence. Yesterday's disaster proved that pretty thoroughly.

Bolton could see that Sullivan was walking the fence perimeter, keeping an eye on el-Jabbar, who was spotting for another one of his people. Bolton started moving closer to the weight yard. Sullivan could probably use the backup with Fischer hanging that close.

Everything happened very quickly after that.

One of the skinheads—they all looked alike— shoved something into a gap in the fence. The bitter taste of adrenaline welled in the back of

Bolton's throat, and he ran quickly toward the weight yard—but it felt like he was moving in slow motion, all of a sudden, even as the hand went between two links in the fence.

Something squirted—it looked like blood. The bitterness in Bolton's throat intensified. Even though he was running at full speed, it felt like he hadn't gotten any closer to the weight yard.

"Shit!"

"He killed him!"

"Son of a bitch!"

Just as Bolton finally got there, the skinheads gathered around each other, like a giant crew-cut sphere. The Muslims started going crazy, banging against the chain-link, the sound of their hands against the metal echoing into the bright sky.

"You're a *dead* man!"

"They killed Vance!"

Sullivan's voice sounded over the din. "Everybody get *down*! *Now*! On the ground!"

Grabbing his radio, Bolton gave the code for a stabbing. "Red dot in the weight yard, red dot in the weight yard!" Then he whirled around. "Everybody down! Now!"

Slowly but surely, everyone in the yard got down on his stomach. They knew the drill.

About half a dozen COs came running into the yard. Two of them, Andros and Jackson, started shoving the Latin Kings to the grass.

Bolton jogged over to the skinheads. "I said get *down*! On your stomachs, hands on head, fingers interlaced, *now*!"

Nobody moved until Fischer nodded. Then they all went down.

As they did so, Bolton noticed a toothbrush on the ground. It was covered in blood and had what looked like a safety razor attached to it.

"I said *down*!" That was Sullivan yelling to the inside of the weight yard.

One of the Muslims said, "There's blood all up in here, yo!"

"Tough," Sullivan snapped.

Looking up, Bolton saw that the tower officer was out on the catwalk, his M16 at the ready. The Blazer belonging to the mobile unit had stopped just outside the yard fence, and Bolton knew the CO inside had chemical agents ready in case a riot broke out—or in case the Muslims didn't listen to Sullivan.

But, just as the skinheads had behaved at Fischer's signal, when el-Jabbar said, "Obey the CO," in his light, pleasant voice, the Muslims obeyed. El-Jabbar was eloquent and charismatic, something you didn't see very often on either side of the fence in RHCF, and Bolton had actually found himself using el-Jabbar as a template for one of the characters in his novel because of the distinctive way he spoke.

Hakim el-Jabbar motivated people. Right now, Bolton was grateful for that, because he motivated them to lie down in the weight yard with the corpse and the blood.

Bolton blew out a breath of relief. They'd had only one other stabbing since Bolton started working here, and it had been a mess—the convicts had rioted for an hour. This one, though, seemed to have calmed down before anything could happen.

Ursitti came running out to the weight yard, breathing heavily. "Talk to me, Sullivan."

"We got a stabbing here, LT," the CO said. "Shivved through the chain-link."

Captain Russell, the superintendent in charge of security, came jogging out to the yard also. Russell was always scowling, so it was usually hard to tell when he was pissed off and when he was just being himself.

Not right now, though. Right now, he was definitely pissed off.

"Sir," Bolton said, pointing down at the toothbrush, "I think we got our murder weapon right here."

"Don't touch it," Russell said. "Don't touch anything. We'll get CERT in here to take the inmates back to their dorms." He took out his cell phone, pushed two buttons, then said, "This is RHCF. We've got a red dot. We need NYPD in here right away."

Some guys from the Corrections Emergency Response Team came running toward the weight yard. Ursitti looked at them and then turned to Bolton. "Get these guys back to their dorms. Once the yard's secure, we'll put the Muslims away."

"Yessir," Bolton said, but on the inside, he was groaning. It would take at least an hour to get all the inmates cuffed and frisked and brought back to their dorms, maybe more, all of it out in this damn heat. And with a dead body, classes would be canceled, so he'd probably wind up outside for the rest of the day anyhow.

"Shit!" That was one of the Muslims.

"Shut the hell *up*, Melendez!"

"There's a dead body up in here!"

"We know," Sullivan said, "shut up and—"

"Not Barker, *Washburne!*"

Bolton felt his eyes go wide, and he ran to the fence and peered in. He saw an array of bodies lying down on the floor of the weight yard, mostly in a row. Two stood out. One was Vance Barker, who was on his back, a gaping, bloody hole in his throat, his big brown eyes wide open. Sweat was still beaded on his bald head, and his mouth hung open, which combined with the slit throat to make it look like he had two mouths and was drinking blood through both of them.

The other body was on its side, with a full head of short-cropped hair, aside from the small round bald spot on the crown. Bolton could see a gash on his forehead, just above his salt-and-pepper beard.

It was Malik Washburne. While Bolton was happy to admit that Barker's death wouldn't be mourned by many beyond his immediate family—if them—he was devastated at Washburne's body lying on the ground. Washburne was one of the good ones—well, as good as a con could be. And he used to be a cop. Bolton's father had known him, back in the day.

Ursitti was wincing. "Damn it."

"Doesn't matter," Russell said. "NYPD'll sort it out. Let's get these people locked down, *now.*"

Jay Bolton really hated his job.

6

STELLA BONASERA HOPED THAT the young women who worked at Belluso's would be understanding of the need for her to take blood and DNA samples from each of them and would let her do so without comment.

Hope, as the saying goes went, springs eternal. They all had questions.

"Why do you have to take my blood?" Jeanie Rodriguez asked. "I mean, I get DNA, that's all over everywhere, but why blood?"

Stella didn't want to admit that they'd found minute traces of blood in the bruises on Maria's knuckles. It could've been Maria's own blood, but if it wasn't, she didn't want to alert any possible suspects to what they'd found. So she just said, "We need to be thorough, that's all. It's best to have as much information as possible."

Dina Rosengaus didn't want her DNA to be in a national database. "It means they can find me anywhere."

"No, really, it doesn't," Stella told her. "It means that if you leave DNA someplace, it's possible for someone to know that you were there. But having your DNA profile doesn't mean we can find you by it."

"Now, maybe. But what about the future? What if they can scan for my—what you call it, DNA profile?"

"If they can do that, they'll already have what they need just from scanning you," Stella said. She had stock answers for all these questions, as she'd gotten them dozens of times.

"But now people can find out where I've been."

"Only if they need to look for it. There are millions of people in the database, with more every day. Nobody could possibly keep track of every single person in there. That's why we only access the information in relation to a crime."

Dina didn't look convinced, but she allowed Stella to take her blood and swab her cheek anyhow.

Annie Wolfowitz backed away from Stella at first. "Don't you need a warrant for that?"

"Only if you don't provide the samples voluntarily. If I can prove to a judge that we need the samples for evidence in a murder investigation— and I have to tell you that it wouldn't take all that much convincing—then I'll have a warrant that will legally compel you to give me blood and DNA samples. But warrants are only needed when the person in question isn't cooperating, and when you don't cooperate, that tends to make cops suspicious."

"Yeah." Annie sighed. "Okay."

After taking a quick bathroom break—which required a key, a level of security Stella thought to be pretty pointless—she finished off with Sal Belluso. The bakery owner spent the entire time muttering in Italian. Stella's own Italian wasn't just rusty, it was oxidized, and Belluso spoke in a dialect Stella didn't know, but she caught enough to know that Belluso wanted the killer very badly and that he wasn't thrilled with all the women cops (the exact term he used was *pola*, which meant both *cop* and *chick*).

She removed the syringe from his arm, grabbed a small square of gauze, and placed it on the puncture. "Hold that," she said.

He obligingly put two fingers down on the gauze. Stella fished out a Band-Aid—the last one she had, luckily; she made a mental note to restock back at the lab—and taped down·the gauze.

"By the way," she said as she packed up her

gear, "you should know that Detective Angell had the best arrest rate of anyone working homicide in the NYPD in 2006. If you want Maria's murder solved, you couldn't be in better hands than that particular *pola*."

Strictly speaking, that wasn't true. Angell only started doing murder in the spring and had only been working on her own for the final quarter of 2006. Any cases she put down prior to that final quarter were credited to her training officer, Detective Benton. However, she *did* have the best rate for anyone in that quarter.

But somehow, saying she had the best arrest rate of anyone for one particular three-month period was less impressive. Besides, it was worth it for the slack-jawed, wide-eyed look of shock on Belluso's face. Whether it was from the fact that Stella understood bits of his rumblings in his native tongue or that Angell was actually a talented cop, Stella couldn't be sure, and it ultimately didn't matter.

She went downstairs, her shoes clunking on the solid wood of the staircase that went down the center of the bakery. Through the picture window, she got an excellent view of Riverdale Avenue. Cars and buses ran in both directions, with plenty of the former double-parked in front of various stores. Up the street, she could see a traffic cop writing a ticket for one of those double-parked cars. Stella thought that they probably hit their quota of parking tickets on this street alone.

This block on Riverdale, north of 236th, was entirely commercial. Across the street from Belluso's, Stella saw a bagel shop, a dry cleaner, a diner, a veterinarian, an insurance office, a florist, a gym, a hardware store, a bank, a comic book store, a pizza place, and a stationery store—and that was just on one side of the street and only halfway up the block. She knew that Riverdale was a heavily residential neighborhood; probably most of the businesses were concentrated in this area, leaving the rest for the nice houses of people like the Mitchums, the deaf family whose daughter's murder had been the subject of Stella's previous trip hereabouts last winter.

One of the buses that went by was a shuttle to the Metro-North Railroad. Between that and the city buses that would take people down the hill to the 1 train on Broadway, this block probably saw a lot of commuter traffic. Stella was willing to bet that Belluso's was a hit in the early morning.

Except today, anyhow.

As she passed by the display cases, she wondered how the cannoli were. Once morning rush hour passed, this place probably got a lot of people in for pastries and more leisurely cups of coffee than that afforded by the morning dash to work. The place even looked like a café in Rome, the way all the places in Little Italy downtown did, and Stella wondered if that was on purpose.

To find out, though, she'd need to talk to Belluso, and she had no great desire to do that just at the moment. If nothing else, it would've spoiled her exit line.

Besides, Angell's departmental sedan was pulling up, which meant she was done with her notification of Maria Campagna's parents.

O'Malley and Wayne were both downstairs as well. "The ME wagon'll be here soon for the body," Stella said. "Even after that, though, we'll have to keep this place sealed up."

Wayne winced. "Sal'll have a conniption fit."

"Sal will have to get over it. It's still a crime scene, and we may need to come back here, depending on what we get from the lab."

Chuckling, O'Malley said, "Joe will be thrilled."

Stella frowned. "Who's Joe?"

"Guy who owns that bagel place." O'Malley pointed at the bagel shop on the corner. "Bagels're great, but their coffee sucks. But any port in a storm, y'know?"

Angell had gotten out of her car. Stella smiled at the two uniforms and said, "Let us know if anything happens."

"Sure thing, Detective," Wayne said.

"Oh," Stella added with the sweetest smile she could manage, "and O'Malley? You call the detective 'angel face' again, and I'll find out about it. And I've got excellent range scores."

With that, Stella departed, pleased with being two-for-two on exit lines this morning. When you waded in dead bodies for a living, you took your victories where you could get them. Besides, Angell was good police, and Stella knew as well as anyone how hard it was for a woman to survive in the NYPD, a degree of difficulty that rose exponentially the higher up the ranks you got. That she was very good at her job helped her cause, but mostly in terms of giving guys like O'Malley less ammunition. If Stella could do her bit to alleviate the razzing Angell got, she'd do it.

Jerking a thumb across the street at 236th, Angell said, "Morgenstern's one block up and around the corner. We can hoof it."

Feeling the morning sun's heat seeping into her skin, Stella asked, "Can't we take your nice air-conditioned car?"

"I haven't been running the AC," she said. "Uses up gas too fast. I got reamed on my gas mileage."

Stella shook her head. "I love bureaucracy. We got similarly reamed on our E-Z Pass usage."

They crossed Riverdale Avenue and started walking up the steep hill of 236th, passing a crafts store, a fish store—which was quite pungent in this heat—a real estate office, and another hardware place before the block gave way entirely to apartment buildings.

"How was Maria's family?"

Angell shuddered. "When I started, Benton said that the worst part of the job was notifying families. Everything else—wading hip-deep in people's blood, talking to scumbags who commit murder for the *stupidest* reason, dealing with idiot lawyers and hidebound judges, too much OT, not enough OT money, no personal life—all that you can deal with, eventually. But nothing is worse than telling someone that their little girl won't ever come home again."

Stella found she could say nothing in response to that.

They walked the rest of the way to Morgenstern's house in companionable silence. And it was a house, not an apartment building. They turned onto Cambridge Avenue to find several small homes with postage-stamp yards in front. One of them apparently belonged to Jack Morgenstern.

As they were about to ring the doorbell, Angell finally broke the silence. "I got the mother—the father died last year. She was apparently worried sick when Maria didn't come home last night, but she didn't report it because Maria'd been out all night a few times before with her boyfriend without calling, so she figured it was that. The mother broke down and cried for fifteen minutes. She said she moved to Riverdale because it was supposed to be a *safer* neighborhood. Then she threw me out and told me to stop wasting time talking to her and to go and capture her daughter's killer."

"Three stages of grief in one shot," Stella said wryly.

"Yeah." Angell rang the doorbell.

The house had a white screen door in front of a white wood door. In front of them was a doormat with the words WELCOME BACK MY FRIENDS TO THE SHOW THAT NEVER ENDS stenciled on it. Gold metal numerals providing the house number were nailed to the inner door. That door swung open to reveal a white male in this thirties with long brown hair— which was somewhat unkempt—and a beard. He was wearing a silk bathrobe and looked bleary-eyed. Stella suspected they'd woken him up.

Stella held up her badge; Angell did likewise. "NYPD, Mr. Morgenstern. I'm Detective Angell, this is Detective Bonasera. We have a few—"

"Just a sec." He closed the door.

Exchanging a glance with Angell, Stella said, "O-o-o-okay."

The door reopened, and Morgenstern then opened the screen as well. He was holding out two business cards. Stella noticed that he was walking a bit stiffly, like he had bruised or even broken ribs. "That's the name and number of my lawyer,

Courtney Bracey. You want to talk to me, set it up with her."

Stella stared down at the cards. If he was law-yering up already . . .

"Mr. Morgenstern," Angell said, "we just have a few questions about—"

"I don't care. I have the right to legal counsel, and I'm damn well exercising that right. Now please, take the cards, go back to your little pre-cinct house, and make an appointment. We're done here."

"Look, Mr. Morgenstern," Stella said, trying to sound reasonable, "we just want to know—"

"Save it, Detective," Morgenstern snapped. "The last time a couple of detectives showed up at my doorstep saying they just had a few questions, I was arrested for rape."

Involuntarily, Stella tensed at the word *rape*. It had been over a year, but the memory of being at-tacked by her psychotic ex-boyfriend Frankie Mala was still so easily triggered. He hadn't actually raped her, though she had felt violated when she discovered that he'd put a recording of their love-making on the Internet. She'd broken up with him after that, and then he broke into her apartment, attacked her, tied her up, cut her, and threatened to do worse.

Sometimes, when she closed her eyes, she still saw him leaping over the partition as she grabbed her Glock out of her handbag, knocking her to the floor.

In only a second, she got over it. She was on the job, not in the office of the department shrink Mac all but twisted her arm into seeing. It had been more than a year ago. She was over it.

She *was*.

Morgenstern was still talking, his voice rising with each sentence, and she forced herself to focus on his words. "Mind you, I didn't rape anybody. But you people put out a description of a white male in his thirties with long brown hair and a beard. I was in jail for *two days* before the real guy raped somebody else. *This* time, they caught the right guy, sprung me without even an apology, not even when the DNA test proved it wasn't me." He gave a bitter-looking half smile. "I suppose I should be grateful—the lawsuit that I won paid for this house." The smile fell, and now he looked furious. "But if you think for one *second* that I have any interest in saying anything to a police officer without my lawyer present, then you're out of your mind. I've been a victim of the NYPD's gestapo tactics once; it's *not* happening again! Good-*bye*!"

With that, he dropped the two business cards on the doormat and slammed the door shut.

"Looks like he gets the best exit line of all," Stella muttered.

Angell was crouched down, picking up the business cards. "What was that?"

"Nothing." Stella sighed. She took one of the cards from Angell, and they started walking back down Cambridge.

"What do you think?" Angell asked.

"He's the last one seen with the victim. He was a rape suspect. He has a temper. He was obviously in a fight recently. He was wearing a shirt that's the same color as the fiber found on the body. I'd say we just talked to prime suspect number one."

7

FOR A LONG TIME, Dr. Sheldon Hawkes never thought much about prison. He'd been a respected surgeon for a few years before one lost patient too many drove him to the medical examiner's office. He couldn't stand to bear even the slightest responsibility for a human being's death, so he put his medical skills to use in trying to catch those who did.

Intellectually, he knew that those who murdered the bodies he examined as an ME—and later, after he moved from the morgue to fieldwork, those responsible for the crime scenes he examined— usually went to prison. But still, that didn't have much meaning for Hawkes.

Then he was arrested, accused of murder, put in handcuffs, and taken to Rikers Island, and prison took on a whole new meaning.

He'd worked in law enforcement for years, but until that day, Sheldon Hawkes had never understood just how *humiliating* it was to be restrained by handcuffs, how helpless you felt with your wrists pulled behind your back, the metal biting into your flesh.

As a black man, Hawkes knew he had to live with the constant suspicion. The little old white ladies who would walk across the street to avoid him, simply because of the color of his skin. The state troopers who pulled him over, ignoring the white drivers who were going much faster down the highway. It didn't matter that he had a medical degree or that he had a badge of his own.

But even so, he'd never quite understood what it was like to be considered the scum of the earth until he was placed in pretrial detention at Rikers. He stopped being a person the moment those cuffs went on.

Hawkes couldn't call it the worst feeling he'd ever had in his life, as that spot was reserved for the way he felt the last time he'd lost a patient on his operating table. But it was pretty damn close.

He had been framed, of course. Shane Casey was a whack-job with a mad-on for the crime lab. Casey's brother had also been accused of murder, but he killed himself in prison. Casey was sure his brother was framed, and so he turned around and framed Hawkes, who had still been an ME at the time of Casey's brother's trial. Hawkes's testimony was part of what led to the guilty verdict.

Regardless of the circumstances, Hawkes never wanted to set foot in a prison again.

So when Deputy Inspector Stanton Gerrard had come by the crime lab that morning, a pit opened in Hawkes's stomach.

Gerrard had been the one leading the charge when Hawkes was arrested. Shortly after that, he was promoted to deputy inspector and placed in charge of the crime lab, just in time to lead a witch hunt against Mac for his role in Clay Dobson's death.

Nobody was ever happy to see Gerrard in the lab, and the feeling was mutual. Mac had dug up some dirt on Gerrard in order to get him to back off on the Dobson thing, but while that had helped Mac in the short term, it also put the CSIs even deeper in the inspector's doghouse.

"Detective Taylor," Gerrard had said, a grimace under his gray beard. "I just got a call from the DOC. We've got two suspicious deaths at the Richmond Hill Correctional Facility. Albany's requested a detective and a crime scene detail." He gave a half smile. "I'd say send your best people, but since you don't have any, I'll settle for whichever one of your screwups is hanging around."

Somehow, Mac had managed not to make a disparaging comment. Instead, he had just told

Hawkes and Danny Messer to suit up and join him.

"Oh, and Detective?" Gerrard had added. "They've ID'd the bodies. One is a scumbag named Vance Barker. The other one's Malik Washburne."

That had brought Mac up short. "Is that who I think it is?"

Gerrard nodded. "The former Officer Gregory Washburne."

"What was he doing in RHCF?"

"Ten years for vehicular homicide. Don't screw this one up, Taylor." With that, Gerrard had left.

"Who's this Washburne guy?" Danny had asked. "Was he dirty?"

"Washburne wasn't a bad cop," Mac had replied. "In fact, he was one of the best. He quit for personal reasons and converted to Islam. That's why he changed his name. I had no idea he'd been arrested."

They'd met up with Flack at the NYPD helipad. Midday traffic would be murder (no pun intended), and it had already been a couple of hours since the crime took place. By the time the Department of Corrections bureaucracy worked its way from Staten Island to Albany and back down to Gerrard's office, the scene had probably already turned into a mess. Speed was of the essence, and they couldn't afford to sit in traffic on two different bridges, nor was Mac sanguine about taking their lab equipment onto the Staten Island Ferry.

But Gerrard had surprised everyone by authorizing the chopper ride. Dressed in his dark blue jacket with the letters csi:ny in white on the back, and carrying his metal case, Hawkes had joined Flack, Danny, and Mac in the helicopter.

The pilot had taken a route that took them over the Hudson River immediately, hugging the New Jersey coast southward, going over the Goethals Bridge, which linked Staten Island to New Jersey, before coming down in the parking lot outside RHCF.

The prison was in the middle of nowhere on the west coast of Staten Island. As he stepped down from the helicopter, head lowered for safety, Hawkes saw a lot of fences topped with spools of razor wire. At the far end of the parking lot was the prison entrance.

Flack gingerly exited from the helicopter. Hawkes offered him a hand down, which he refused to take. "Flack, they prescribe Percocet for a reason," he said.

"What, you're my mother, now?"

"No, but I am a doctor, and my medical advice to you is to take the painkillers."

"As I recall," Flack said with a smirk as they walked toward the entrance, "your medical advice was for me to stay off my feet for another month. I'm fine."

Hawkes considered pressing the point, then decided it was a waste of time. He'd known Don Flack long enough to be quite familiar with his ability to be as stubborn as a jackass, with a personality to match if you pushed it.

They walked across the parking lot to the entrance, where a man with thinning white hair and a thick white mustache greeted them. He was dressed in a white shirt with a badge, which indicated a higher rank in the prison. With him were two COs wearing blue shirts; one had lieutenant's bars on his collar, and the other had three chevrons, indicating a sergeant.

"Gentlemen, my name is Captain Richard Russell. I'm the superintendent of security." The man in white offered his hand.

"I'm Detective Taylor from the crime lab," Mac said, taking the handshake. "This is Detective Flack, Detective Messer, and Dr. Hawkes."

"Pleased to meet you all. This is Lieutenant Ursitti and Sergeant Jackson. I'm going to have to ask you to leave your cell phones and weapons at the arsenal." Russell pointed at a sign, which read ALL ARMAMENTS MUST BE LEFT AT THE ARSENAL. Under those words was an arrow that pointed away from the front entrance to an alcove at the end of the building.

As Russell led them to the alcove, he continued: "You'll also each have a CO assigned to you while you're in my facility."

Danny leaned to Hawkes and muttered, "What, they think we're gonna steal the silver?" ·

The alcove had a window, a CO sitting behind it. A metal tray similar to those used at bank drive-throughs was under the window, and it slid out as they approached.

"If you place your weapons and phones there, Officer Simone will place them in lockers, and you'll keep the keys."

Hawkes reached into his holster and took out his nine millimeter. Mac did likewise. After a second, shaking his head, so did Danny. They also handed over their Treos. They each placed them in the tray as it slid out, then it slid back in. Moments later, the tray slid out again bearing three keys. Hawkes felt a little better about the whole thing once he realized he got to hold the key to the locker that held his weapon. He hated carrying the damn thing—it contravened the Hippocratic oath, to his mind— and he couldn't shoot it worth a damn, anyhow, but he was still responsible for it.

Flack asked, "What happened, exactly?"

Before Ursitti could respond, Russell said, "Detective, you have to hand over your weapon and phone as well. No exceptions."

"Fine." Flack's tone indicated the opposite, but

he placed his weapon, his backup weapon, and his flip-top phone in the tray. His key came out a moment later.

Ursitti, meanwhile, said, "Both bodies are in the weight yard. It's a fenced-off part of the yard. There were forty-five Muslims in there, and one of the skinheads stabbed one of the Muslims through the chain-link."

"That's Vance Barker?" Flack asked.

Ursitti nodded. "Yeah. He's in on a drug charge, same as most of these guys. One of those organizational soldier types that'd rather do time than flip on their buddies."

"Looks like he took one for the team once too often," Mac said.

They walked inside. Hawkes felt the blessed cool of air-conditioning as they stepped through the double doors to the entryway.

Mac asked, "How do you know there were exactly forty-five in the yard?"

"That's the yard's max capacity. We had to keep two guys out 'cause they hit the limit."

Another CO sat behind a long desk inside. In front of the desk, in the center of the narrow entryway, was a metal detector. The CO pulled out a battered notebook and flipped white pages until he reached a blank one. "Sign in."

"You've gotta be kidding me," Danny said.

"Procedure," the CO said with a shrug.

"We have to keep track of everyone who comes in and out of here, Detective Messer," Russell said primly. "I would think you of all people would appreciate that."

"We do," Mac said quickly before Danny could respond. He grabbed the pen and signed his name, as well as the time and the purpose of his visit (he wrote NYPD INVESTIGATION in neat block letters; Hawkes intended to do likewise).

Ursitti continued: "Other body's Malik Washburne. Nobody saw what happened to him, but we figure somebody took him out while everyone was watching Barker bleed out."

Each of them in turn emptied his pockets, put the contents in a red plastic bin, and walked through the metal detector. Nobody set it off, for which Hawkes was grateful. He wouldn't have put it past Flack to have a third weapon on his person.

Once that was done and they each had the back of his hand stamped with fluorescent ink, a steel door started to slide open.

"Cameras can only be used in the weight yard and the immediate area around it," Russell said. "Any of my COs sees you taking any other pictures without authorization, your equipment will be impounded and you'll be escorted from the premises."

Hawkes frowned. "And why is that?"

Russell turned on him. "You have a problem

with that, Dr. Hawkes, you can take it up with Albany. I'm just following the rules here. I suggest you do the same."

"Okay." Hawkes noticed that Sergeant Jackson was rolling his eyes behind Russell's back. Captain Russell apparently had a reputation.

They all walked into the alcove and were asked to place their hands on a tray with a hand-shaped indentation. Ultraviolet light was shone on their hands, and the fluorescent ink turned up blue where they'd been stamped. Hawkes thought that was a nice touch—putting something on visitors that they couldn't easily get rid of because they couldn't even see it.

Once they had all shown their hands, the door they had come through slid slowly shut, and a facing door slid slowly open. They walked back outside, the heat and humidity hitting Hawkes like a hammer.

They walked down a path that was lined with neatly arranged flowers; there was even a koi pond. Hawkes assumed that the landscaping was done by the inmates.

Mac said, in a tone that suggested he'd been simmering for a while, "Captain, *you* asked for *us*. I don't appreciate being told how to do my job."

"I'm not," Russell said. "I'm telling you what's allowed in my facility. Again, if you have a problem, take it up with Albany."

Going through another set of double doors put them back in the AC. Three COs, all with one stripe on their sleeves, were waiting for them.

Ursitti said, "Detective Flack, I'll take you to our interrogation room—you can start interviewing witnesses there."

Flack nodded, then looked at one of the COs and smiled. "Hey, Terry, we gotta stop meeting like this."

One of the COs—a big guy with a baby face—smiled and said, "Donnie."

Russell looked back and forth between the two. "You two know each other, Officer Sullivan?"

The CO with the baby face dropped the smile. "Yes, sir. Detective Flack's dad and my dad used to bust heads together in the one-one-two back in the day."

"Swell," Russell said with a scowl. "Officer Sullivan, you'll accompany Detective Taylor. Officer Andros, you'll accompany Detective Messer. Officer Ciccone, you'll go with Dr. Hawkes."

The six of them proceeded through a few more corridors, past several checkpoints and guard posts, and finally again went out into the heat and humidity. Hawkes wryly thought he was going to get pneumonia at this rate, although the AC inside the prison wasn't exactly what you'd call high-level. That was what Hawkes liked about both the morgue and the crime lab—high-tech equipment and dead bodies both needed to stay cool, so New York summers were bearable at work.

Except when you went out to a crime scene.

There was no shade to speak of in the open field between the building and the weight yard, so the sun was beating down mercilessly on the ground from the cloudless sky.

As he crossed the yard, the sun hot on the back of his neck, Hawkes tried not to think about the fact that he was, once again, in a prison, with a CO dogging his every step. With this Ciccone guy walking right behind him, Hawkes almost felt like he was in prison for real again, not just visiting. Like he wasn't a person anymore.

He really hated that.

After a long walk across the grassy field, they reached the weight yard. Behind the weight yard was a copse of trees, which provided shade for a batch of picnic tables. Beyond the cluster of tables was a basketball court.

The yard was completely empty, save for a few COs who were standing around the weight yard. Hawkes assumed that the place was currently in lockdown, with all the inmates confined in their cells.

An African-American man with a goatee very much like the one Hawkes used to wear stood at the gate. The CO with Mac, Flack's friend Sullivan, said, "Jay, these're the crime lab guys. Uncle Cal said they can do whatever they want in the weight room."

Jay nodded and took the keys out of his belt, then flipped through several before coming to the one that unlocked the padlock on the chain that kept the gate shut.

Hawkes took in the entire crime scene with a practiced eye as the gate swung open with the metallic whining of hinges. Inside were several weight benches, half a dozen barbells, and a huge number of round metal doughnut weights of various sizes.

One body was lying on the ground near the fence. There was blood all around him, splattered and smeared.

Mac asked, "Can someone describe exactly what happened?"

The man named Jay stepped forward and described the events of that morning, including forcing all the convicts inside the weight yard to lie on their stomachs. There were forty-five of them—the maximum occupancy, as Ursitti had said—and with them all lying down in there, it was a little cramped.

When he was finished with his account, Jay pointed to the ground outside the weight yard. "Found that shiv. Nobody touched it after I found it, I made sure."

"Thanks," Mac said as he walked over to where Jay was pointing. He yanked a latex glove out of his pocket and held it between his fingers, using it to pick up the item. "A toothbrush with a safety razor attached—and covered in blood."

Sullivan said, "They don't get points for originality 'round here, Detective."

"Good thing," Mac muttered. He pulled out an evidence envelope and dropped the makeshift murder weapon inside. "Blood's probably our vic, and this'll have the murderer's prints." He looked up. "Danny, you take Barker. Sheldon, check out Washburne."

Hawkes nodded. As he entered the weight yard, Ciccone on his heels, he muttered, "Reconstructing's going to be difficult in this mess."

"The hell you gotta reconstruct for?" Ciccone asked. "One of the skinheads killed Barker."

"It was Mulroney," Sullivan added.

Hawkes whirled around. Mac and Danny were looking at him, too. Mac asked, "How do you know that?"

"I saw him. I already gave my verbal report to the LT. Hell, half the Muslims in here probably saw it, and so did the gangbangers hangin' around outside. Skinheads won't say nothin', but they don't have to."

"Who's Mulroney?" Mac asked.

"Jack Mulroney," Sullivan said. "He's in for assault—bar brawl, him against two homosexuals." Smirking, Sullivan added, "Not the fairest of fights."

Ciccone muttered, "More like a fairy fight." Hawkes shot him a disgusted look, which the CO ignored.

"Anyway, this is a step up for him," Sullivan said. "He's a brawler, but this is the first time he's actually killed someone."

Hawkes nodded and walked toward the free weights, his mind already racing ahead to the true conundrum he had to solve: the death of Malik Washburne.

He asked Ciccone, "Anybody see what happened to him?"

The CO shrugged.

From the gate, Sullivan said, "We were all busy lookin' at Barker getting shivved. I heard a clunk, turned around, and Washburne was on the floor."

Hawkes knelt down next to the body. Here, at least, he was in his element. No matter how he was feeling, he knew that what he was good at—what he was here for—was using his medical degree and his experience to glean answers from dead bodies.

Like everyone else here who wasn't a CO, Washburne was wearing the green dickies of a convict, though he had removed the shirt and was wearing only a white tank undershirt for weight lifting in the hot summer sun. He had apparently been growing his hair long in a seventies-style

Afro—but it wasn't enough to hide the giant gash in his forehead.

Putting on his latex gloves—and sighing with the inevitablility of spending the next twenty-four hours with his hands smelling like sweat-drenched latex, a stench that grossed Hawkes out even more than the smell of dead bodies—Hawkes examined the gash. It looked about the right size to have been caused by one of the weights.

Standing up, he took out his Nikon D200 and started photographing the body from every angle. Once that was done, he took out an L-ruler and balanced it on Washburne's cheek, to record the size of the abrasion on his forehead.

Lying near the body was one of the free weights: a twenty-pound doughnut weight, based on the number stenciled into it. It had blood on one part of its edge.

Looking up, Hawkes saw that barely two feet from the body and the fallen weight was a bench press. One side of the barbell had three doughnut weights.

The other side had two. On the end with three doughnuts, the outermost weight was also a twenty-pounder.

Hawkes photographed the bench from as many angles as he could think of, then did the same for the doughnut free weight, both with and without the L-ruler.

"Jesus Christ," Ciccone muttered. "You need a

freakin' diagram, Doc? The weight came off that barbell. Whoever wasted Washburne probably conked him on the head with it. Hell, one of the cons figured that out while lying on his belly. In case, y'know, it ain't obvious."

"It is obvious, but we still have to document it," Hawkes said, kneeling back down beside the body. "Prosecutors like it better when we're thorough. So do juries."

"I done jury duty, Doc. Only thing we liked was to go home fast."

Blood had pooled near the wound, but there was more blood on various parts of Washburne's body, all near the head or in spots where the gash could, conceivably, have dripped. Head wounds tended to gush, after all. Still, there was enough blood all over the place in here that it was best to collect as many samples as possible.

Reaching into his kit, Hawkes took out several Q-tips and meticulously swabbed blood from the head wound, from several other parts of the body, and also from the doughnut weight. Each swab went into a separate evidence bags, which Hawkes labeled with a Sharpie. Hawkes noticed that one area of blood was significantly drier than the others. He noted that that batch should be tested first—in both mathematics and forensics, the discrepant part of a set usually provided the most useful information.

As he was swabbing, he noticed a thread on the victim's shoulder. It looked like a green fiber. It probably belonged to Washburne's own prison outfit. Still, Hawkes grabbed his tweezers and pulled the fiber off, bagging and labeling that as well.

"Y'know, I thought the most boring thing in the world was the overnight shift, when the convicts are asleep," Ciccone said, shaking his head, his arms folded. "Looks like I was wrong, 'cause this is *way* more boring. Don't know how you do it, Doc, this is the boringest damn thing."

Hawkes didn't respond. Having established that Ciccone found what he did for a living dull, Hawkes found it easy to disregard the man and continue silently with his work.

Danny Messer had been surprised when Mac had tapped him to be on this detail, since Danny had some relatives who were incarcerated at RHCF. The Messer family had a significant number of members in the Tanglewood Boys. Danny had managed to stay out of that quagmire, graduating at the top of his class at the Academy, after which Mac had specifically requested him for his team.

Being in the crime lab was the best thing for him. While nobody had said anything—and several people, including Don Flack, had said it wouldn't matter—Danny didn't think he'd be entirely trusted on the street. He'd grown up with his family under surveillance by the feds, after all.

Besides, he liked working in the lab.

Still, he tried to avoid his home borough of Staten Island as much as possible. Danny hated coming back home, a feeling he seemed to share with most people who'd grown up on the island and left it.

Today, though, it wasn't possible. Stella and Lindsay were in the Bronx, and that left Danny and Sheldon to go with Mac—and all three of them would be needed. This was two bodies in a case that came down from on high: Albany to Deputy Inspector Scumbag Gerrard his own damn self.

At least he could take heart in the fact that the place was locked down. All the convicts were in their dorms. They had stopped calling them "cells" in medium- and minimum-security places a while ago, for no good reason that Danny could see. Probably for the same stupid reason they started calling them "corrections officers" instead of "prison guards," and "sanitation engineers" instead of "garbage men," and "flight attendants" instead of "stewardesses." And, for that matter, "crime scene investigators" instead of "police scientists." Danny thought it was stupid. He knew that the term *corrections officer* was created to apply to licensed state peace officers, as opposed to guards, who were minimum-wage hacks with no authority outside the prison—and, for that matter, that *flight attendant* was more accurate and non-gender-specific. He still thought it was stupid.

But he could do a George Carlin routine on the degradation of language on his own time. Right now, Mac trusted him on this case, and he would give it his best. Danny hadn't always given Mac good reason to trust him, so he appreciated those occasions when he did.

Of course, he gave Sheldon the whodunit. Nobody had seen Washburne get iced. Danny's guy, though, everyone saw what happened.

Still, people lied. Evidence didn't. That was why Danny rejected the life of lies that came with being a Tanglewood Boy and joined the crime lab.

So he worked the scene.

First was pictures. You had to record the scene as it was before you started touching things.

Once he got the full Vance Barker photo album, he looked more closely at the wound. Whoever did it nailed him right in the carotid. It was almost a perfect kill shot; anybody who got that artery sliced open would be dead in seconds. Whoever did this was professional or very lucky.

Since this place was medium security, Danny

tended to think it was the latter. But that wasn't his problem right now.

Looking at the rest of the vic's face, he noticed that Barker had a split lip. Danny had almost missed it thanks to all the blood. Glancing up at the CO with him—Andros?—he asked, "When did our boy get into a fight?"

"What day is it?" Andros said with a snort. "I've only been here a month, and this guy's gotten into twelve fights."

"This one was recent."

"Oh, yeah—yesterday's ball game. There was a brawl after Barker did a takeout slide at second."

"Party never stops around here, huh?"

"Tell me about it."

Danny shook his head and stood up. He looked around at the chain-link fence, taking pictures of the blood spray on the metal.

From the other side of the fence, Mac was inspecting the outside. "Looks like our killer reached in here." He pointed with a gloved finger through one of the holes in the chain-link.

"Yeah," Danny said, "that tracks with the splatter I'm getting here."

Mac said, "There's blood smeared on the lower part of this hole. It's smeared moving outward, and that's consistent with a hand being yanked back. Probably rubbed against the chain-link with his pinkie." He looked at Sullivan. "I'm going to need to see your suspect. You haven't changed his clothes, have you?"

Sullivan shook his head. "Nah, they're all safe and sound and not moving."

"Good. Can you take me to him, and anybody who might've been standing around him?"

"Sure," Sullivan said. "They're all in Alpha Block."

"Good." He looked through the chain-link at the weight yard. Danny thought Mac's ultraserious face looked comical broken up by the metal. "Danny, Sheldon, you two finish up here. Once you've bagged and tagged everything, meet me back at the captain's office so we can arrange to have the bodies shipped to the morgue."

"Sure thing, Mac," Danny said.

8

IN THE SUMMERTIME, STELLA loved coming to the morgue.

Like far too many things in her life, it was something Stella tried not to examine too closely. Still, there was a certain logic to it. Summers in New York could be absolutely brutal, heat in the eighties and nineties and high humidity. It wasn't as bad as, say, Florida, but it still wasn't any fun. Today was one of the nastier days. Just the walk from Belluso's to Morgenstern's house and back had exhausted her and left her dripping with sweat.

So coming to the morgue was a breath of, if not fresh air, at least cool air. In the wintertime, it was less than pleasant, but on days like this, Stella loved coming here.

Even with the dead bodies.

She also was happy to see that Dr. Sid Hammerback was the ME assigned to the Campagna case. Over the past few weeks, she'd felt protective of Sid, after she walked in on him on the floor of the autopsy room. He'd gone into anaphylactic shock from a sandwich, the contents of which he hadn't checked closely enough (he hadn't set foot in that particular deli since), and Stella had performed CPR to help revive him.

"How's my slave for life doing?" she asked with a cheeky grin as she entered the lab.

"At your service as ever," Sid said with mock solemnity. Then he broke into one of his infectious grins.

He removed his glasses, which were on a chain around his neck and separated at the nosepiece. Every time he pulled the glasses apart, Stella winced, thinking for a moment that he'd broken his glasses, despite Sid having had those glasses for years now.

The body of Maria Campagna was laid out on the table. Sid had already completed the autopsy: the body was naked, with the telltale Y-shaped stitching of a chest that had been opened.

Handing Stella his preliminary report in a manila folder, Sid said, "COD was strangulation. Her throat was crushed. Based on body temp, I'd say she died late last night."

Stella took the report and nodded. "That fits with Belluso's closing time."

"Lividity was consistent with position. She probably died where you found her."

With a slight bark of laughter, Stella said, "Good, because the scene was *no* help in that regard. Her body was on a floor that had been walked on, tripped on, and had things dragged over it for years now."

"Didn't find any prints or finger indentations on the neck." Sid walked to the big screen that hung over the table. Using a latex-gloved hand, he used the touch-screen interface to call up the X-rays of Maria's neck. "The anterior of her hyoid was splintered inward. There's also damage to the larynx, pharynx, thyroid, and two of the parathyroid glands. The pattern of the hyoid break and the collateral damage is consistent with an arm being wrapped around the neck and squeezing. Based on our victim's height, and based on the strength necessary to do this, I'm guessing our killer is a man who's taller than her and is right-handed."

Staring at the screen, with the points of impact highlighted in green by Sid, Stella saw that the pattern of damage to Maria's neck was at a slight downward angle as you went right to left. She nodded. "It fits—our guy grabbed her in a headlock from behind and literally squeezed the life out of her."

"I didn't find any trace on the neck, aside from that fiber you had in your report. Our guy was probably wearing a long-sleeved shirt when he did the deed."

"Yeah. It was certainly chilly enough late last night. What about the bruises on her knuckles?"

"They look to be antemortem. Safe bet that they're defensive wounds, though that's just between you and me until the labs come back on the blood. If it's hers, then I can't say for sure that the bruises had anything to do with the killer. If it's someone else's—"

"Then we've got something to work with." Stella sighed. "Anything else?"

Sid reattached his glasses over his nose and pointed at the area just above the Y-stitching. "Minor irritation of the skin in the pattern of a necklace, which tracks with the divot in her skin on the back of the neck. She definitely wore a necklace of some sort. It could've come off in the struggle."

"Or we could be looking at a robbery." Again Stella sighed. Still too many questions, not enough answers. But not all the evidence had been examined yet. There was the trace on the knuckles and the fiber they had found. "Thanks, Sid. And watch what you eat."

Chuckling, Sid said, "Always. Thanks, Stell. Oh, hey, listen, I'm having a cookout Saturday night. I'm going to start marinating the steaks on Friday."

Stella felt her mouth water. Sid had given up a career as a chef in order to become a medical examiner—a career choice Stella had never entirely understood, considering his culinary talents—and his steak marinade was the stuff of legends. The only ingredients Stella knew for sure were Worcestershire sauce, white pepper, and olive oil, and she only knew those because she'd guessed them and Sid reluctantly admitted she was right. (She was especially proud of guessing the white pepper.) Danny had jokingly threatened to take a sample back to the lab and was deterred only by the threat of Sid putting all his autopsies at the bottom of the priority list. Mac expressed concern about Sid compromising the integrity of the lab, prompting Sid's fellow ME (and Mac's girlfriend) Peyton Driscoll to punch him playfully on the arm. Sid and Danny had assured Mac that they were both kidding.

"Peyton and Mac are already coming, and so's Sheldon. Danny and Lindsay had to beg off, though. What about you?"

"Wild horses couldn't keep me from your marinade, Sid. I'll be there with bells on."

"Good, then I'll know you're coming," Sid said with a smile.

Rolling her eyes, Stella departed the lab with the autopsy report in hand.

Upstairs, she found Lindsay talking with Adam

Ross. Both were wearing their white lab coats with NY: CRIME LAB stenciled on the breast.

"Please, they don't know what winter *is* around here," Lindsay was saying. "They get a few inches of snow and everyone hides in their apartment like it's the second coming. We'd have to get four feet of accumulation in Bozeman before we'd even notice it's snowing."

"Which is why I stay away from Montana," Adam said with a shudder. "People weren't meant to live in the cold. Remember, humanity started out in Africa, where it's nice and toasty." He smiled under his beard. "What I love is when they bitch when it goes over ninety. That's a cold snap where I come from in Arizona."

As she approached the pair, Stella said, "Yeah, but it's a dry heat."

"Which is as it should be," Adam said without missing a beat. "Humidity just messes with my hair."

"Right," Lindsay said, "because hair care is at the top of your list of priorities."

"Damn right." Adam couldn't hold the straight face. On a good day, he might remember to comb his unruly brown hair, and that was done in by his habit of running his hands through it.

"If a native New Yorker can join this out-of-towner conversation about what weather wimps we are . . ." Stella said.

Adam straightened, immediately all business. Or as all business as Adam ever got. He was the prototypical lab rat. Occasionally, Mac or Stella would drag him out into the field, usually kicking and screaming. He'd confided in Stella once on the subject. "Going into the field," he'd said, "makes it too real, you know? Out there, it's people being hurt. In here, it's a puzzle to be solved. I can focus better on puzzles."

Now Adam said, "Well, I've got good news and bad news."

With a sigh, Stella said, "Bad news first."

"As usual." He held up a printout. "Ran the fiber and found a match almost instantly."

Stella winced. Fast matches meant common matches. The bane of evidence-gathering was the common fiber, the standard shoe print, the fashionable piece of jewelry. The holy grail of the crime lab was finding something unique to the victim and/or the perp. To Adam, she said, "That's never good."

"And today's not the exception. The fiber is a standard cotton/polyester blend. Nothing particularly unique about it, no trace of anything else—just black cotton/poly."

Stella muttered a curse. "So our killer was wearing, on a cool night, a black sweatshirt."

"Yup. I have officially narrowed the suspect list to three quarters of the population of New York City."

"More like seven eighths," Lindsay said. "I remember when I first moved here, I thought everyone was depressed all the time." She smirked. "They don't wear that much black in Montana."

"Still," Stella said, taking the report from Adam, "at least we know our killer was wearing a black sweatshirt. If we find a suspect who was wearing one, it gives us something to work with." She looked at Adam. "What's the good news?"

Looking sheepish, Adam said, "Er, well, I lied. There is no good news."

"Swell."

The sound of a twelve-bar blues song emitted from Stella's jacket pocket. Reaching inside, she pulled out her Treo, which displayed the words DETECTIVE JENNIFER ANGELL and Angell's cell number. She touched the screen to answer the phone and put it to her ear. "Heya, Jen."

"Stell. Listen, I got good news and bad news."

"Do you really have good news, or are you and Adam using the same gag writer?"

"Huh?"

"Never mind—what's up?"

"Well, I just spent ten minutes on the phone with Jack Morgenstern's lawyer, Courtney Bracey. That's ten minutes I'll be begging for on my deathbed. I've decided to beat the Christmas rush and start hating her now. They're coming in this afternoon, and it looks to be as much fun as root canal."

"Sounds like a blast. What's the good news?"

"I left a message for our vic's boyfriend, Bobby DelVecchio? He called me back while I was going ten rounds with Bracey. He's also coming in this afternoon, and he says he knows who the killer is."

9

MAC TAYLOR WALKED THOUGHTFULLY across the prison yard, contemplating the life of Malik Washburne.

He'd been born with the name Gregory Washburne, and he'd been a uniformed cop, assigned to the one-oh-eight in Long Island City, the neighborhood in Queens where he grew up. Mac had met him once or twice, and he'd struck Mac as a good, conscientious cop. He always made sure that crime scenes were preserved and took some of the best notes of any uniform Mac had worked with.

Mac also knew that he, like far too many cops, was fighting alcohol addiction. He'd worn an AA pin on his uniform, which was against regulations, but his sergeant let him get away with it in light of his good work.

Four years ago, though, he had been instrumental in nailing a drug gang working out of the Robinsfield Houses. The gang had been led by one of Washburne's childhood friends.

Mac knew how difficult that could be.

Once the trial ended and Washburne's friend was convicted, Washburne handed in his shield and his weapon and became a community activist. He'd already converted to Islam, mainly because of its provisions against drinking alcohol, and after resigning from the department, he also changed his first name to Malik. He'd been doing good work helping to keep Long Island City clean after the arrest of their main drug gang. Last Mac had heard, he was volunteering at the Kinson Rehab Center on Queens Boulevard.

Turning to the CO escorting him—Flack's friend Sullivan—Mac asked, "How did Washburne wind up in here?"

Sullivan shrugged. "Fell off the wagon. Way he told it, one of the kids he was workin' with at that rehab center in Queens he volunteered at OD'd on him. He just *lost* it. Went to a liquor store, bought the first bottle he could grab off the shelf, and started guzzlin'. Then he got behind the wheel, ran a red light, and killed two people."

"That's a damn shame." And Mac meant it. Washburne was a good man, and it saddened him to see such a man brought so low by his addiction.

"Model prisoner, though," Sullivan said. "He did lotsa mediatin' between the Muslims and the skinheads. Honestly, he did more good than the damn ball game did."

The pair of them had now walked most of the way across the yard and were heading into the long building that housed Jack Mulroney.

"It's funny, Detective, me and Donnie were just talkin' about you today."

"Oh?" That surprised Mac.

"Yeah, we had breakfast—catchin' up, y'know? He told me you were the best."

"That was good of him." Mac knew the words sounded inadequate, but taking compliments had never been his strong suit. Besides, lately he didn't really feel like the best. How much of that was due to the way he lost control with Clay Dobson and how much was due to the way he was stumbling through his relationship with Peyton Driscoll, he couldn't say.

"Look, Donnie don't pay compliments that don't mean nothin'. He's got sincerity oozin' outta those blue eyes of his. So if he says you're the best, I'm inclined to believe him." He hesitated. "Which is good—'cause I can take or leave Barker, but Washburne was a good guy."

"We'll find out who killed him, Officer." Those words were said with more confidence. Barker's stabbing had distracted attention from Washburne, but Mac knew the evidence would point to his killer.

Just as Sullivan moved to open the door to A Block, the door opened from the inside. Another CO, a small, pale man with a large hook nose, was escorting a prisoner outside. Said prisoner was in leg irons. Mac was surprised a medium-security prison even *had* leg irons, since those were generally reserved for maximum-security facilities.

"Jesus, Grabowski, we were just comin' to see this asshole."

"This Mulroney?" Mac asked.

The other CO, Grabowski, said, "Yeah. I was told to bring him to interrogation."

"Perfect timing," Mac said. Mulroney's right arm was covered in blood. "Hold him still, please." He held up his camera and took several pictures. "I'm gonna need those clothes. I'll clear it with Flack," he added quickly when Grabowski started to object. "Just take us to where he can change. I'll bag his clothes, he can change into fresh ones, and then we'll talk to him."

Grabowski shrugged. "Fine, whatever."

Mulroney was quiet throughout these proceedings. He wasn't smiling, exactly, but he wasn't frowning either. Based on what Sullivan had said earlier, this was Mulroney's first kill. Mac remembered the first time he was responsible for taking a human life, when he served in the Marines in

Beirut. He hadn't thought it would be a big deal—
they'd trained him in this, after all—but the image
of the bullets from his M16A1 slicing into an
enemy soldier's body had been seared on his brain
ever since. He didn't sleep for several nights after
that.

Killing a person changed you. Jack Mulroney
was about to learn that lesson the hard way.

But while Mac had taken a life in the service of
his country, Mulroney had done so for personal
reasons. He would be punished. Mac would see to
that.

The procedure took several minutes: Mulroney
had to have the leg irons removed, the dickies
were taken off his person and put in one of Mac's
evidence bags, Mulroney put on fresh dickies, and
then Grabowski reapplied the leg irons. Sullivan
and Grabowski then escorted them both to interrogation, where Flack and Ursitti were waiting.

The interrogation room was a bland room that
they got to by walking down a bland corridor.
Most municipal buildings in New York City had a
similar look to them: off-white brick walls, brown
or green molding (brown, in this case), and filthy
linoleum floors. RHCF was no different.

Sullivan and Grabowski led them through a
wooden door into a small room that had a Formica
table with one chair on one side and two chairs on
the other. It looked like most every other interro-

gation room in the world: no clocks, no windows, no hint that there was a world beyond the room, aside from a small video camera in the corner. (Thanks to television, everyone knew that there was somebody watching on the other side of the two-way mirror, so most places had abandoned the pretense and lost the mirror, just sticking with a camera to record the interview. Besides, having a recording made things easier at the trial phase.)

Grabowski sat Mulroney down, leaving the leg irons on. A single handcuff was attached to the table, but the leg irons made that redundant.

Ursitti dismissed the other COs, leaving Mulroney alone with Flack, Ursitti, and Mac. Flack sat down across from Mulroney and started to remind him of his rights, but Mulroney cut him off.

"Let's cut the crap. I killed the asshole, all right?"

Flack looked up at Mac. "Damn, I'm good."

"Very funny," Mulroney said, "but what's the point of playing coy? El-Jabbar and the rest of his towelheads all saw me shiv the prick, and you guys probably got eighteen kinds of tests you can do on the shiv to show that I held it."

"Why'd you do it?" Flack asked. "You're just a garden-variety gay-basher. Why'd you graduate to murder?"

Mulroney shrugged. "Sonofabitch did a take-out slide."

"This was at the ball game?" Flack was taking notes now.

"Yeah." Mulroney looked up at Ursitti. "Some genius thought it'd help 'foster a commonality' between us and the towelheads if we played a nice friendly game of baseball. National pastime and all that shit." He snorted. "I don't even know what 'foster a commonality' *means*."

"So what happened?" Flack asked.

Mulroney shrugged again. "It was the top of the third. The towelheads were up. I was playing second, Hunt was at short."

"Brett Hunt," Ursitti added. "He's in for gay-bashing, too."

"Good guy," Mulroney said. "We made a good keystone."

"Yeah, I'm sure Derek Jeter and Robinson Canó bonded over beating up gay guys, too," Flack said sarcastically. "Get on with it."

"So Barker gets up and he draws a walk. Next guy was Yarnall."

"Ryan Yarnall," Ursitti said. "He's in for check fraud."

Mulroney laughed. "He hits like an accountant, too. He struck out on three pitches. Swings through every damn thing, it was hilarious. Then Yoba gets up."

"Greg Yoba, in for robbery."

"Right, and he grounds it to Hunt. I run to second, Hunt flips it to me, and I'm all set to turn around and throw to first, when, wham! The sonofabitch picks up his leg as he's sliding into second. My shin *still* hurts."

"That when the fight broke out?" Mac asked.

"Yeah. Bastard shouldn't have done that."

"So you killed him," Flack said.

Mulroney shrugged. "It wasn't right. And the COs broke it up before I could get my own back."

"In the majors," Flack said, "they don't shiv guys who do that."

Smiling, Mulroney said, "Well, maybe they should."

"This isn't a laughing matter," Mac snapped. "A man is dead. Before, you were getting out of here in a couple of years. Now, assuming you don't get the death penalty, you'll be spending the rest of your life in those green dickies, and not in as nice a place as this."

"Maybe," Mulroney said. "But he deserved it. At least I showed that sonofabitch what for. It was worth it just for that."

Flack had a few more perfunctory questions for Mulroney, but the interview was essentially over. The man had confessed. Mac would make sure the evidence supported that confession—and if it didn't, he'd find out what Mulroney was hiding.

But the Barker murder wasn't the real mystery here—Washburne was. To Ursitti, Mac said, "Lieutenant, I'd like to interview some of your COs."

"Well," Flack said, "we're definitely interviewing one of 'em. See, they're really not supposed to be able to *make* those toothbrush shivs."

Mac looked at Ursitti. "How would one of the inmates get their hands on a razor?"

"When they shave. They try that crap all the time, putting tinfoil in the safety razor so it looks like the blade's in there."

Frowning, Mac said, "Don't they use magnets to test that?"

"In max security, yeah. I, uh, managed to finagle getting us one." Ursitti suddenly was interested in the pattern on the linoleum floor.

Mac regarded the lieutenant. "You're not supposed to have one of those?"

"Ain't in the budget, and if it ain't in the budget, it ain't in the prison." Ursitti said those words as if they were a mantra he'd heard over and over again—probably from Russell. "But—well, let's just say we got us an electric magnet under the table."

"So who handled shaving this morning for Mulroney's block?"

Flack said, "According to the duty roster, it was Ciccone."

"That's the guy guard-dogging Hawkes."

Ursitti said, "Well, your guy's getting a new guard dog, 'cause Ciccone's ass'll be in that chair in a minute."

Sure enough, Ciccone came in a few minutes later, palming sweat off his forehead. No doubt he was grateful to be in the air-conditioned interview room after being outside for so long. Looking for all the world like an eight-year-old who'd been summoned to the principal's office, Ciccone fell more than sat in the chair.

Flack flipped through the pages of a clipboard that Ursitti had handed him. "According to this, you had shaving duty this morning in A Block."

"Yeah, that's right." Ciccone studied the table intently, not looking into Flack's, or anyone else's, eyes.

"You gave them each a safety razor."

"That's the procedure, yeah. They go inside, they do their business, then they gimme back the razors."

Mac said, "Isn't procedure also to check each of those razors when they give them back to make sure that the razors are intact?"

"Yeah, but there's, like, sixty guys in there, and they start pissing and moaning when you stop to check every single one. 'Sides, most of 'em don't bother, so I just check 'em randomly. That's SOP around here."

Flack put the clipboard down on the table. It only made a mild clack when he did, but Ciccone flinched.

"SOP is also to use a magnet to check the razor,"

Mac said. "According to Lieutenant Ursitti here, you've been issued an electric magnet that you're supposed to place every safety razor on to make sure that the blade's still in there."

Now Ciccone rolled his eyes, and Mac couldn't help but notice how bloodshot they were. Fresh sweat was beading on his forehead even though it was still nice and cool in the interrogation room.

"Right, SOP, sure. I wasn't 'issued' anything, and there ain't no procedure for that. Yeah, we got the magnet, but it ain't on any list of prison equipment, right, Lieutenant?"

Ursitti had remained calm throughout, but his eyes were blazing now as he said, "You know damn well we got that on the down-low, Ciccone—that doesn't change the fact that I ordered you to *use* the thing."

"Order? How can you order me to use something we ain't supposed to have?"

"I swear to you, Ciccone, there will be a disciplinary hearing, and—"

"Knock yourself out, Lieutenant." Ciccone was now looking straight at Ursitti. "But I didn't do anything wrong by not using that magnet."

Mac said, "Nevertheless, Officer Ciccone, Jack Mulroney was able to create a weapon used for murder thanks to your negligence. Even if you hadn't used the magnet, you didn't actually *check* Mulroney's razor."

"I told you, I was doing a random—"

"It didn't occur to you to check the razor of the man who got into a brawl the previous day?"

Ciccone had nothing to say to that, which didn't surprise Mac, so he continued: "I don't suppose the fact that you didn't use the magnet had anything to do with your four-alarm hangover?"

At that, Ciccone tensed. So did Ursitti, though it was due to anger rather than nervousness. The CO said, "I don't know what—"

"You're sweating, your eyes are bloodshot, you're sensitive to noise. The magnet's electric, so it makes a humming noise—that probably would've driven you crazy." Mac leaned forward, his palms resting on the table, and stared right at Ciccone. "A man's dead because of your negligence, Officer Ciccone. Maybe we can't nail you for not using the magnet, but I intend to make sure that you pay for your role in this."

"Fine," Ciccone said, "then I ain't saying a god-damn thing without my lawyer."

"Then we're done here," Flack said. He looked at Ursitti, who sent Ciccone to wait in the captain's office.

They talked to a few more COs, among them Sullivan. They all more or less repeated the same story, corroborating what the evidence seemed to indicate.

At least as it pertained to the Barker murder.

The details of the Washburne murder remained elusive.

"I didn't see a damn thing," Sullivan said. "And I don't mind tellin' you, I'm really pissed off about it. Washburne was a good police back in the day, and he was what you call your model prisoner. I mean, mosta these guys, the ones that aren't stone-cold assholes, they try to be polite, y'know? They figure it'll help with parole and all that— but Washburne was genuine. He was—what's the word—repentant, that's it."

Mac smiled. "That's where the word *penitentiary* comes from. A place intended to make a criminal repent."

"Yeah, that's prob'ly why they changed it to *correctional facility*, 'cause these guys mostly don't go in for repenting." Sullivan snorted. "Course, they ain't all that correct, neither."

When they were finished with Sullivan, a final CO came in: Randy Andros.

Flack was looking at a different clipboard this time. "You've only been here a month?"

Andros nodded. "Worked in Sing Sing for the last few years. My wife got a job in Jersey, so we moved to Elizabeth, and the commute to Ossining from there sucks." He shook his head. "I'm sorry I bothered."

Ursitti said, "They'll get over it."

"Over what?" Mac asked with a frown.

"The COs," Ursitti said. "They assume any new guy is a rat."

Mac hardly needed that bit of slang to be translated: a new CO was assumed to be a mole from Internal Affairs. Having recently been subject to the whims of the NYPD's own Internal Affairs Unit, Mac could understand the disdain.

"So I get treated like crap. Kind of a comedown after actually getting *invited* to weekly poker games and dinners and stuff."

As much as Mac sympathized, he really wasn't interested in this man's personal life. Neither was Flack, as he immediately started asking questions about Mulroney, about Barker, and about Washburne.

Andros had nothing new to add about the former two, but he had a radically different perspective on the latter: "He was just another asshole. Probably pissed somebody off and got himself conked on the head."

"You didn't like him?" Mac asked.

"We're not supposed to *like* the convicts, Detective, we're supposed to *guard* them. I don't get why this guy was supposed to be treated differently just because he used to be a cop. He's just like all the rest." Andros barked a bitter laugh. "He even tried the usual crap with his meds."

"What do you mean?" Flack asked.

"Most of these guys are on medication. Some

of them try all sorts of tricks to not take their pills. This morning, I was supervising the distribution of meds in Charlie Block, and Washburne tried to palm his Klonopin."

"That's used to treat anxiety," Mac said. "Not surprising for a morally centered man who committed vehicular homicide."

"Morally centered, right," Andros said with a shrug. "If he's so damn morally centered, why'd he start drinking again? And don't give me that 'alcoholism is a disease' crapola. You get a disease, you don't have a choice, but you *choose* to walk into the bar and order a beer, know what I mean?"

Mac was starting to suspect that there was more to Andros's socialization troubles than just the COs' belief that he might be a rat, but said nothing.

Once they finished with Andros, Danny and Sheldon joined them in the interrogation room. Danny said, "Hope that 'copter ain't got a weight limit, 'cause we packed up half the yard to bring back with us."

"Plus two bodies," Sheldon said. "I'll do up the receipt for that."

Mac nodded. RHCF would need receipts for the bodies of both Washburne and Barker. Normally, it would have to be from the medical examiner, but Sheldon's time as an ME meant he was authorized to provide it in the absence of someone currently attached to the ME's office.

Flack leaned back in his chair. "I've got about eight million more people to talk to."

"I'll stay and give you a hand." Mac turned to his subordinates. "You two, get back to the lab, start processing everything. And tell Peyton, or whichever ME's on duty, that Washburne's the priority of the two."

Sheldon nodded. "Sure thing, Mac."

They headed for the door. Mac followed them both into the corridor. "Sheldon, any thoughts on what happened to Washburne?"

"Looks like somebody hit him on the head with a weight. Beyond that . . ." Sheldon shrugged. "With any luck, we'll find something on the weight, but there were forty-five people in there, and it's a public place. It's going to be hard to find any trace evidence that'd be meaningful, especially with a murder weapon that's been touched by so many people."

"Well, Flack and I will be talking to all forty-three suspects. See what you can find."

"We're on it, Mac."

With that, the pair of them headed down the corridor, accompanied by two COs.

Mac knew that convictions usually came from a combination of eyewitness testimony and forensic evidence. One was good, but both were better. With that in mind, he trusted Sheldon and Danny to find the latter, while he stayed behind to help Flack with the former.

10

STELLA HAD ALREADY TAKEN an instant dislike to Jack Morgenstern, and she found that she could easily extend that sentiment to his lawyer.

Courtney Bracey was a very attractive woman: pale skin, short dark hair, perfect teeth, a cleft chin, and penetrating brown eyes. She wore an Armani suit that practically advertised how expensive it was.

Morgenstern, though, didn't bother dressing up. He was wearing a red T-shirt with what looked to Stella like a Southwestern Indian design in black on the chest, black jeans, and black Rockports. His long brown hair was tied back in a ponytail.

"My client," Bracey said as soon as the two detectives entered the interrogation room, "is willing to cooperate with you up to a point. If at any stage it looks as if he is being accused of a crime, I will end this interview until such time as you place my client under arrest."

"By the way," Morgenstern said, "nice touch coming in twenty minutes after our appointment was for. Courtney wanted me to get up and walk out after five, but I'm in a good mood today."

"The delay was unavoidable," Angell said as she sat down. "We—"

Morgenstern held up a hand. "Spare me. I know all the techniques—you let the perp stew in his own juices for a while before coming to talk to him, figuring the boredom might drive him to talk. Bravo, you learned Interrogation Technique Number One. Let's move on, okay?"

Stella shot Angell a *this is gonna be fun* look.

"Are you aware of the fact that Maria Campagna is dead?"

Looking confused, Morgenstern said, "No, but that's mostly by virtue of not having the first clue who Maria Campagna *is*."

"She was one of the young women who worked at Belluso's Bakery."

Now his face fell, his eyes growing wide. His surprise certainly seemed genuine. The majority of killers were dumb as posts and bad actors, but Stella had met plenty of good fakers on the job, too.

"Jesus, *Maria*? She's *dead*?"

"Yes."

"Oh my God. I—I didn't know her last name, but—"

Angell took out some of Lindsay's crime scene photos. Unsurprisingly, she'd chosen the grisliest of them. "Someone strangled her. Someone wearing a black sweatshirt. Someone who went into Belluso's just before closing time."

Morgenstern refused to look at the pictures. "I really don't need to see that, and I don't appreciate Interrogation Technique Number Two, either." Now he seemed to be over the surprise. "Oh, and for the record, yes, I was wearing a black sweatshirt last night. So was half of New York."

"So you knew the victim?" Angell asked.

"Yes. Maria was a friend of mine."

"So good a friend," Stella said, "that you don't know her last name?"

"Believe what you want. I went into Belluso's all the time, but it was all first names. I don't think any of the people there know my last name, either."

That was actually true—O'Malley only knew it because he had Morgenstern's business card—but Stella saw no reason to share that.

Angell said, "Witnesses saw you going into Belluso's right before closing."

"I assume by *witnesses* you mean Annie, since the only people who saw me were her and Maria."

"Answer the question," Angell said tartly.

Bracey was equally tart. "You didn't ask one, Detective, you made a statement. If you ask a question, my client will be happy to respond to it."

"All right, then, how much is he paying you to be a pain in my ass?"

Her eyes flickering over Angell's T-shirt and jeans, Bracey said, "More than you could afford, I'm sure."

"Saucer of milk, table one," Stella muttered.

"I'm sorry, Detective?" Bracey said.

"Never mind."

Morgenstern, Stella noticed, was smiling and leaning back in his chair—and then he winced. She recalled how stiffly he was walking when she and Angell saw him at his house earlier.

"Mr. Morgenstern," she said, "why were you coming into Belluso's so late?"

"I just got out of fighting class. I take karate at a dojo that's just around the corner from Belluso's—it's called Riverdale Pinan Karate." He smiled. "*Pinan* is Japanese for 'peace and harmony,' by the way."

"So naturally," Stella said, "you take fighting classes there."

"A great way to achieve peace and harmony is to blow off steam, Detective."

Stella couldn't actually argue with that—she'd abused many a punching bag in her time after a particularly stressful day.

Morgenstern went on: "I'm usually dehydrated after class, and the dojo only sells Gatorade, which I can't stand. So I come into Belluso's and get a bottle of water. I saw Annie leaving, and Maria was behind the counter. I asked for water, she gave it to me, I paid for it, I left."

"Did you like Maria, Mr. Morgenstern?" Angell asked.

"Sure. I like all the women who work there. I flirt with them all the time—it's fun. Part of the atmosphere."

"You do know that many of them are underage, right?"

Bracey tapped a finger on the table. "Don't even *think* about going there, Detective. This department has already tried to make my client into a rapist—you try making him into a pedophile, and he'll be able to buy a much bigger house this time. Stick with what happened on the night of Ms. Campagna's death."

"Fine," Stella said. "Did you flirt with Maria last night?"

"Probably." Morgenstern shrugged. "I honestly don't remember. I was exhausted."

"So you don't remember getting into a fight with her? Maybe her punching you?"

"What?"

Bracey started, "Detective—"

But Stella barged on. "How'd you hurt your ribs?"

"*Senpai* John kicked me in the ribs. He's seventeen years old and doesn't know his own strength, and I didn't block his side kick in time."

Angell smiled. "You got beat up by a teenager?"

"A teenager who's a black belt, Detective, that's why I call him '*Senpai* John.' The word *senpai* is Japanese for 'senior student.' He's been taking karate since he was four. I've been taking karate since I turned thirty-five, and I'm only a green belt. He's just a little bit better at it than I am—for now."

Stella reached into her bag and took out her Nikon. "I'm going to need to take pictures of any bruising on your chest. If you want to make this difficult, I'll get a warrant—we're already getting one for your apartment, so . . ."

Morgenstern and Bracey exchanged glances. Bracey said, "I don't think it's a good idea."

"They're getting a warrant anyhow," Morgenstern said with a shrug. "She brought her camera and everything." He lifted his shirt.

The beginnings of bruises were forming over Morgenstern's sternum. No obvious impressions from a fist, but the Nikon's resolution was a lot better than Stella's eyes. They'd examine the photo in the lab.

As she took the pictures, Stella asked, "Do you wear protective gear in fighting class?"

"Yeah. Boxing gloves over wrist wraps, full headgear, foot protection, jockstrap. I usually wear shin guards, too, and some of the women wear chest protectors."

Once she was finished photographing and Morgenstern lowered his shirt, Stella said, "We'll also need your clothes from last night."

"You're welcome to them, but I already washed them—and before you start screaming 'smoking gun!' at me, I was sweating like a stuck pig last night. As soon as I walked in the door, I tossed my clothes and my *gi* into the washer."

"Ghee?" Stella asked.

Angell answered. "His karate uniform."

"Is there anything else, Detectives?" Bracey asked.

"Not yet," Angell said, "but after we search your house, we may have more questions."

"Assuming you get the warrant," Bracey said, "that's fine."

"They'll get the warrant," Morgenstern said dismissively. "There's hundreds of judges in the city—at least one of them has to owe one of these two a favor. Besides, their probable cause actually doesn't suck too badly."

"Gee, thanks," Stella said.

"I'll be present when you serve the warrant,"

Bracey said as she and Morgenstern rose to their feet.

"Thanks for the warning," Angell said with a sweet smile.

After they left, Angell looked at Stella. "Whaddaya think, Stell?"

"I think we need to take a trip back up to Riverdale and talk to the people at Riverdale Pinan Karate, and see if we can get a piece of footgear. I want something to compare those bruises to."

"Yeah, and I want to talk to this *Senpai* John kid."

"To verify his story?"

Angell nodded. "And if he really did kick that jackass in the ribs, to shake his hand."

"*Oh* yeah," Stella said.

"I'm liking this guy more and more for our killer," Angell continued. "He washed the clothes—and he knows procedure enough that he knows it's suspicious, but it's also reasonable for him to have done so after a fighting class." She smiled. "I love perps like him—they think they're smarter than they really are. Makes it that much more fun to take them down."

"Assuming it *is* him," Stella said. "The only trace we've found so far is the world's most generic fiber."

"Well, we'll see what happens when we toss his

house—not to mention when you guys get the results back on her bruises."

A uniform stuck his head in the door. "Detectives, I got a guy here, says he has an appointment—Robert DelVecchio?"

"Yeah." Angell brightened. "Show him in."

DelVecchio was a tall man with no discernible neck and a barrel chest that would've been more impressive without the developing beer gut. Stella figured him to be in his early twenties, yet his brown hair was already showing the beginnings of male pattern baldness. He was wearing a T-shirt with the words MT. ST. VINCENT FOOTBALL emblazoned on the front and knee-length white shorts, revealing tree-trunk-sized legs. Stella knew the type: school jock whose glory days were already in the rearview mirror.

"Mr. DelVecchio? I'm Detective Angell, this is Detective Bonasera."

"Pleased to meet ya." DelVecchio was holding a sheaf of papers in his hands, which he plunked down on the table before he sat down. "Here's your murderer. Find this guy, you find who killed Maria."

Stella picked up the papers. They were all letters addressed to Maria, but unsigned. All were printed on a laser or ink-jet printer of some sort. "Who sent these?"

"Hell if *I* know. That's why I brought them to *you* people."

Angell muttered, "Knew this was too good to be true."

"Look, all I know is, it was someone at Belluso's."

"How do you know that?" Stella asked.

" 'Cause that's what Maria told me. She said it was no big deal, but I knew this guy was nutsy-cuckoo, y'know?" He slapped one meaty hand on the table. "I kept trying to get her to quit that damn place, but would she listen? That girl had a mind of her own, y'know?"

"Yeah, I hate when that happens," Angell said dryly. "When did the letters start coming?"

"I'm not sure. I only found out about them a couple weeks ago, and she wouldn't tell me when it started, but I figure at least six months. She's been at Belluso's eight months, so it couldn't have been more than that."

Stella started reading one of the letters aloud. "'Dear Maria. How do I love thee? Let me count the ways that I could love you. Number one—'"

"Do you have to read that out loud?" DelVecchio asked plaintively.

Flipping to the next one, Stella said, "He misquotes Shakespeare on the next one, too." She started riffling through them. "Ooh, he does a haiku here—and the next one's got a detailed description of what he wants to do to her in the bakery bathroom."

"It's disgusting!" DelVecchio cried.

"Can we keep these?" Stella asked.

DelVecchio recoiled. "I sure as hell don't want them."

"Do you have any guesses who it might be?"

"How the hell should *I* know? I mean, sure, there were lots of guys who went in there, and Maria's a hottie, y'know? If she wasn't already my girl, I'd have been hitting on her too. But I didn't know none of those guys. I don't like those kinds of places—too froofy. Gimme a Starbucks any day of the week."

"So noted. While you're here, Mr. DelVecchio," Stella said, "we're going to need some blood and DNA—if you don't mind."

DelVecchio shrugged. "Why should I mind? You do that, you can eliminate me as a suspect, right?"

Relieved, Stella took out her kit. DelVecchio had struck her as the type who would give her a hard time about it just on general principles. "Exactly."

"If it makes it easier to find Maria's killer, I'll give you my left arm."

Angell asked DelVecchio a few more general questions while Stella took his blood and swabbed his cheek. Then he left.

After he was gone, Stella thwapped the letters into a neat pile and said, "I'm gonna take these letters to the lab to see if we can trace the provenance of the printer that made it."

"Good luck."

She snorted. "We're gonna need it. Handwriting you can trace. Even typewriters would sometimes have something distinctive about different models—especially the old manuals, they went off-kilter when you looked at them funny. But printers? They're mass produced. There might be DNA on the more recent ones, though."

"Let's hope so," Angell said.

11

FINGERPRINTS WERE FIRST USED as a tool for identification purposes in criminal investigations in the nineteenth century. The first known instance of fingerprints being discussed was in an anatomy text published in Breslau in 1823. It wasn't until the later part of the century that people started applying them to criminalistics—though the idea didn't take at first. Sheldon Hawkes remembered the first time he'd read with surprise that Dr. Henry Faulds—who'd published a paper on prints in 1880 in *Nature*—offered the notion of using fingerprints to identify criminals to the Metropolitan Police in London. They refused, dismissing the entire notion as fanciful.

Hawkes often wondered if the people who rejected the notion realized their mistake. It was like the person who wanted to close the U.S. Patent Office in the early part of the twentieth century because he thought everything that could be invented had been invented, or the people in the 1940s who saw television as a passing fad, or the people in the 1970s who couldn't imagine what possible use people would ever have for a computer in their homes.

The definitive work on the subject was *Finger Prints*, a book published in 1892 by Sir Francis Galton, which included all ten of Galton's own fingerprints as an illustration on the title page.

Hawkes had actually found a leather-bound copy of the book in the Strand one day last year and bought it for Mac as a combination Christmas and belated thank-you present for moving him over to fieldwork. It had been two years, and Hawkes had no regrets about leaving the morgue. Besides, he knew the place was safe in Peyton Driscoll's hands.

For one thing, it meant he got to play with fingerprints. Although Hawkes had wanted to be a doctor since he was a kid, he'd always had an interest in forensic science, going back to when he read *Pudd'nhead Wilson* by Mark Twain, one of the first works of fiction to make use of the nascent field of dactyloscopy.

From a forensic perspective, the good thing about fingerprints was that they were everywhere.

The same papers that first postulated the uniqueness of fingerprints in the nineteenth century also
pointed out the uniqueness of palm-, toe-, and
soleprints. All of those extremities secreted oils
from the eccrine glands that were often left behind
on things touched by that particular body part in
the pattern of the dermal papillae (ridges) that
made up the prints.

But people touched things with their fingers
considerably more often than they did their palms
or any part of their feet, so fingers became the
focal point.

The bad thing about fingerprints was that
while they were everywhere, they were often
incomplete. Criminals weren't always considerate
enough to leave perfect impressions of their entire finger whenever they touched something at a
crime scene.

And sometimes they touched things that had
already been touched repeatedly by others. Case in
point: the weights in the yard from RHCF.

The actual method for making latent prints visible hadn't changed overmuch since Galton's day:
you used powder of some kind. In the old days,
you'd cover the surface with the powder, then
gently blow it away. What remained behind had
adhered to the eccrine gland secretions, which
were left in the pattern of the fingerprint.

At least in theory. Sometimes those prints were

smudged, particularly when several people in succession had touched the thing and left plenty of sweat on it. That sweat also tended to make regular powders clump, messing up the latent print. For that reason, Hawkes went with contrasting powder, which he applied gently with a magnetic brush. One of the advantages of his years as a surgeon was that it made it easier for him to keep his hand steady while applying the magnetic powder. Danny had been particularly cranky when Hawkes got the hang of it after only a few hours—it had taken Danny months to get it right.

Hawkes had taken the doughnut weight that appeared to have been used to kill Malik Washburne, as well as the barbell and the other doughnut weights on it. The latter were really for comparison purposes, to see if he could figure out who had been using the weights besides the vic.

After taking photos of the powdered weights, Hawkes used acetate stickers to pull up anything that even resembled a fingerprint. The porous nature of the metal in the weights was such that the stickers might not work, so he had the photos as backup. As he pulled each print, he placed the sticker on his flatbed 1000-DPI scanner. The slowness of the scan was offset by the small size of the image being scanned, so it took about an hour for Hawkes to get everything that looked even vaguely like a print onto the lab computer's mainframe.

Unfortunately, some of the prints were very vague indeed. The vast majority of them were too smudged and/or incomplete to get enough of an arch, loop, or whorl to even attempt a match.

The only place where he got anything solid was on the barbell itself—unsurprising, since that had to be gripped tightly in order to be used properly.

Ursitti had provided a list of the forty-five inmates who were in the weight yard at the time of Washburne's death, and since they were all obviously in the penal system, their prints were conveniently on file. Another issue with fingerprints was the sheer volume of prints to compare them to, a number that grew larger every day, particularly in this post-9/11, security-conscious world. While having a larger field of people to compare to increased the chance of a match, it also increased the time it took to do comparison scans.

Luckily, Hawkes had a good starting point. If the prints weren't a match for any of the forty-five in question, then he'd expand the search to the inmates and employees of RHCF. If *that* didn't match—well, then they had a mystery on their hands, and he'd expand the search further.

While he waited for the search to run its course, he called up the digital photos of the crime scene, selecting the ones he'd taken of Washburne's head wound with the ruler next to it. He got up, double-checked the size of the doughnut weight, then called up the photo of the weight and resized it so its image was proportional to that of the picture of Washburne. Using the mouse, he cut out the weight from one photo and then dragged it over to the wound.

The weight fit perfectly in the wound. (Instinctively, he kept thinking of the weight as the murder weapon, but his years as an ME had taught him never to make assumptions until the cause of death was determined, and Dr. Driscoll hadn't done the autopsy yet.)

He'd saved the images at various stages and now appended all those images to his report, quickly typing in the results.

Shortly after he finished that task, the computer finished its comparison of the fingerprints. Hawkes had recovered seven decent prints from the barbell and one from the doughnut weight. Two of the barbell prints belonged to Malik Washburne.

The one on the doughnut weight and the other five on the barbell belonged to Jorge Melendez. Alt-Tabbing to another window, Hawkes called up Melendez's sheet from the database. He was doing time for possession with intent to sell.

Pulling his Treo out of his pocket and removing his plastic-frame glasses, Hawkes called Mac.

Then he hung up after the first ring, remembering that Mac's own phone was still sitting in the arsenal at RHCF.

Putting his glasses back on, he Alt-Tabbed his desktop computer over to an Internet browser and accessed the phone directory on the NYPD's intranet. It didn't take him long to find RHCF's number, and he called that, asking for Captain Russell.

"Captain Russell can't come to the phone right now," he was told.

"This is Dr. Sheldon Hawkes of the New York Crime Lab. I actually need to speak to Detective Mac Taylor or Detective Don Flack. They're both on-site interviewing witnesses in the incident you guys had today."

"Can I have your badge number, please?"

Hawkes gave it.

"Hold, please."

Adam popped his head into the lab and saw that Hawkes was on the phone. "I'll come back," he whispered.

Hawkes removed the Treo from his ear, put it on speaker, and set it down on the table. "S'okay, I'm on hold. What is it?"

"I ran that dried blood first, like you asked." Adam said. "It wasn't Washburne's, and it wasn't Barker's."

Hawkes nodded in acknowledgment. It made sense to run those two comparisons first, especially given how much of Barker's blood had splattered all over the yard.

"It's AB negative." Adam held out a sheet of

paper. "I sent it to DNA, but in the meantime, I checked it against the other forty-three guys in the yard, and only three people had that blood type."

Hawkes took the paper from Adam and saw the three names on the list: HAKIM EL-JABBAR, JORGE MELENDEZ, TYRONE STANLEY.

"Sheldon?" That was Mac's voice on speakerphone.

"Yeah, Mac, it's me. Listen, have you talked to an inmate named Jorge Melendez yet?"

"Not yet—but he's on the list. Why?"

"Melendez's prints, along with Washburne's, are on the barbell Washburne was using, and Melendez's was the only usable print on the weight that cut Washburne's head open."

"All right, thanks. And write this number down." Mac read out a phone number with a 718 area code. "I already gave it to Danny when he called. Call that number directly if you need to reach me or Flack."

Hawkes made a note of it. "Got it. What did Danny tell you?"

"Plenty of clear prints on the toothbrush, and they all belonged to Jack Mulroney."

"So we've got one dunker, at least." Dunkers, or slam-dunks, were the cases that law enforcement lived for: where the perp confessed, the evidence all agreed with the confession, and the case could be put down with a minimum of fuss and effort.

"Yeah," Mac said. "Let me know what else you find."

After Mac hung up, Hawkes picked up the Treo and entered the new number in his contact list. Looking up at Adam, he said, "Let me know when that DNA comes in."

"Will do. Oh, yeah, I also ID'd that fiber you found on the vic's shoulder."

Hawkes Smirked. "Let me guess—comes from prison dickies, right?"

"Yes and no. You see, I am smarter than the average bear, and I determined that the thread you found specifically is a thread used to sew the seams on the pants of New York State Department of Corrections convict uniforms—and *only* the pants. They use a different kind of thread for the shirt seams."

At that Hawkes frowned. "How did a thread from a pair of pants get on our guy's shoulder?"

Smiling beneath his beard, Adam said, "That, my friend, is *your* problem."

"A problem for later. Right now, I'm gonna go bug Peyton."

"I'm sure she'll love that," Adam said dryly.

Grinning, Hawkes removed his glasses, dropped them in his white lab coat pocket, and headed downstairs to the morgue.

Hawkes had succeeded Peyton Driscoll as the chief medical examiner when she left the job to take a teaching position at Columbia University. In the interview she had conducted with Hawkes before he took over, she'd said, in that clipped British tone of hers, that she needed "a spot of mundanity." When Peyton finally returned, a year after Hawkes moved to the field, Peyton claimed to have decided that teaching was too "routine." Hawkes had asked her what happened to the spot of mundanity, and Peyton had replied, "I got it out with some detergent, and I'm back in the saddle."

As he approached the morgue, Hawkes saw the perfectly coiffed silver hair of Deputy Inspector Gerrard opening the door ahead of him.

With a due sense of anticipation and dread, Hawkes jogged to catch up to him. "Inspector."

Turning around, Gerrard said, "Dr. Hawkes. I'm guessing we're both here for the same reason."

Gerrard had already been the one to bring them this case, and now he was checking on the ME personally. Hawkes saw no way in which that could be construed as a good thing. He squared his shoulders and followed Gerrard into the morgue.

"Dr. Driscoll," Gerrard said in what he probably thought was an amiable tone, "what can you tell me about Malik Washburne?"

Peyton looked up, and her face went sour. "Inspector. At the moment, I can't tell you much, as I haven't started the autopsy yet."

"Well, whatever you do find, trace-wise, put a

rush on it, and use my name. This case gets top priority."

"It does?"

Gerrard glared at Hawkes with penetrating eyes. "Yes, Doctor, it does. What possible problem could you have with that?"

Gerrard's defensiveness might be understandable given his recent sparring with Mac, but that didn't mean Hawkes had to like it. "I was just surprised, that's all. I wouldn't think two deaths in custody would get this kind of heat."

"Well, it does, and for two reasons. For one thing, Washburne was a member. He did wrong, but he was doing his time like a good soldier, and he deserved better than what he got."

Hawkes couldn't argue with that.

"Not to mention, RHCF hasn't had a DIC in twenty years, and now they got two in one day. Albany's nervous."

Peyton smiled insincerely. "And it's budget time, so naturally you wish to stay on Albany's good side."

"Staying on Albany's good side gets you geeks all your fancy toys, Doc," Gerrard said. "Speaking of which, what do those toys say about Washburne?"

"Not much so far," Peyton said, "again, by virtue of my not having begun the autopsy yet. However, I can say this much: the vast majority of the blood that we found on his body wasn't his. I sent it for DNA analysis."

"Did you type it?" Hawkes asked.

Peyton nodded. "O-positive."

Hawkes rubbed his chin with his right hand. "That's Barker's type, so it's probably spatter from his wound. I'll double-check the pattern of the O-positive blood on him with his position and Barker's."

Gerrard folded his arms over his coffee-stained tie. "How much of the blood was Washburne's own?"

"Just what I found near the head wound."

"That doesn't make sense," Gerrard said. "Head wounds gush like a sonofabitch."

Hawkes regarded Gerrard. "Right."

"Don't give me that look, Hawkes—I *have* been a cop for a bunch of years now. I picked up a thing or two."

"Well, I've sent blood to the lab for tox," Peyton said, "and I'll check stomach contents and the rest. As soon as I have something, I'll let both of you know. However, I won't have anything with you two standing here playing mother hen."

Having always hated it when people kibbitzed over his own autopsies, Hawkes put up both hands and backed away from the table. "Sorry. I'll get out of your way."

"I'll ride herd on the lab," Gerrard said, following Hawkes toward the exit. "Get those results."

"Thank you, Inspector," Peyton said as she grabbed her scalpel.

As he left with Gerrard, Hawkes said, "Thanks for the help."

"I figure you guys need all the help you can get," Gerrard said with an obnoxious grin. "Besides, Sinclair wants this one, too. He and Washburne rode a blue-and-white together back in the day."

Brigham Sinclair was the chief of detectives and the other person who had raked Mac over the coals during the whole Dobson mess. It probably killed him to know that he had to rely on Mac to solve this case. But Hawkes knew better than to say anything. His usual solution to office politics was to keep his head down and duck the shrapnel.

Gerrard asked, "We have anything like a suspect?"

"We might," Hawkes said. "The weight that caused the head wound had a lot of smudged prints, but one was clear—guy named Jorge Melendez. Flack's questioning him now." Hawkes thought it more politic to only mention Flack, who had served under Gerrard's command, rather than Mac. "He was in the yard at the time, and he was probably the last person to touch the weight that smashed Washburne's head in. But we're a long way from proving that," he added quickly, so as not to get Gerrard's hopes up.

But Gerrard, as he had so snidely pointed out,

had been a cop for a while now. He nodded as they got to the elevator bank. "Good. Keep me posted, Hawkes. I don't want this one getting screwed up."

"We're on it."

"That's what worries me," Gerrard muttered.

Hawkes managed to force himself not to say anything. He knew the best revenge would be to put the case down, and soon.

Jorge Melendez really had no idea that the guy was an undercover cop.

He'd thought he'd had good cop radar. Twice, he'd figured some junkie for a UC, and he'd been right both times. Two of his *hermanos*, Pablo and Jimmy, had gotten popped selling to the same guy that Jorge wouldn't go near.

Jorge was strictly independent. He didn't want to get caught up in that gang shit. He had a source that sold him decent shit for a decent price. It wasn't nothing huge, wasn't nothing he could build an empire with, but it allowed him to make himself a living, and in this world, what more could you ask for, really?

Mostly he sold to college kids. Some years he figured he could just sell during finals week and he'd be able to pay the rent for six months. The best part about selling to students was that he had turnover. Meant the cops couldn't find patterns, at least not without looking too hard. Plus, they were all focused on the gangs. They usually left a small-time entrepreneur like Jorge alone.

Then he found out the hard way that the cops knew all about him, they just didn't give much of a damn—which suited him fine—until they needed someone to drop a dime on someone called Ray-Ray. Jorge had heard about Ray-Ray—ran heroin out of Alphabet City, but that was all he knew. The cops had figured they'd bust Jorge, get him to flip on Ray-Ray. But he didn't have anything to flip.

Nothing pissed off cops more than messing with their plans. Since they couldn't use Jorge to trade up to Ray-Ray, they went crazy on him. He couldn't afford a good lawyer, so he got stuck with some white chick of a public defender who didn't know her skinny ass from her bony elbows and landed Jorge in RHCF.

His only hope was parole. Then he'd be back on the streets before his hair went gray. He figured the best way to do that was to go all Malcolm X and become a Muslim. When he saw that one of the other cons—dude named Malik Washburne—was offering a Koran class, he figured that was the best way to start.

But just like the UC cop, Jorge misjudged seriously on that one.

Now, after both Washburne and Vance got

themselves iced in the weight yard, the whole place had gone into lockdown. That meant everyone was in his dorm, and the TVs were only showing one thing. Jorge hated it. Only thing he ever watched on TV outside was pay-per-view porn, and they didn't let them watch anything that good inside, so Jorge mostly ignored it.

Then one of the COs—Jorge didn't know his name on purpose; bastards didn't deserve names, they were just bullies with nightsticks—took him out to talk to a detective.

Actually, he was talking to two detectives. They both had dark hair. The one in the suit who was sitting had blue eyes and smirked a lot. The other one was standing up, wearing just a suit jacket and button-down shirt without the tie, and he looked like he scowled all the time. They introduced themselves as Detective Flack and Mac Taylor.

"Flack and Mac," Jorge said. "That's cute. You two should go onna road or somethin'."

"Glad you approve," Flack said. "So tell me, Jorge—what were you doing in the weight yard yesterday?"

If the questions were all *this* stupid, this might actually wind up being fun. There was a CO in the room, too, but Jorge ignored him like he did the COs most of the time. "Liftin' weights."

"Anything else?"

"Not till one of them skinheads shivved Vance."

"What about Malik Washburne?"

"What *about* him?"

"You see him die?"

"Saw him on the ground. Shit, I was the one told the COs he got iced."

Flack—or was it Mac? Jorge had already lost track—smiled. "And damn neighborly of you that was, too. Did you interact with him at all prior to that?"

"Yeah, I used the bench 'fore he did." Jorge was glad they were just talking about the yard. As long as they didn't talk about the damn Koran class, he was okay.

"Before him, huh?" Flack said. "You figure you could get back into his Koran class if you gave up the bench for him?"

Shit. "I don't know what you mean."

"Yeah, you do. You signed up for Washburne's Koran class. Probably figured if you wore a dashiki and knelt to Allah a few times, the parole board would go easy on you."

Jorge snarled. "That's interferin' with my religious rights, yo!"

Mac talked for the first time. "Which way do you kneel when you pray to Allah?"

Suddenly, Jorge got nervous. He was pretty sure he knew that one. Had something to do with the sun, he thought. "East—the way the sun rises."

"Actually," Mac said with a smile, "it's toward Mecca. Nice try, though."

Flack was holding a folder and was flipping through it. "I got a report here from Officer Sullivan. He said that yesterday, during Malik Washburne's Koran class, he informed you that trying to fake a religious conversion to improve your parole chances was, and I quote, 'an insult to Allah.'"

"And that was when you hit him," Mac said.

It wasn't like he could deny it, so Jorge said, "Yeah, I took a swing at him, but I didn't hit him or nothin'. He hit me, though. *Pendejo* got me right in the nose!"

"According to the infirmary report," Mac said, "it wasn't broken, but it did bleed a lot. Some of that blood got on Washburne, and we found it on his body."

"Yeah, so we got into it, so what? That don't mean I killed him."

"And yet," Flack said, "you got the trifecta: means, motive, *and* opportunity. We got your prints on the weight that killed him."

"I told you I *used* that weight right before he did! And yeah, I figured I'd suck up to his sorry ass so I could get back in the Koran class. There ain't nobody but Allah in my life now."

Flack looked up at Mac. Unless it was the other way around. "You can just *feel* the religious fervor, can'tcha?"

"Oozing out of his pores," Mac said. Then he leaned forward and stared at him with his scary-ass eyes. "The evidence is piling up against you, Jorge. Malik Washburne had a lot of friends in here. It'd go easier if you confess now."

Jorge was no fool. Cops only said that when they didn't have anything. If they were sure, they'd arrest him. Not that it mattered that much—he wasn't going anywhere for another two years, and then only if he made parole—but he wasn't making their lives easier, either. "Screw you, cop. I didn't kill Washburne. I ain't a killer."

"Yeah, well," Flack said, "neither was Jack Mulroney."

"Yeah, but white folks is crazy. I'm just a businessman bidin' his time in the service of Allah."

Flack and Mac looked at each other, then Mac said, "We're done here. For now, anyhow."

As the CO took Jorge back to his dorm, he wondered what would happen next. He was nothing but a wannabe Muslim, and el-Jabbar had been giving him static on the subject. Getting into it with Washburne didn't help. If word got out that he was prime suspect number one, he was seriously screwed.

Luckily, cops weren't the type to go gossiping. Jorge figured he was safe as long as the cops didn't say anything, and they wouldn't unless and until they actually *had* something. If that happened, they'd arrest whoever they had, and he'd be safe then.

At least, Jorge hoped that would be how it worked.

· ·   ·   · · · ·   ·   ·

After Melendez was taken out, Mac asked who was next on the list.

Ursitti consulted his clipboard. "Karl Fischer. He's—"

"I know what he's in for." Mac shook his head. Fischer had shot three young men in a subway car, killing one, leaving one in a coma, and paralyzing the third for life. All three were African-American. "What the hell's he doing *here*?"

Holding up a hand, Ursitti said, "I know, Detective, I know, but his lawyer made a motion and the judge granted it—as long as his case is on appeal, he gets to stay in medium. And he carries a lotta weight around here."

"Using the system for his own benefit," Mac said with disgust. Of course, Mac himself had done something similar to get Gerrard and Sinclair off his back, but that was only because his back was against the wall.

Besides which, Mac was on the side of right there. When Clay Dobson was first arrested, the officers failed to secure his belt. Dobson tried to hang himself with that belt. Gerrard, then a lieutenant, covered up both the failure to secure and the suicide attempt. Mac hadn't wanted to use that against Gerrard and Sinclair (who was the inspector in charge of the precinct at the time of Dobson's arrest), but he had little choice. While the DA's office had cleared Mac of any wrongdoing in Dobson's death, Sinclair had started an internal investigation to please the media and raise his own profile, no doubt in an attempt to make his bid for the commissioner's chair more realistic.

Mac had thought him to be a fool in any case. Gerrard, at least, used to be a good police. Sinclair, though, was a political animal with delusions of grandeur—and also no sense of history. Most NYPD commissioners were brought in from outside, and the job tended to chew people up and spit them out. Theodore Roosevelt had one of the most distinguished careers of anyone in American history, a successful soldier, a well-regarded New York State governor, a popular vice president and president. The one failure in his entire career was his disastrous tenure as the commissioner of the NYPD.

Sinclair was no Teddy Roosevelt. Thoughts like that kept Mac warm at night.

And sights like Karl Fischer kept him up at night. One of the COs Mac hadn't seen before brought Fischer in. He was shorter than Mac was expecting him to be, with a monk's fringe of hair that was part blond, part silver; a hook nose; and wide, penetrating blue eyes. They were the same color as Flack's.

Most of the inmates who'd come into this room were either defiant or overly solicitous. The former were the harder criminals who didn't give a damn about anything; the latter were the ones who were doing everything they could to be model citizens in order to make parole.

Fischer didn't fit either one of those types. He had a superiority complex about him, a vibe Mac hadn't gotten off any of the other inmates so far. "Detective Flack, Detective Taylor," he said in a bourbon-smooth voice with just a hint of a Southern accent, "what can I do to help y'all today?"

Where others had asked that question as if eager to please, Fischer was acting as if he were doling out indulgences. Neither detective had introduced himself; Fischer must have gotten their names from one of the other inmates, a neat trick with the place in lockdown. Obviously, he wanted to show off how good his information network was.

Mac found he couldn't help himself. "How'd you swing getting remanded here? You were convicted of, among other things, first-degree murder."

"That's arguable, Detective Taylor. You see, the law says I'm entitled to a jury of my *peers*. That jury was pretty much all my inferiors." He smiled. "Pity that particular nuance doesn't carry much weight with New York judges, but I've got other things to base my appeal on. For one thing, the evidence was truly spotty. Obviously, Detective Taylor, you weren't the one on the case. I can't imagine you allowing an arrest to proceed with the pissant evidence they had on me. If'n you were, I daresay this would've had a much better end for all concerned."

"Somehow I doubt that," Mac said tightly.

"Don't sell yourself short, Detective. I've been hearin' about your trials and tribulations with that Dobson fella. Now *there's* a hardcore sumbitch, if you'll pardon my French. It's a travesty of justice that a man like him gets to go free while an innocent man such as myself rots away in prison."

Flack got the interview back on track, for which Mac was grateful. "What can you tell us about the two murders that happened this morning?"

"Not a thing, sorry to say, Detective. They both happened in the weight yard when I was not present in that facility."

"So you didn't know that it was Jack Mulroney who killed Vance Barker."

"I was deep in conversation with Mr. William Cox. We were discussing the Gospel according to St. John and the discrepancies between it and the other three Gospels, which I attribute to John actually being present."

Mac raised an eyebrow. "Really? Most religious scholars have come to the conclusion that John was actually the farthest removed from the lifetime of Jesus Christ and that Mark was the most likely to be an eyewitness. That's a very old-fashioned viewpoint you have, Fischer."

"Well, I'm an old-fashioned kinda guy. I'm surprised to hear an officer of the law espousing knowledge of scripture, particularly from a scholarly perspective." He smiled, an expression that was wholly without warmth. "But then, you were a Marine, weren'tcha, Detective? I guess it's true that there are no atheists in foxholes, huh?"

Cursing himself for allowing Fischer to direct the interview, Mac saved Flack the trouble of getting them back on track. "What did you see?"

"I'm afraid that I was sufficiently engrossed in my spiritual discourse with William to see much of anything. I only noticed something was going on when the, ah, *gentlemen* in the weight yard started screaming obscenities. I noticed that there was a considerable amount of blood on the fence, but beyond that, I'm afraid I didn't notice any particulars."

Ursitti stepped in for the first time. "So Mulroney didn't come to you? Asking permission?"

"I'm afraid I have no idea what you're talking about, Lieutenant. Nobody in this prison needs my permission to do anything. I'm just an inmate hereabouts."

"Cut the crap, Fischer," Ursitti said, "everybody knows you run the white people here."

"That's an unsubstantiated allegation, Lieutenant. And I'd say it's slanderous besides. Within the confines of the regulations of this facility, Jack Mulroney is free to do whatever he wishes with or without my consent."

"So the fact that he talked to you in the mess right after he stole his razor blade is just a coincidence."

Fischer looked studiously thoughtful. Mac felt nauseated all of a sudden.

"I do recall," Fischer finally said, "that Jack and I had a conversation over breakfast. I believe it was about the unfairness of Mr. Vance Barker's take-out slide during yesterday's baseball game."

Flack asked, "Did Mulroney mention retribution?"

"In fact, he did, but I cautioned him against it. Such retribution, as you call it, very rarely has any kind of good end. It would seem he didn't follow my advice—assuming he was the one who stabbed Mr. Barker. As I said, I didn't see it."

This was getting them nowhere. Besides, Mulroney had confessed, and they had physical evidence to back it up. While trying to nail Fischer on conspiracy to commit murder would have given Mac great joy, he doubted someone who'd finagled remanding to medium security while appealing a murder charge would have any trouble sliding out of additional charges here. So Mac moved on to the other case. "What about Malik Washburne?"

"What about him?"

"Did you see who killed him?"

"Again, Detective, he was in the weight yard. I wasn't. And I don't much pay attention to the comings and goings of heathens. They'll all get theirs when the Kingdom of Heaven arrives, worry not."

"I wasn't worried," Mac said.

Flack asked, "Were you aware of any disagreements Washburne may have had with any of the other inmates?"

"Far as I could tell, folks seemed to like him well enough. So did I, truth be told. He was a decent sort of fella—for a heathen, leastaways. Whoever killed him will surely burn in the fires of hell for his sin." Again, the smile. "Not that most of those imprisoned here were likely to avoid that destination in the first place."

"Except you, of course," Mac said, "being innocent and all."

"Perfection is God's prerogative, Detective Taylor. We mortals can only aspire to it, and that means that sometimes mistakes will be made, such as my incarceration. It is a mistake that I will rectify, worry not."

"Still not worried." Mac looked at Flack. "We're done here."

"Definitely."

Fischer stood up. "I'm sorry I couldn't have been more help, gentlemen. I hope you find both of the murderers in our midst."

After Fischer left, Flack started looking at the floor on either side of the table.

"What're you looking for, Don?"

Flack looked up at Mac. "I figure after all the manure that was being shoveled, we oughta be seeing a rose pop out of the floor any second now."

Mac chuckled. Ursitti didn't. The lieutenant said, "Fischer's no laughing matter, Detective. I really hope his appeal finishes, one way or the other, soon, 'cause the sooner he's out of here, the smoother everything'll go around here." He sighed. "It's no coincidence that our first DIC in two decades is while that asshole's here. El-Jabbar's bad enough, but at least he keeps things together, y'know? Fischer's just bad news. Usually the white guys here keep their heads down, but he's got 'em all riled up. And I'll tell you something else, no way Mulroney even *thinks* about doing what he did without runnin' it by Fischer first."

"Unfortunately," Mac said with a sigh, "the only evidence we have points to Mulroney acting alone."

"Yeah." Ursitti shook his head and looked at his clipboard to see who the next interview was.

12

SERVING THE WARRANT ON Jack Morgenstern's house hadn't been nearly as painful as Stella had feared it would be.

Bracey was present, as promised. Morgenstern wasn't, which was something of a relief. Then again, Stella knew how invasive the execution of a search warrant could be, and so, probably, did Morgenstern, from his previous experience with the NYPD. She couldn't blame him for not wanting to be around for it.

Stella had made a list of what they needed from the house—the clothes from the night before and Maria's necklace, if it was there—and the uniforms from the five-oh knew their stuff, so she figured they'd grab anything they thought would be suspicious. A lot of them patronized Belluso's and knew

Maria, so they were motivated to find her killer. As Angell had said on the drive up, you didn't mess with a cop's source of caffeine. They'd be thorough.

So once Bracey read over every word of the warrant and let them into the house on Cambridge Avenue, Stella and Angell left the uniforms to it and walked over to Riverdale Pinan Karate, which was located in a modest storefront on Fieldston Road, off Riverdale Avenue.

As they walked over, Angell asked, "You get anything from the love letters?"

Stella sighed. "No epithelials, and the only usable print hits were DelVecchio and our vic, but we know they both touched them. The paper itself was Georgia-Pacific eight-and-a-half-by-eleven printer paper that's readily available at every Staples, Office Max, CVS, Duane Reade, and Hallmark store in town. The printer looks to be a Hewlett-Packard laser jet, which is only the most popular printer on the market." She shook her head. "Hell, it's what *we* use. For all we can prove, *Danny* wrote those letters."

Angell smiled. "Somehow, Messer doesn't strike me as the type to write a haiku. Dirty limerick, maybe."

Stella chuckled. "The point is, though, we're nowhere. We might—*might*—be able to match it with a specific printer, but it's a long shot. Best we could do is use it as an interrogation tool—throw it in the perp's face and hope he doesn't realize how weak the evidence is."

"I don't see that happening with Morgenstern as long as he has Shark Lady by his side."

They walked down Fieldston Road, the late-afternoon sun blazing at Stella's back. The dojo had just opened when they arrived. Based on the schedule, which was on a brochure that Stella grabbed on the way in, they only taught classes in the late afternoon and evening. Most of the dojos Stella knew of in Manhattan had early morning classes, but the later schedule tracked with the more residential nature of Riverdale. Stella bet that the majority of their students were kids who came after school.

Coming inside, Stella saw a small reception desk, several chairs in front of a waist-high divider, and a bench. Beyond the divider was the polished wood floor of the dojo, which extended back several dozen feet. A floor-to-ceiling mirror along the north wall made the place look bigger than it was; the south wall had both an American and Japanese flag hanging from it.

Behind the reception desk were several shrink-wrapped uniforms, T-shirts, and pieces of fighting equipment that she assumed were for sale.

A young woman named Donna Farr was already there—a student, she worked part-time as the dojo's receptionist. She did verify that Jack Morgenstern attended the *kumite* class the previous night and that he left at about 10:50 P.M. That tracked with everything else they'd heard. Donna even verified that Morgenstern was wearing a black sweatshirt.

Shortly, a very tall dark-skinned man came in. As he entered, he put his fists in front of his chest and bowed from the waist, saying, *"Osu."* Then he came the rest of the way in.

"Sensei," Donna said, "these people are from the NYPD."

Angell pulled out her badge, and Stella did likewise. "I'm Detective Angell, this is Detective Bonasera. We're here to talk to you about Jack Morgenstern."

"I'm Allen Portman—this is my dojo. How can I help you?"

Stella said, "We just need to verify that Mr. Morgenstern was part of the fighting class last night and that he was at one point kicked in the ribs."

"May I ask what this is regarding?"

Quickly, Angell said, "An ongoing investigation that we can't talk about in detail."

"Jack is one of my better students. If he's under investigation—"

"We really can't talk about it," Stella said mildly.

Angell added, "I'm sorry, but we have to ask these questions."

Portman folded his arms over his well-muscled chest. "All right. During one of the later rounds in the class, Jack fought with *Senpai* John."

"How many rounds do you usually go?" Angell asked.

"Fifteen—fourteen two-minute rounds, then one that's three minutes. This would've been either round thirteen or fourteen—we were still doing kick and punch both. The last round is always just punches. Jack missed with a *mawashi giri*—that's a roundhouse kick—and that left him open for a *yoko giri*, a side kick. He caught Jack right in the rib cage. After the round, I told him he could rest, but he insisted on continuing." Portman smiled slightly. "Jack can be stubborn that way."

Somehow, Stella managed to keep from making a snide comment. Instead, she asked, "You always wear footgear during fighting classes?"

"Of course."

"Everyone wear the same kind?"

"Generally. We sell fighting gear, and most of the students purchase from us."

"Is *Senpai* John one of the 'most' in question?"

Portman nodded. "He wears the standard footgear, yes."

Stella nodded back. "We're going to need one

set of footgear for comparison purposes, Mr. Portman."

"Of course." Portman didn't sound happy about it, but he was obviously still willing to cooperate. Then again, Stella couldn't imagine that having one of his students under suspicion for a crime was anything that sat well with him. "Donna, could you please give the detectives a set of footgear? The large size, please."

"*Osu, Sensei.*" Donna, who had been working on the computer at the reception desk, hit a few more keys, then got up and pulled down some footgear from the shelves behind her.

"Detectives," Portman said, "I want you to know that I've known Jack for three years now. He's a good man and a good student. I'm aware of the history he has with your department, and I'd ask you to please not hold that against him. He can be abrasive, it's true, but I don't believe that he has it in his heart to commit a murder."

Stella took the footgear from Donna. "Thanks." Then she turned to Portman. "What makes you think this is a murder?"

"Deductive reasoning, Detective Bonasera," Portman said with a small smile. "I know all the detectives that work the day shift in the Fiftieth Precinct, and you two are not among them. I do a good deal of community outreach, and that requires coordination with the local precinct," he added by way of explanation. "Also I know that a young woman was killed in Belluso's Bakery this morning. It isn't that difficult to put two and two together. You think that Jack killed Maria."

While Riverdale was a large community, the businesses were all clustered in a small area. Stella therefore couldn't bring herself to muster up surprise that one business owner would be aware of what happened in one around the corner. New Yorkers minded their own business, but murder was bad for business.

Angell had a few more questions about the dojo—Stella soon learned that she had guessed right, eighty percent of Riverdale Pinan Karate's enrollment was children between the ages of four and eighteen—and then they prepared to go. Stella and Angell both left business cards with Donna.

"If there's anything else I can do to help, Detectives," Portman said, "please don't hesitate to call. Our number's on the brochure."

Angell and Stella both expressed their gratitude, then left the dojo.

They stopped at the crime lab's SUV to put the footgear in the trunk, then proceeded on to Morgenstern's house.

O'Malley was standing in the foyer holding up a large blue plastic evidence bag filled to bursting with clothes. "This is what our guy wore last night, we think."

"You *think*, Deej?" Angell asked with an undertone of annoyance that was creeping its way into being an overtone.

"They were still in the dryer, along with a karate uniform. I figure he put 'em in the dryer last night 'fore he went to bed and left 'em there." He shrugged. "I do it all the time."

Stella looked at Angell. "What is it with men that they can't fold laundry until they absolutely have to?"

"Hey, don't turn this into a men-women thing, Detective—my wife doesn't even remember to *do* the damn laundry half the time, all right? Anyhow, you want this stuff or not?"

"Want." Stella held out her hand. "What about the karate uniform?"

"Bagged that, too. Bats has it."

"Any sign of the necklace?" Stella asked.

Shaking his head, O'Malley said, "Nada."

"Where's the dryer?"

O'Malley led her back through a hallway and kitchen to a small alcove off the kitchen. Angell went upstairs to see how things were going in the bedroom.

Reaching into her jacket pocket, Stella pulled out her penlight. She had once joked with Mac that they all wielded their penlights like weapons, and Danny had said that if Mac lost his penlight, he'd get the shakes from the withdrawal.

Still, they were useful, especially when you were searching the inside of a dryer for an errant purple-painted fingernail.

Unfortunately, while she found plenty of dust and lint, she found no fingernails. Nothing in the washer, either. It might have still been on the clothes—she'd check that once she got them back to the lab—but it was more likely that it was knocked off in the wash.

"Hey, Stell!" That was Angell calling from upstairs.

Stella leaned her head outside the washroom. "Yeah, Jen?"

"You should come up here."

Pocketing the penlight, she went up the stairs, her shoe heels clunking on the bare wood. She was surprised that he hadn't put a runner down to mute the noise.

Turning left at the landing, she saw that one of the house's three bedrooms had been converted into an office. At a large wooden desk sat a Dell desktop computer, a mouse pad with the New York Yankees logo on it, and a printer.

A Hewlett-Packard laser jet, to be precise. Two of the five-oh's uniforms were disconnecting it.

Angell walked over to the desk and opened a drawer. "And looky here."

Following her, Stella peered into the drawer,

which included all manner of detritus—envelopes with bills; some booklets; a passport; a few rulers; various office supplies, such as paper clips, binder clips, and staples; and, finally, a ream of paper from Georgia-Pacific.

Stella tilted her head. "Well, it doesn't actually prove anything, but it also means that we can't eliminate him, either."

"Works for me," Angell said.

Sighing, Stella went back downstairs. The evidence all *supported* the notion that Morgenstern killed Maria, but did nothing to *prove* it.

At least not yet.

Still, Stella hated this part of it. While it was true that evidence didn't lie, it didn't always tell the truth.

Sometimes it just sat and taunted you, and didn't actually *tell* you anything.

"Jen," she called back upstairs, "I'm gonna head back—get to work on some of this."

Angell poked her head over the banister. "Will do. I'll send over everything once it's collected."

Bracey appeared out of nowhere and said, "I expect an itemized receipt, Detective."

Putting her hand to her chest and trying to get her breathing under control, Stella said, "You scared me."

"I *said* I expect—"

"—an itemized receipt, I heard you the first

time, Ms. Bracey. Don't worry, you'll get it. Excuse me."

With that, she left the Morgenstern house. She needed to get back to the lab and find out once and for all if the house's owner really was a killer.

13

IT SEEMS TO BE a routine crime scene check. You and Mac follow a blood trail that starts at the dead body and leads upstairs into a corporate office hallway.

There's a ladder on the floor where the trail ends and an open panel in the ceiling. Mac holds a latex glove in his hand and straightens the ladder, then he climbs it to see what's up there.

While Mac does that, holding that penlight he always carries like it's a spear or something, your mind starts to wander. You're testifying in the Howard case in a week, and you're supposed to go over your testimony with ADA Maria Cabrera this afternoon. Even though the evidence against Howard's partner in the plastic surgery business is overwhelming, the jackass still pled not guilty and hired an expensive mouthpiece.

Worse, the DA gave it to Cabrera, the snottiest person

in the prosecutor's office. She still has a grudge against you for the Balidemaj case, which means this meeting will be as much fun as your last trip to the dentist, only without the cute hygienist, Abby. If the ADAs were less like Cabrera and more like Abby, you'd enjoy testifying more. You should call her, actually . . .

Suddenly, Mac practically jumps off the ladder. "We gotta check the building. If there's anyone here, get 'em out." *You wonder what the hell he's talking about, when he says three fateful words:*

"There's a bomb."

All thoughts of Abby's hourglass figure and the Howard case and Cabrera's obnoxiousness flee from your brain at the sound of those words.

Instead, you think that the last thing this city needs is another building blowing up.

"Hit the alarm!" *Mac yells, and you reach out with one long arm and yank on the white handle of the fire alarm.*

It's craziness after that, the alarm blaring in your ears. "Call central," *Mac screams over the alarm,* "no radio!" *But you already have your cell phone out and flipped open.*

"Suspicious package," *you cry as you run upstairs,* "621 Greenwich. A bomb."

Central, as usual, is staffed by morons. "Did you say a bomb?" *the guy says. You're pretty sure it's Soohoo. Probably half asleep like usual.*

"Yeah a bomb!"

You and Mac get to the next floor, and sure enough, even though it's Sunday, there are workaholics in the building who just can't wait until Monday to do what they have to do. Of course, you're working on a Sunday, but never mind.

Used to be that evacuating a building was like pulling teeth, only without the sexy hygienist. Since the fall of 2001, though, all you had to do was say the word bomb, *and every New Yorker knew exactly what to do.*

You're not sure if that's a good thing or not.

Mac calls Monroe—who had gone outside to get more crime lab toys from the SUV—and tells her to evacuate the area.

Finally, you're checking the last of the doors, making sure that the building's been completely emptied. It's just you and Mac left, looks like.

"All right," Mac says, "c'mon, let's go."

You both turn and head to the stairwell.

"Hey, what's goin' on?"

You whirl around, and there's some schmuck wearing noise-canceling headphones who looks confused. You start moving toward him.

"Hey, get the hell outta here!"

And then the world explodes in a fiery conflagration. Your ears pop from the deafening report of the bomb's detonation, and you feel the impact of shrapnel slicing into your chest.

You don't remember anything after that . . .

Flack sat up quickly, his bare chest drenched in sweat. "Son of a *bitch*."

Though the dream had ended, the pain in his chest hadn't died down.

It took Flack a few seconds to extricate himself from his sheets, which had gotten tangled in his legs.

It had been a while since he'd had the dream.

He wasn't sure what prompted it this time. Usually, there was some kind of trigger, but he'd spent all day today at Richmond Hill interviewing surly convicts and brain-dead COs. That wasn't a hundred percent accurate, of course. Many of the COs were just fine, especially Terry, and a surprisingly large number of the cons were polite, but Flack didn't remember the decent ones with anywhere near the same clarity with which he remembered the jackasses.

Flack liked the look of Melendez as their guy. Mac would say it was because of the fingerprint on the murder weapon, but Flack put more stock in the fight in the Koran class. Guys like Melendez were always searching for a way to get out early, and Washburne had put up a roadblock to that. And the incident in the weight yard had provided him with a golden opportunity: everyone was busy looking at Barker. Melendez could get his revenge without anybody even seeing him.

He even pointed out the dead body so people wouldn't suspect him. The classic stupid person's rationale: *If I point out the dead body, I can't have done the murder.*

He looked over at the clock radio next to his bed. 3:52.

Then he looked down at the network of scars on the left side of his chest.

Knowing he wouldn't get back to sleep, and not relishing the idea of possibly having the dream again anyhow, Flack got up.

That proved to be a mistake, as the twinges of pain in his chest turned into white-hot knives of agony. He fell back down, staring at the ceiling, trying to get his breathing under control.

After a few dozen eternities, the pain started to die down. Slowly, very, very slowly, Flack got up from the bed. He gingerly walked to the closet, where his suit jacket was hanging. Opening the closet door proved to be even more painful than getting up had been, and he almost stumbled to the floor with the pain.

Taking a second to let the pain subside, he stood upright and reached into the inner pocket of the jacket he'd been wearing yesterday.

He heard the clatter of a Percocet against plastic as he pulled out the pill bottle.

He also heard Terry Sullivan's voice: *"Will you please take the pill, for the love of Christ?"*

Walking into the kitchen, he pulled open the refrigerator door. His memory hadn't betrayed him: there was an open bottle of Chianti Classico, the cork sticking up out of it.

Under normal circumstances, Flack would've gotten a wineglass out of the china closet, but—with all respect to an excellent Tuscan red—he needed this sooner rather than later. Besides, opening and closing doors was proving to be agonizing. He could just get a regular milk glass out of the dry rack next to the sink without having to open or close anything.

Pouring out the remainder of the Chianti, he then put the pill in his mouth and downed a mouthful of the wine.

Peyton Driscoll usually got in early. She had promised a full autopsy report on Malik Washburne first thing in the morning. For all Flack knew, she'd had a prelim the night before, but after a full day at RHCF, he'd come straight home. If something important came up, Mac or somebody would've called him. Or not—it wasn't as if anybody involved in the case was going anywhere, and Mac had even commented to Flack that he looked like he needed a good night's sleep.

A pity he didn't get one.

The pharmacy opened at eight, he knew. Flack intended to be there as soon as the gate went up.

So what if it was weak. Sometimes weakness was a strength.

Seeing the video on the web, watching herself making love to a man she thought she knew.

"So I broke up with Frankie right then and there. Told him I never wanted to see him again."

Sneaking up on her in the parking lot, wondering why she wouldn't return his phone calls, as if he didn't know.

"Did you think it was funny? Did you think it would turn me on?"

Walking into the apartment to find him standing there, lighting candles, as though it were the most natural thing in the world.

"It's one of my rules: no men in my place. Just in case things go bad, I always have a safe place to go to."

Rushing to the phone to call 911—or Flack or the landlord, somebody—only to have him rip the phone out of the wall and throw it across the room with a clatter. Suddenly everything changes: a seemingly harmless guy who won't take no for an answer has become dangerous.

"All right, that's it. I'm making a phone call."

Feeling the phone cord bite into her wrists behind her back as he ties her up, angrily wondering how she could treat him like one of the suspects she meets at work, never mind that he's acting just like one himself.

"I loved your statue—so beautiful. And I loved all the I-love-you messages. And I really meant to call you—I did."

Sitting in the bathtub, her fingers slick with her own blood as she tries desperately to grip the blade that she'd managed to pry out of her leg razor so she could slice the phone cord apart and be free.

"I remember the doorbell ringing—but I don't know why."

Digging through the handbag with bloody fingers, trying desperately to find and hold her Glock, when he comes leaping over the divider, knocking her to the floor with a bone-jarring impact.

"You caught me off guard. Can you blame me?"

He grabs the Glock and tries to shoot her, but he doesn't know how to shoot a handgun and never takes the safety off. She takes advantage of his confusion and grabs the weapon from his hand.

"That's the name and number of my lawyer, Courtney Bracey. You want to talk to me, set it up with her."

Stella bolted upright.

It wasn't the first time she'd dreamed about that terrible night when Frankie Mala broke into her apartment and held her captive. Usually, any mention of a rape or kidnapping or sexual assault triggered that reaction.

But this time, it had been Jack Morgenstern in the dream, taking Frankie's place. Morgenstern who tied her up, Morgenstern who tried to shoot her, Morgenstern whom she was about to shoot three times in the chest.

Rubbing her eyes while sitting in the very bed

where Frankie had tied her up, she looked over at the clock radio on the end table, which told her that it was a little before five.

She was getting up in a few hours anyhow. This morning, she had a meeting with the ADA to go over next week's testimony in the Osborne case, then it was back to the grind with the Maria Campagna murder—which was obviously preying on her mind if the prime suspect was showing up in her dreams.

As she padded to the kitchen—the same kitchen where she'd found Frankie blithely setting the table—she reflected with frustration on how little useful evidence they actually had. There was no sign of Maria's fingernail on Morgenstern's clothes, nor anywhere in his house. The bruise that was forming on Morgenstern's chest was shaped vaguely enough that it could have come from the impact of a teenager's protected foot, or a woman's fist, or both.

Everything at the lab was getting bumped for Mac's prison case, so Stella didn't know the results of the trace left on Maria's knuckles yet. She just had to hope they'd discover something definitive there.

They also hadn't found Maria's necklace in Morgenstern's house. Angell had double-checked with Maria's mother, and she said Maria had indeed worn the necklace when she left for work the previous day.

Any decent lawyer would blow through that evidence like a shotgun through cardboard, and Bracey—no matter how annoying she might be—was more than a decent lawyer.

They needed the proverbial smoking gun.

Stella liked it better when criminals were stupid. Then they were easy to intimidate with circumstantial evidence. Morgenstern, though, wouldn't intimidate easily, especially after what he went through on that rape case.

She had read up on Morgenstern's case. The actual rapist didn't look anything like Morgenstern, but he did match the general description. The victim never got a good look at her attacker, so her ID of him wasn't solid, but Morgenstern's alibi for the time of the rape had simply been that he was alone in his Belmont apartment, which hadn't helped his case.

In all fairness, Stella could see how he would be wary of the NYPD after being put through the wringer like that.

But at the end of the day, he was still the most viable suspect they had.

They just needed to prove it.

She needed to prove it.

Walking to the counter, she put on a pot of coffee. No sense trying to get back to sleep now. She'd down some caffeine, shower, and maybe go to the gym. She suddenly felt the need to take out her frustrations on an innocent punching bag.

I'm jogging, just like I do every night.

The night wind is blowing in my face.

The car takes the place of the wind, shining light that blinds me.

I know the drill. I don't stop them from searching me.

I think it's insane, but I know better than to resist.

That's what they taught me, you do what the cops tell you to do.

I don't know where the money in my pocket came from. I don't know why they're handcuffing me.

I do know how it makes me feel. I'm helpless. No control. Just like in the ER, when the patient won't come back to life no matter what I do.

No control.

A man says I shot someone. I don't know what he's talking about.

A lawyer tells me he's on my side, even though he questions me the same way a suspect is questioned.

I'm put in jail, forced to wear a prison uniform instead of my own clothes.

I'm handcuffed if I'm taken anywhere outside the prison.

And then he comes to visit me.

Shane Casey.

He did this to me.

He took my control away. And no one will believe me.

Hawkes woke up as his alarm went off. He was still having the dream.

Part of him figured he should talk to that departmental shrink. Mac had recommended it after he was released, but it wasn't a requirement. Maybe he'd ask Stella how it worked out for her after Frankie attacked her.

Or maybe he'd just talk to Stella. She'd been tied up and threatened, her wrists bound as if they were handcuffed. She knew what it was like to be helpless.

To lose control.

Sitting in his darkened apartment, the lights of the city that never slept casting odd shadows in his bedroom, Sheldon Hawkes was willing to admit that the thing that scared him more than anything else was losing control. He became a doctor so he could control life and death, only to find that life and death weren't anywhere near as easy to wrangle as he'd led himself to believe.

It had been too much, so he fled the hospital for the morgue. His patients were already dead, so he couldn't kill them there. He had his control back.

Then Shane Casey took it all away from him. Just so he could clear the name of his brother— who turned out to be exactly as guilty as the jury had found him.

It was all for nothing.

Sometimes, Hawkes thought that was the worst part of it all. Casey's loyalty to his brother was touching but misplaced.

And all it cost was a little piece of Sheldon Hawkes's soul.

He hadn't gone running since that night. It wasn't that he was afraid to, exactly, he just didn't want to risk reliving it.

That was a sort of fear, wasn't it?

Maybe he did have things to discuss with the shrink.

However, that could wait until after this case was put down. Peyton had said when he left for the day that she had to check a few things against Washburne's medical records at RHCF before she would release the autopsy report. She was also being cagey about her findings, not even filing a prelim. At the time, she had said it was because, with Gerrard breathing down her neck, she didn't want to jump to any conclusions, and that excuse certainly had the ring of believability about it.

But Hawkes had been an ME too long not to know the signs. Peyton had found something that didn't make sense, and she didn't want to tell anyone about it until she had an answer or had proven to herself that an answer was not to be found.

He hoped it was the former.

Hawkes performed all his morning ablutions and rituals, then hopped the R train uptown to work.

Stella was waiting in the elevator bank when he arrived. "Morning, Stella."

"Hey, Sheldon. How's your prison riot going?"

"One's a dunker—guy confessed, evidence matched up. Unfortunately, the other one's Washburne. We've got a suspect, but I'm still waiting for Peyton's report."

She smiled. "I envy you. I've got a suspect, too, and Sid's *done* his report, but it's all way too circumstantial."

Unable to miss the fact that Stella wasn't making eye contact, Hawkes stared straight at her and said, "You okay?"

Finally, she met his gaze.

Hawkes recognized the haunted look in her eyes. It was the same one he saw in the mirror after waking up from that damn dream.

"Bad dreams?" he asked.

"How'd you guess?" She didn't actually sound that surprised.

"Experience. Wanna get a drink after the shift's over and compare night terrors?"

She smiled. "You're on, Doc."

With a telltale ding, the elevator arrived. They both got on, went to their floor, and disembarked.

As soon as they got off, Stella's Treo rang. She looked down at the display, said, "Angell," then put the phone to her ear. "What's up, Jen? Really? Okay. I've got a meeting, but I'll send Lindsay up to meet you."

"What is it?" Hawkes asked.

She gave him a grin. "The proverbial break in the case. Our vic was missing a necklace, and Angell said it just turned up. I gotta go find Lindsay. I'll see you later, Sheldon."

Stella peeled off and went in search of Lindsay. Hawkes continued toward the break room to get some coffee, only to find Peyton Driscoll waiting for him. She was holding what looked very much like an autopsy report in her hand.

"I'm afraid I have some disturbing news," she said by way of greeting.

"I had a feeling."

She frowned. "Are you becoming a psychic, Sheldon?"

"No, but when you don't file a prelim, I know *something*'s up," Hawkes said. "Give it to me straight, Doc, I can take it."

"I have a cause of death for Malik Washburne, né Gregory Washburne, and it is most assuredly *not* blunt force trauma to the head. Rather, it was asphyxiation due to the closing of the throat as a result of an allergic reaction."

Eyes wide, Hawkes took the report from Peyton and started flipping through it. "Allergic to what?"

"That," she said with a sigh, "is the question. I haven't the foggiest."

He looked at her, then led the way out of the break room toward Mac's office. "C'mon, we'd better talk to Mac. And, if we're really unlucky, to Gerrard, too."

14

TAYVON OLIVERA WAS REALLY looking forward to putting the beat-down on Jorge Melendez.

Truth be told, he wanted a piece of Jack Mulroney, too. But Mulroney had half the COs in RHCF all over him, and he'd probably be arrested soon for knifing Vance Barker. The bastard would get to see the outside just long enough to go through the cop house again. Then maybe he'd get sent to some max-security place like Sing Sing.

They were hard-core there. Mulroney would get his, Tayvon was sure of that. He wouldn't last three seconds.

Tayvon just wished he could be the one to bring him down.

Meantime, he'd get his shot at that bastard Melendez.

In some ways, Tayvon was in RHCF because of Malik Washburne. But he figured he was still alive because of him, also. Back in the day, Tayvon was doping and getting into fights. He tried to box but got his ass thrown onto the street after the first time he peed in a cup.

Things got so bad, Tayvon ran out of money for his coke fix, so he started stealing. When he got caught, the judge ordered him to go to the Kinson Rehab Center.

That was where Tayvon met Malik Washburne. At first, Tayvon didn't want anything to do with a cop, even if he wasn't a cop anymore. But Malik kept at him, helping him through the rehab, sitting up with him while he went through the DTs.

Tayvon didn't really go for religion—it wasn't his thing—but after spending so much time with Malik, he did respect the Nation of Islam. In particular, he respected what they had done for the Original Man. He didn't really believe in it, but folks like Malik and Hakim el-Jabbar, he had mad respect for them and people like them who preached the word. Even if the words didn't really mean anything to Tayvon, they meant something to other people.

Black folks who listened to people like Hakim and Malik, they felt better about who they were. They weren't ashamed of the color of their skin. Tayvon was down with that.

Like Malik before him, Hakim respected Tayvon's lack of faith, because Tayvon didn't do bullshit. He didn't try to pretend to be faithful because it might do him some good. Nah, Tayvon just did his business, and he got caught. Yeah, he was off the coke, but he was still a big dude who was good at beat-downs. So he started working for folks he used to buy his dope from—as well as taking legit bouncer and bodyguard jobs. One time, he beat up somebody that actually filed a police report, and for the second time, Tayvon got nailed by the cops.

No rehab—he had to do his time, but that was cool. He'd be out in the street once he did his bit, and then it'd be back to business.

Until then, he was more than happy to put a beat-down on some fool who had earned it.

And Melendez had. That little punk-ass fool didn't believe in Allah or Mohammed or none of that other stuff any more than Tayvon did, but Melendez tried to make like he did. Even went to Malik's Koran class.

That was why Tayvon wasn't surprised when word came down from Hakim: Melendez killed Malik. Well, okay, he was a *little* surprised that a punk like Melendez had had the balls to do the deed. But after that throw-down they had in Malik's class, Tayvon figured Melendez had enough of a mad-on to take Malik out. Besides, he did it while everyone was watching Mulroney ice Vance.

And that was *weak*. Vance didn't do nothing wrong. Okay, so he slid hard, so the hell what? Tayvon saw somebody pull that on Derek Jeter just last week, and Jeter didn't go stabbing the guy with a razor.

Tayvon had no idea how Hakim knew that Melendez was the one who did in Malik, but Hakim was always knowing things he wasn't supposed to. His word was good enough for Tayvon.

The deed would be done in the shower that morning. He wouldn't have long, but the shower was the best time, especially since it could wash away blood. Besides, Tayvon had been doing push-ups on his knuckles for twenty years. As long as he punched with the first two knuckles, nobody would even know he'd punched anyone.

Bolton was the CO watching the showers, but he kept his distance. There were two other COs in sight, too, which was weird, but Tayvon figured after what went down in the yard, everyone was a little squirrelly.

Tayvon grabbed the soap and lathered himself up. It had been a long night stuck in the dorms, which weren't air-conditioned, and the COs decided to be assholes and keep the fans off, too. Tayvon spent the whole night sweating like a mother.

Of course, the water was practically ice cold and

the pressure was down. Tayvon figured that was
on purpose, too. Damn hacks, always messing with
them.

"Yo, Bolton," somebody yelled, "what's with the
damn water?"

"Is it wet?" Bolton asked.

"Well, yeah, but—"

"Then shut the hell up."

Even dribbly cold water felt good after sleeping
in an oven all night, so Tayvon enjoyed it while he
waited for the right moment.

After yelling at the guy who mouthed off, Bolton turned away from the showers, shaking his
head in annoyance.

Tayvon took advantage of this opportunity to
move closer to Melendez. It wasn't hard—ever
since he and Malik got into it, nobody'd been all
that fond of Melendez. Hakim had accused him of
being a carpetbagging Muslim. Tayvon didn't know
what that meant, but it didn't sound very good.

Then Tayvon looked around until he caught Hakim's eye. At his nod, several other people moved
so they were standing in Bolton's line of sight.
Even if Bolton turned around, all he'd see would
be a dozen wet bodies, and not Tayvon beating the
holy crap out of Jorge Melendez.

First Tayvon closed his eyes, slowing his breathing down. That was something they taught him in
martial arts school back when he was a kid, which

was where he got started doing the push-ups on his knuckles. Hurt like hell, but it was worth it. Sometimes, Tayvon thought he should've stuck with martial arts, but at the time, he liked cocaine more.

Once his breathing was nice and regular, he placed one of his massive hands on top of Melendez's head. Tayvon was almost a full head taller than Melendez, so it was like grabbing a golf ball on a tee and turning it around.

Rearing back with his other hand, he punched Melendez in the solar plexus.

While Tayvon remembered very little of the specifics of his martial arts training, he did remember a few things. One was how useful it was to do push-ups on your knuckles in order to toughen your fists and make your punches more effective. In a life spent beating people up, both as a bouncer in legit bars and strip clubs and working for slingers and bangers, that lesson had stuck real good.

The other one was a Japanese word. He'd studied *shotokan,* and he'd had to learn all kinds of Japanese words, but the only one he really remembered was *suigetsu.* It meant "solar plexus," but that wasn't why Tayvon remembered it. The literal translation of the word was "moon on the water." According to the old guy who ran the school, there was an old story about a monkey who would see the moon reflected on the water and try to grab the moon, but he couldn't because it was just a reflection, and monkeys were stupid.

The solar plexus was called *suigetsu* because trying to catch your breath after being punched there was like that monkey trying to grab the moon.

In Tayvon's line of work, it was good for your first punch to be one that kept the guy you were beating up from making any noise. That was especially handy in the echo chamber of a prison shower. Even with the water going—and that wasn't as useful a masking sound, as the pressure was down today—if Melendez started screaming, it would all be over.

Instead, Melendez was kneeling on the wet floor of the shower, cold water dripping down his face, eyes wide, mouth open, trying to catch his breath like the stupid monkey in the story.

Next Tayvon grabbed his head a second time, yanked his head up by his hair, and brought his knee up into Melendez's jaw.

Bone on bone was always risky, but it would hurt Melendez a lot worse than it would Tayvon, and that was what mattered. Besides, if he broke the jaw, Melendez couldn't talk.

Several of Hakim's people started milling around, closing the circle so that no one outside would see what was going on.

Tayvon got a few more punches in, including

one to the ribs that resulted in at least a couple of broken bones.

Then he heard Bolton's voice. "Hey!"

As soon as he heard that, Tayvon disappeared into the crowd. Several people moved aside to let him blend in.

Bolton started wading into the shower, bellowing, "Kill the water, now!" As soon as he got to Melendez, who was now curled up in a fetal position on the wet floor, bleeding from his mouth and nose, Bolton said, "Ah, *shit*!" He pulled out his radio and called for medical.

Tayvon smiled. He got to throw down on the asshole who killed Malik. And Hakim had said that Tayvon wouldn't have to worry about any heat.

After over a year inside, Tayvon hadn't gotten to beat anyone up. He'd forgotten how much *fun* it was.

Of course, beating people up was what got him in here in the first place, but whatever. Putting a beat-down on some fool who deserved it—there wasn't anything better in the world.

15

MAC TAYLOR HAD SPENT last night alone.

There was a time when that wouldn't have been unusual. Since September 2001, after the loss of his wife, Claire, and so many others, he'd had to adjust to sleeping alone, on those rare occasions when he *could* sleep.

After five years, though, he found himself at last able to take someone else to his bed. Peyton Driscoll was someone he'd always liked and admired back when she had served as ME, and when she returned to the job a year ago, Mac had found that he liked and admired her even more. And then he found out that the feeling was mutual.

It had been a difficult road for Mac—and for Peyton, who had gone into the relationship knowing that she had competition from a ghost. Plus it seemed that the only feelings Mac had been able to tap into these days were negative ones: anger, frustration, vindictiveness. Others—humor, tenderness, affection, and yes, love—those were harder to come by.

When Stella had been attacked by her ex-boyfriend and forced to shoot him, Mac had been there for her as best he could. He had worked the scene, and he had taken her home. But he hadn't been able to be there for her emotionally—that had fallen to Flack. Mac couldn't even be there for himself emotionally, so how could he help Stella? The answer was by doing his job and letting Flack, who was better equipped to handle emotional breakdowns, be the shoulder to cry on.

Peyton was slowly reminding him how to do that. That didn't mean he didn't occasionally roll over expecting to see Claire there, and it didn't mean that he had gotten rid of the one item of hers he had kept (a beach ball she'd blown up, because it still held her breath), and it didn't mean he could fly over lower Manhattan (as he'd done on the way back from Staten Island yesterday) without a cold, icy hole opening in his stomach.

But he was getting there.

However, last night, Peyton had begged off their date because she wanted to make sure that the Barker autopsy was done properly. She anticipated exhaustion upon completion, so she went home, leaving Mac to sleep alone.

Or, at least, lie awake alone.

His first thought when he sees the report on channel 5 that a plane hit one of the WTC buildings is fear. Claire works in World Trade, and after a horrible accident like that, evacuating would be difficult. Still, after the bombing in 1993, the occupants of the Twin Towers had evac plans in place. Mac tries to call Claire, but he can't get through at her office or on her cell. The towers and phone lines are probably overloaded. Besides, it's just an accident, nothing to worry about.

That thought remains right until the second plane hits.

Up until then, this is a tragedy, a horrible accident, a plane going horrendously off course.

When the second plane hits, everything changes.

It's like a switch is thrown. Now it's no longer an accident—it's an attack.

Mac Taylor feels the change in his gut, the instincts of a detective, the instincts of a Marine. But in his heart there is still only one thought: Claire.

He will spend that entire horrible Tuesday trying to find out if she survived.

He will never hear from her again.

The memories were always there, but today—when the chopper to and from Staten Island had flown over Ground Zero—they were particularly intense.

Almost six full years later, and it was still a hole in the ground. They still hadn't recovered all the remains, and the remains they had found had yet to all be identified. Mac had no idea if finding Claire's genetic material on the site would make a difference to him. Was there a part of him still holding on to the possibility that she was alive somewhere?

It was ridiculous, of course. Mac was a rationalist, through and through, and there was simply no way that Claire would have stayed away all this time if she had survived, no matter what she might have gone through. She definitely died when the towers collapsed.

But why was there a part of Mac that held on? It was hard to say. Mac had been working murders for years now, and if he'd learned one thing in all that time it was that everyone reacted differently to the death of a loved one.

This morning, he came into the lab alone, cup of coffee in hand, only to find Peyton waiting in his office, along with Sheldon and Deputy Inspector Gerrard.

Opening the glass door to his office, he said without preamble, "I'm going to go out on a limb here and say this is about the Barker case."

"I'm afraid so," Peyton said. Her apologetic tone set the mood for Mac: something had gone wrong, or at least sideways.

Peyton simply handed him the autopsy report.

Mac flipped through it, then looked back up at her. "Anaphylactic shock?"

"That's my medical diagnosis, yes. The head wound was postmortem, which is why it bled so little."

"So how'd it happen?"

Sheldon stepped forward. "I actually have a theory on that, Mac. I haven't tested it out yet, but—"

"Then it's a hypothesis," Mac said, setting the report down on his desk. He walked around it, briefly looked at the view of Broadway out his large window, then sat in his leather chair. "Once you test it successfully, then it becomes a theory."

Hands on hips, Gerrard said, "Can we have grammar class some other time, please?"

Mac shot Gerrard an annoyed look, then said, "Go ahead, Sheldon."

"We found a thread on Washburne's shoulder, one that Adam identified as coming from RHCF prison dickies—but from the pants, not the shirt."

"So how'd it get on his shoulder?"

"My guess," Sheldon said, "is somebody bumped him when Barker got stabbed. Let's say he was lying on the weight bench when he went into anaphylactic shock. He could've died right there while lying down and nobody would've noticed."

"You think they'd miss that?" Gerrard asked.

"It's possible," Peyton said. "He stopped breathing when his throat closed up. He'd only be able to make incoherent whispery grunts."

Mac nodded. "Which wouldn't be all that different from the sounds people would be making while lifting weights."

Sheldon continued. "Besides, he had to have been dead for a few minutes before he got hit on the head in order for the wound to have had so little bleeding. Now when Barker got stabbed, it was chaos in there. Maybe someone bumped up against Washburne's body, knocking him off the weight bench, hitting his head on the weight hard enough to cause the gash and also knock the weight onto the ground."

Gerrard now folded his arms over his chest. "It's also possible that Melendez took the weight off the bar and hit Washburne over the head with it, not realizing he was already dead."

"I've met the man," Mac said, "and I can't say with a straight face that he wouldn't be that stupid."

"I'll run some simulations," Sheldon said, "see which scenario fits the evidence."

"All right," Gerrard said, "then what did Washburne react to?"

"That's the problem," Peyton said. "I haven't the foggiest. All his stomach contents were long digested, so it couldn't have been something he ate. The tox report only showed Klonopin. Accord-

ing to his prison record, he's been taking Klonopin
since his trial, so it couldn't have been that."

"People develop allergies as they get older," Gerrard said. "When I turned forty, I suddenly became
allergic to powdered detergents."

Peyton shook her head. "It's possible, but there
would have been a sign of it. According to the
prescriptions in prison records, Malik Washburne
was taking one hundred milligrams of Klonopin
every day for almost a year. That violent an allergy
doesn't develop overnight."

Mac's Treo rang in his suit jacket. Pulling it out,
he saw it was Flack. He put the call on speaker and
said, "Don, it's Mac—I've got you on speaker with
Peyton, Sheldon, and Inspector Gerrard."

Flack's tinny voice said, "I just got off the phone
with Ursitti. Seems somebody beat the crap out of
Jorge Melendez."

"What? Why?"

"Ursitti tells me that it's retribution for Washburne's death."

Gerrard said, "How the hell did anyone there
know Melendez was a suspect?"

"That's the sixty-four-thousand-dollar question,
Inspector. I'm headin' back there now," Flack
said.

"I'll meet you there," Mac told him.

"I'm stuck in traffic on the BQE, so you'll probably beat me there."

Mac looked at Gerrard, who said, "You will—you can have the chopper again."

"Thanks." He looked down at the phone. "I'll see you there, Don."

After hanging up, he looked at Sheldon. "You and Danny do a re-creation, see if you can figure out exactly how Washburne would've received his wound and gotten onto the ground."

"On it," Sheldon said, and left.

Before Mac could say anything else, Peyton said, "I'll run some more blood tests, see if we can find something exotic that a standard tox screen wouldn't find." He nodded in thanks, and Peyton also took her leave.

That left Mac and Gerrard in the room together, which wasn't particularly comfortable for either man. Though Mac found he didn't give a good goddamn what was comfortable for the deputy inspector.

"Can I help you with something else, Stan?"

"That's 'Inspector Gerrard,' Detective Taylor. You lost the right to use my first name when you stabbed me in the back."

"*I* stabbed *you* in the back?" Mac was incredulous. "I wasn't the one who sicced Internal on me after the DA had already cleared me!"

"Yeah, and neither was I—that was Sinclair. *I* was the one who did you the courtesy of meeting with you and informing you of the investigation.

Sinclair didn't even want that much—he would've been happy for you to hear about it on New York 1 with the rest of the city, but I thought you deserved the consideration of a face-to-face. Your response to this courtesy was to insult me, and then, when you felt like the hearing wasn't going your way, you decided to dig up dirt on me." Gerrard stepped forward and leaned over Mac's desk, his palms flat on the wood surface. "If you think for a second that I'm going to forget what you did to me, Detective, you are sadly mistaken. From here on in, I'll be taking permanent residence up your rectum, and you'd better for *damn* sure walk straight and fly right. That goes for your usual gang of idiots out there, too. If Messer goes whacko again, if Monroe bolts a crime scene—yeah, I know about that—or if you decide to go vigilante again, I will be there with a giant hammer, and I will use it to nail your ass to the wall."

Gerrard seemed to think that was a good exit line, because he chose that moment to walk toward the door. Then he stopped and turned around. "Washburne was a member, Mac. Do right by him."

"That was always my intention," Mac said tightly. "Is there anything in my history that suggests I'd do otherwise?"

"Six months ago, I'd have said no, but now? Now you're going around threatening the chief of detectives. That's a special kind of stupid, Mac. I don't want you to screw up, but if you do, you will pay for it. Oh, and one more thing—you said you were getting the hang of playing politics, but politics is like poker. You don't show your hand till all the betting's in."

"The betting *was* in, Inspector," Mac said angrily. "You and Sinclair were railroading me."

"How do you know? The investigation wasn't over yet. How did you know you wouldn't get the same get-out-of-jail-free card the DA gave you?"

Not buying the notion for a second, Mac said, "Was that likely to happen?"

Gerrard smiled. "Oh, I could tell you, Mac—but that would be doing you a favor. I'm not inclined to do favors for detectives who blackmail me. So I'll just let you stew on that one and remind you that I know what you have in your hand now."

Then Gerrard finally left.

Mac turned his chair around and stared out the window. He looked at the cars moving slowly down Broadway. It was a long drop from Mac's office to the street.

Even longer than the drop Dobson took.

Unbidden, his mind turned back to Dobson's smirk as he jumped off the roof, preferring death to another prison term. He'd already tried to kill himself once rather than go to jail, a fact that Gerrard himself had covered up.

Mac was going to have to live with that smirk for the rest of his life.

Gerrard was right about one thing—Mac wasn't all that great at playing politics. He preferred the simplicity of the lab: you found out what happened through evidence, through facts. Politics was all about obfuscation.

He'd been lucky with the dirt he had on Gerrard. Mac had no faith that a politically motivated witch hunt would find him anything other than guilty, no matter what mind games Gerrard was playing now.

Shaking his head, he turned back toward his desk. Gerrard didn't matter. Sure, he'd be taking up residence in his rectum, as he so indelicately put it, but he'd been living there ever since Gerrard's promotion when the inspector decided to throw his weight around during the UN translator case. Gerrard being an irritant was already a given part of the equation, so Mac wasn't going to concern himself.

His job was to solve the variables.

Getting up from his desk, he called ahead to the copter pad, requesting a lift to Staten Island.

16

LINDSAY WOULD MUCH PREFER that Stella had done this.

Angell had called Stella, asking someone from the crime lab to meet her at the Rosengaus apartment on West 247th Street, a bit farther into Riverdale than Belluso's. But since Stella had her meeting with Cabrera, she fobbed it off on Lindsay, who was not looking forward to navigating through the steep hills and twisty-turny roads that characterized Riverdale.

Sure enough, after getting off the Henry Hudson Parkway (even with its toll—Stella's exact instructions: "Screw the E-Z Pass memo, just get where you need to go") at 246th Street, she made several wrong turns. The numbering of the streets up here didn't seem to make any sense; they twisted every which way, and not for the first time, she found herself missing the straight, perpendicular roads of Bozeman.

Eventually, she found the place. It was a three-story house with a two-car garage of a type she'd seen often in the outer boroughs. Perpendicular to the garage was a screen door that led to a ground-floor apartment. Said door was set under a staircase that led to a porch overhanging the garage, where there were another two doors. One would lead to the second-floor apartment, with the other leading to another staircase that took you to the third floor.

Two cars were parked in front of the garage, preventing Lindsay from pulling in there. Instead, she found a parking spot halfway down the block and across the street, between two driveways, so she didn't have to parallel park. She'd never acquired the parallel parking skill—it was the only part of the driving test she'd failed back home—and she rarely had need to practice it. The only time she drove was on official business, and most of the time, she could park wherever she wanted.

She supposed she could have parked in the driveway, but that seemed like an abuse of privilege, somehow. If she put her NYPD ID on the dashboard, she wouldn't be hassled; it still felt wrong to Lindsay. If Danny were here, he'd probably tease her about her bumpkin ways, but there was more to it than that. After what Mac went through with Sinclair, Lindsay felt that even the perception of wrongdoing would hurt the crime lab right now, and any kind of bad press would just get in the way of the work. Even though she'd been with the crime lab for over a year, she was still the rookie, and she wasn't about to be the one to get Mac in trouble.

The address Stella had given her was for apartment three. After retrieving her case from the trunk, she crossed the street and walked up the outside staircase of the house, her shoes clacking on the stone steps. Assuming that the leftmost door was the one for upstairs, she rang that bell. Moments later, she heard the muffled sound of feet coming down a flight of stairs, then the creak of the door opening.

An older woman who was dressed up in a silk blouse and slacks, her face elegantly painted with makeup, opened the door. Lindsay instantly saw the family resemblance between her and Dina Rosengaus.

Holding up her badge, she identified herself.

"Come in, please," the woman said.

Lindsay followed her up the wooden stairs through a door that led to a hallway that continued straight ahead, with a doorway leading to a dining room on the right.

Seated there was an overweight man with a

large nose, wearing only a white undershirt and shorts; Dina Rosengaus, whose cheeks were wet and puffy with crying; and Angell.

In the center of the dining room table, on a white tablecloth, was a gold chain.

Angell said, "Look what we found. Nobody's touched it since Dina came out—we were waiting for you."

Wasting no time, Lindsay pulled a latex glove out of her back pocket—she always kept several there—and placed her case on the dining room table. Clacking it open, she pulled out a small evidence envelope, labeled it with a red Sharpie, and then put the glove on with a rubberized snap. Picking up the chain, she took a quick look at it. It was actually rather a nice necklace. She had already been told back at Belluso's yesterday that it was eighteen-karat gold, and so she handled it gingerly, as higher-karat gold was softer and more malleable. It was eighteen inches long, a standard length of braided rope chain, a beautiful butter-gold color typical of Italian eighteen-karat work, with a lobster-claw clasp. At a glance, at least, the clasp seemed to match the abrasion on the back of Maria's neck.

Peering more closely at it, she saw a tiny bit of discoloration on one of the links. Praying that it was dried blood, she dropped the necklace into the envelope and sealed it.

The older man said something in Russian. Dina muttered something back.

Angell said, "So, Dina, you want to explain why you have Maria's necklace?"

"I didn't kill her," Dina said, her voice breaking. "I just—" She swallowed. "Jeanie was calling 911. While she talked to them, I reached down and—and I took necklace."

"Why?" Lindsay was horrified.

"I—I never like Maria much. I know that is not right, but is true." Dina's English grammar was worse than usual, Lindsay noted, which was a normal sign of stress. "She was always talking about how wonderful her boyfriend was. I have not had boyfriend since coming to this country. When I did have boyfriend, Sasha was never able to buy me anything as nice as this. And the necklace—*always* the necklace. Never did Maria pass up opportunity to remind us that Bobby got her necklace."

Angell shook her head. "So you took it."

The man said more in Russian. The woman put a hand on his shoulder and said a single word.

"It was stupid, I know, and I'm sorry."

"Yeah, well," Angell said with a wince, "that's really not gonna cover it. You've opened yourself to criminal charges."

"What do you mean?" the man asked, speaking English for the first time. His voice wasn't as deep in this language.

"I mean she interfered with a murder investigation. And Detective Monroe here is going to take that necklace back to her lab, and she's going to see if there's anything on there that proves that your daughter committed the murder. And even if she doesn't, I could arrest her right now on charges of desecration of remains and obstruction of justice."

The tears started pouring down Dina's cheeks now. "I'm—I'm sorry, I didn't—"

Dina's father stood up. "Are you threatening my daughter, Detective?"

"Alec, *please*, calm down," the mother said, still sitting, looking up at him with a pleading expression.

"No, Raya, I will not calm down. My daughter came to *you* with this!"

"She also took the necklace in the first place," Lindsay said in a gentle voice, hoping to play peacemaker. Angell looked like she was ready to go ten rounds with Mr. Rosengaus, and that wouldn't do anyone any good—least of all Angell.

"I not kill her," Dina said in a small, sob-choked voice.

Lindsay thought that tone sounded eerily familiar. "We'll find that out."

Angell got up. "I'm not going to arrest anybody right now, but I will come back, rest assured. C'mon, Lindsay."

Closing her case, Lindsay removed the glove and put it back in her pocket—she preferred to dispose of it back in the lab instead of in the Rosengauses' garbage—and followed Angell downstairs.

"You were a little hard on her, weren't you?" Lindsay waited until they were outside to ask the question.

"I barely got started," Angell said with a snort. "The father was giving me attitude before you got there. He wanted to know when the 'real' detective was showing up. And I'm not convinced that our girl didn't do it. She's tall enough, and she might have the strength."

"Maybe," Lindsay said. "It's kind of a long shot, though."

"Well, do your lab thing, then. If that little stain really is blood, then we may have our killer."

"Keep in mind that it may be Maria's blood."

Angell sighed as she walked down the outer staircase to her car, which turned out to be one of the ones in the driveway. "I hope not. I need something definite here. As long as Morgenstern has his shark on retainer, we can't do anything with him unless the evidence is a *lot* more solid than what we have."

Nodding, Lindsay said, "I'll get right on this and get back to you."

Angell nodded as she got into her sedan.

17

WHEN MAC ARRIVED AT RHCF, he went immediately to the arsenal and checked his weapon and his Treo. After being handed the key by the CO on duty, he went inside, signed in, and waited while the CO behind the bench looked over his large metal case. It wasn't the same CO who was at the bench yesterday—this time it was a short man with thick glasses resting on a small nose, which in turn was over a thick mustache. All he needed were bushy eyebrows to complete the Groucho Marx look.

"What's this?" the CO asked, holding up Mac's Nikon.

Thinking it might be a trick question, Mac slowly said, "It's a camera."

"I don't think you're allowed to have that in here."

Mac sighed. He understood that the officer was just doing his job, but he really wasn't in the mood for this today. "I'm a detective with the New York Crime Lab—I need my camera in order to do my job. When I was here yesterday, I had all this equipment with me."

"Well, that's fine for yesterday, sir, but that was then and this is now. I can't allow you to take that camera in with you."

Mac doubted he'd even need the camera, but he hated the notion of being without it—especially if he *did* need it for a reason he couldn't predict.

After a brief pause, Mac said, "Call Captain Russell up here, he'll vouch for me."

Peering at Mac through the thick glasses, the CO said, "Sir, this is policy—there's no need to bother the captain with this. I can't allow you to take the camera inside."

Before Mac could object further, he heard the metallic hum of the outer door opening. Turning, he saw Ursitti walking through it, then waiting for the inner door to open.

When it did, he stepped through and said, "Detective Taylor. What's the holdup?"

"This officer won't let me bring my camera inside."

Ursitti gave the CO behind the desk a pained look. Mac had the feeling he'd used that particular look on that particular CO many a time. "What the hell is your problem?"

"LT, it's policy that—"

"It's policy that people don't die in custody. Let him take the damn camera."

With the utmost reluctance, the CO said, "If you say so, LT."

"Yeah, I *say* so." As Mac collected his case, Ursitti added, "I'm sorry, Detective."

Not wanting to create ill will, Mac said, "It's all right. The officer was just doing his duty."

After Mac had his hand stamped, Ursitti took him through both sets of doors, had his hand checked under the black light between them, then led him to a part of the prison he hadn't been to the last time: the infirmary.

The nature of his job was such that Mac had visited many hospitals, from various state-of-the-art facilities in the city where assorted victims had been taken, to the patch-'em-up makeshift field hospitals in Beirut when he served in the Marines. Involuntarily, Mac's hand went to his heart, where he was wounded in 1983; he'd been patched up in one of those field hospitals. The scar had faded, though it was still very visible, and it didn't twinge anymore when it rained, but he was always aware of it.

The infirmary at RHCF was somewhere between those two extremes: not as fancy as Bellevue, Cabrini, St. Luke's–Roosevelt, or the other Manhattan places he frequented, but not quite as depressing as the field hospital. There were two rows of beds lined up, some with patients, others empty and neatly made.

Ursitti brought him to a far corner, where a doctor was waiting, along with Russell. Lying on the bed was Jorge Melendez. Mac immediately noticed bruising on Melendez's jaw. He appeared to be asleep—Mac assumed he was on morphine, which had turned his lights right out.

Russell introduced the doctor, whose name was Patel.

"What happened?" Mac asked.

"He was assaulted in the shower," Dr. Patel said as he pulled the sheet down to reveal multiple contusions on Melendez's chest, some of which were obscured by bandages. "Cracked three ribs. No internal bleeding, though."

Mac nodded. "I'm not surprised. Whoever did this knew exactly what he was doing."

"What do you mean?" Russell asked.

"He was hit hardest in the solar plexus, right where the breath would be knocked out of someone, preventing him from calling for help. Based on those bruises, the blows were landed solidly, despite both the first and the target being dripping wet. This is the mark of an experienced pugilist."

Russell shrugged. "Well, we already know who did it."

This was news to Mac. "Who was it?"

"El-Jabbar. He confessed to it an hour ago. Said he wanted to mete out justice to 'Brother Malik's' killer."

"There's just one problem," Mac said.

"What's that?"

"Melendez didn't kill Malik Washburne."

Russell's white mustache twitched. "What?"

"Washburne died of anaphylactic shock. We're not sure from what yet, but Jorge Melendez isn't a strong suspect right now. Nobody is until we figure out what killed him." He looked at Ursitti. "What I want to know is how el-Jabbar knew that Melendez even *was* a suspect."

Frowning, Ursitti said, "I was kinda wonderin' that myself."

"I think we need to talk to Mr. el-Jabbar."

"He's in the box," Russell said. To Ursitti: "Have him brought to the interview room."

Ursitti's radio crackled, informing him that Flack had arrived.

"Have him meet us at the interview room," Mac told Ursitti, who nodded to him and Russell.

It took several minutes for Mac and Russell to get to the interview room, which was halfway across the prison. The walk was a much different experience today then it had been yesterday, when the place was in lockdown. Inmates walked casually through the corridors and outside. Most of them respectfully greeted Russell, and the captain gave them each at least a nod back. Some he talked to, asking how they were doing. A couple tried to engage him in conversation, but he politely put them off to another time. One even said, "This is about Malik and Vance, right?"

Russell said, "I can't really say," even though it was obvious that it couldn't be anything else.

Several more minutes passed after they arrived before Flack showed up, escorted by Ursitti.

"Glad you could make it," Mac said with a wry smile as the pair entered.

Shaking his head, Flack said, "Ran my damn siren on the BQE, and I *still* couldn't move more than ten miles an hour. I'm half-tempted to leave the car here and fly back with you."

Mac felt Flack's pain. It was less of an issue for the crime lab, as they generally weren't needed until after everything was over, but New York City traffic had always been a major impediment to cops' ability to arrive at a crime scene in a timely manner. Mac knew that Flack felt that frustration keenly. It was even worse for FDNY, for whom time was always of the essence. Fire truck drivers, he knew, hated navigating the city streets with a passion.

While waiting for el-Jabbar's arrival, Mac filled Flack in on Melendez's condition.

Flack's eyebrows formed a V over his blue eyes. "How the hell did el-Jabbar find out about Melendez?"

"We'll know soon," Russell said confidently.

Mac hoped that confidence was warranted.

Eventually, Officer Andros brought in Hakim el-Jabbar. The inmate wore a knit red-and-white skullcap on his head, but otherwise sported the usual prison dickies. Yesterday he had been one of Mac and Flack's many interviews, but he claimed not to have seen anything. He wasn't a very big man, but he had wide, expressive brown eyes, an aquiline nose, and a broad mouth surrounded by a thin beard.

He spoke in a soft, insistent voice. "What can I do for you gentlemen today?"

"For starters," Flack said, "why'd you beat the crap out of Jorge Melendez?"

"Jorge was a pretender. He used the word of Allah for his own purposes. And when Brother Malik exposed his lie, Jorge killed him. He needed to pay for that." As he spoke, el-Jabbar folded his handcuffed hands neatly in front of him on the table.

Mac stared at those hands while Flack continued the questioning.

"What makes you think that Melendez killed 'Brother Malik'?"

El-Jabbar smiled, showing a wide array of perfect teeth. "There is no need to be coy, Detective. I'm aware of the fact that he is your primary suspect."

Flack leaned forward. "Fine. We'll drop coy. How the *hell* did you find out Melendez was a suspect?"

"I prefer to protect my sources. Let us just say that information comes my way."

Mac spoke up. "You're not a journalist, Mr. el-Jabbar, and you're not a lawyer. You're a prisoner. Privilege doesn't apply."

"Perhaps not. But the punishment for noncooperation would be solitary confinement—which I am already enduring."

That elicited a snort from Andros.

"So," Flack said, "when this information came your way, you took it upon yourself to take care of business?"

"Brother Malik was a respected member of the community—both inside this prison and outside it. Jorge needed to pay, so I administered justice in the shower this morning."

"Yeah." Flack leaned back and folded his arms over his dark tie. "Administering justice is kind of *our* thing." El-Jabbar was about to speak, but Flack unfolded his arms to raise one hand, cutting him off. "I know, I know, it's just 'white man's justice.' That doesn't really count for you, does it?"

"Something like that." Again, el-Jabbar smiled.

Mac decided he didn't like that smile and so was determined to wipe it off his face. "There's just one problem, Mr. el-Jabbar—you didn't beat anybody up."

Sure enough, the smile fell, which gave Mac a measure of satisfaction. "I beg your pardon, Detective?"

"Beg all you want, you're not getting it." Pointing at el-Jabbar's hands, still folded neatly, Mac said, "Your knuckles are smooth and clean. No abrasions, no calluses. Whoever attacked Melendez was experienced and would have evidence of that experience on his hands. Evidence doesn't lie, Mr. el-Jabbar—and in this case, neither does lack of evidence. Who are you covering for?"

"I do not need to 'cover' for anyone, Detective. It was my wish that Jorge pay for Brother Malik's death."

Mac shook his head. So now he was changing his story—he ordered the beat-down. "Unfortunately, you collected your debt from the wrong man." At el-Jabbar's confused expression, he added: "Malik Washburne died of anaphylactic shock. Jorge Melendez didn't kill him."

"What? But I was told—" He cut himself off.

Flack stared at him. "Who told you?"

"It does not matter."

"Yeah, it kind of does. See, info about suspects isn't something we like to have advertised in the middle of an investigation."

"Probably one of the COs," Andros said.

Russell drew himself up. "What makes you say that, Officer?"

Andros shrugged. "Most of the other COs liked Washburne for whatever stupid reason."

Defensively, Flack said, "He used to be a good cop."

"Maybe—I don't know about that. I do know that everybody liked him."

Pointedly, el-Jabbar said, "Except for *you*, Officer Andros."

Ignoring him, Andros said, "The point is, I could see one of the COs telling 'Brother Hakim' here that Melendez was the suspect, 'cause they know just how he'd respond."

"That doesn't make sense," Russell said. "And besides, if Detective Taylor is right, and el-Jabbar didn't do it, why take credit when it means going into the box?"

"Please." Andros snorted. "For *him*, solitary's a vacation. It's quiet, he gets food brought to him, and he can meditate."

Flack turned to el-Jabbar. "So how 'bout it, 'Brother'? Who gave Melendez up?"

"Again, Detective," el-Jabbar said placidly, "I prefer to protect my sources."

"And protect yourself," Mac said. "Assuming Officer Andros is correct, and you give up a CO, there might be retribution."

Archly, Russell said, "That doesn't go on here."

Mac didn't see any need to press the issue—though Andros did give another derisive snort. El-Jabbar wasn't going to talk. Mac wasn't thrilled, but it was also beside the point.

And they were no closer to finding out how Malik Washburne had died.

Danny Messer just loved the NYPD Crime Lab's proprietary computer-aided design program, which they used to reconstruct crime scenes.

The programming geeks had streamlined the whole thing, so all you had to do was enter in the height and weight of a person. If you wanted to add further details, you could, or you could just use the generic body. Then you entered the dimensions of the figure's surrounding environment.

It was all pretty basic stuff, but the streamlining was what made the difference. In particular, Danny loved the fact that it could cross-reference with the autopsy records, so all you had to do was enter the case number and it would provide an image of the body right away.

As soon as Sheldon came to him saying that

they needed to reconstruct Malik Washburne's
murder with the new information that showed he
died from his throat closing up, Danny immediately ran to the computer like a kid on Christmas
morning. Sheldon, of course, let him, knowing
that Danny would piss and moan if he ran the program without him.

Danny could be a magnificent pain in the ass.
He viewed it as one of his finest qualities.

Sheldon didn't, which was why he let Danny
run the program.

"Okay," Danny said, cracking his knuckles as
he sat down at the ergonomic keyboard that Mac
insisted on them using. He hated the stupid things,
but every time he complained, Mac would e-mail
him multiple studies on repetitive stress injuries
until Danny shut up. Mac could also be a magnificent pain in the ass when he put his mind to it,
only he was more subtle about it.

Danny didn't do subtle. It wasted too much en-
ergy.

First he called up the autopsy records for Malik
Washburne and entered it into the CAD program.
Immediately, an image of a generic male human
figure of Washburne's height, weight, and build
appeared on all three monitors in front of him.
Then he created a second, identical image.

Sheldon had his full report from the crime scene,
and he read out the dimensions of the weight

bench, the barbell, and the doughnut weights that were on it. The crime-scene photos placed everything, including the doughnut weights that were on the barbell and the one on the ground.

"Hang on," Danny said. "Why would the weight be on the ground?"

"That's where we found it," Sheldon said.

"Yeah, but why would Washburne have an uneven number of weights?"

"Dunno, but let's start with it there and see where it goes."

"Yeah." He placed everything where it belonged, putting one of the Washburne figures on the weight bench in the standard position and the other one where the body lay, based on Sheldon's photos.

Next they had to enter more precise information. Danny created another generic male figure. "Where'd you find the thread on Washburne's body from the guy's pants?"

Sheldon reached over and grabbed the mouse.

"Hey! Who's doing this?" Danny protested.

"I could take half an hour to explain it, or I could just point the damn mouse," Sheldon said with a good-natured grin.

Sighing dramatically, Danny leaned back and said, "Fine, fine, steal my thunder."

Shaking his head, Sheldon said, "You are *such* a geek."

"Yeah, bite me, Doc."

Once Sheldon clicked on the spot where they found the thread, Danny gently pushed him out of the way and started entering in the trajectory he needed the second figure to take in order to leave the thread.

"Now for the real important question—how hard does he have to hit in order to knock Washburne onto the floor?"

"Average foot speed for someone walking is three miles an hour," Sheldon said. "Well, actually, it's between two-point-eight and three-point-two miles an hour, but we should start with that."

"You know that off the top of your head, but *I'm* the geek?"

"Absolutely," Sheldon deadpanned.

Danny chuckled. "That's probably too slow, but you're right, it's a good start." He entered three miles per hour and had the second body walk in such a way that his left hip (where the seam was) would hit Washburne in the right spot in the shoulder.

The figure moved across the screen, and Washburne barely budged.

Sheldon rubbed his chin. "If he was reacting to Barker getting stabbed, he probably wasn't walking at a leisurely pace."

"Didn't I say that?" Danny asked with a cheeky grin. "Let's make it eight."

"I was thinking ten," Sheldon said.

"Well, you're the expert on foot speed," Danny said dryly, "but that weight yard wasn't *that* big, and it was filled to capacity. Even if he was motorin', he wasn't gonna be able to go much more than eight."

Tilting his head to the side, Sheldon said, "Yeah, okay, let's go with eight."

"Glad you approve."

"Hey, this is *my* half of the case. You got the dunker, remember?"

"Oh yeah, exciting stuff. The guy confessed, and I got prints on the murder weapon that matched the guy who confessed. Wasn't exactly breakin' my brain, y'know? Flack may like the dunkers, but me? I like a challenge."

"That why you chased Lindsay to Montana?" Sheldon was grinning as he said that. "What's happening with you two anyhow?"

"We're friends and colleagues," was all Danny would say, not wanting to give Sheldon the satisfaction of sharing gossip, especially when the gossip was about him. After a rocky start, Danny and Lindsay Monroe's relationship had taken a turn for the better ever since he took personal time and flew out to Bozeman to lend moral support when Lindsay testified against Kadems.

But Danny was still pissed that he was the last to know about Mac and Dr. Driscoll, so he intended to keep everyone in the dark as long as he could get away with it.

"Okay," he said, dragging them back to the subject at hand, "eight miles an hour. Let's see what we got."

This time the second figure collided with Washburne hard enough to knock the body off the bench. He hit his head on the edge of the barbell and fell to the ground, but not in a position that matched that of the second Washburne.

Sheldon was shaking his head. "That doesn't work. The body's in the wrong place—and even if you figure it's been moved, or we got a variable wrong, there's also the fact that there's no blood on the barbell, and the barbell couldn't have caused that wound in the first place."

"Yeah, but look at the placement." Danny pointed at the spot on the barbell where Washburne's head had hit in the second simulation. "Let's try putting the weight where it's supposed to be, on the end of the barbell." Using the mouse, Danny moved it from the ground to that spot.

He ran the sim again, at the same speed. Again the second figure hit Washburne. Again Washburne hit his head on the barbell and fell in the wrong spot.

"Move the weight," Sheldon said. "Maybe they weren't on evenly."

Nodding, Danny shifted the weight so it would

be right where Washburne's head hit. Again he ran it at eight miles per hour.

Washburne hit this time, but in the wrong place on his head, and he didn't fall to the ground anywhere near the second Washburne.

"I'll make him go faster. Guy just got shivved, I bet he's runnin'. 'Sides, the faster he goes, the more likely there is to be that thread transfer."

Sheldon shrugged. "Fair enough. Worth a shot, anyhow."

Upping it to eleven miles an hour, Danny ran it again. This time Washburne's head hit the spot between two of the weights, so he moved the weight back to its first position and ran it again.

This time, not only did Washburne's head hit the weight in the right spot, but the weight fell off in the right spot *and* Washburne's body fell in the same location as the second body. It wasn't a one hundred percent matchup, but it was close enough to establish that that was likely what had happened.

"So that's it," Sheldon said. "Washburne's throat closes up. He can't call for help, and he dies on the bench. Mulroney stabs Barker. Everyone in the yard comes running to see what's going on, and one of them bumps Washburne, transferring a fiber to his shoulder and knocking him into the weight, which causes the wound and also knocks the weight to the ground."

Danny nodded. "Only one problem—how'd Melendez's print get on the weight?"

"He probably used the weight. Hell, so many people touched that thing, the print hit was always going to be circumstantial just by virtue of Melendez being one of the people in the yard. He had every reason to touch it."

"Yeah." Danny saved the latest simulation to the folder for the report on the Washburne-Barker double homicide. Another advantage of the CAD program was that it recorded all the information that had been entered, so it could be used in court. Danny wasn't sure how useful this would be, or even if the case would go to trial—with anaphylactic shock as the COD, it was more than likely there *was* no murderer to try—but the file still needed to be complete.

Stretching his back so a couple of vertebrae cracked, he got up and said, "Pleasure workin' with you, Doc. Now if you'll excuse me, I gotta see a man about a dog."

In fact, he had a date with Lindsay, assuming she was done with whatever she and Stella were doing for the Campagna case.

If she wasn't, he'd wait. She was worth it.

18

LINDSAY MONROE OPENED THE evidence envelope and plucked out the gold necklace.

The first thing she did was lay it down gently on the white surface of the big table in the crime lab, with the tiny stain visible, and photograph it. After taking several shots of it as a whole, she attached the Sigma telephoto lens to the camera and zoomed in on the stain itself.

She grabbed a sterile cotton swab and moistened it with distilled water, then applied it to the necklace where the stain was. The blood obligingly came off on the swab.

She applied part of the sample on the swab to a plastic container. Then she brought the swab over to the matrix-assisted laser desorption/ionization (MALDI) mass spectrograph. The MALDI would measure the mass-to-charge ratio of the ions, which would enable Lindsay to discover the molecular nature of the sample. In this particular case, it would allow her to identify the species of the sample's source from the hemogloblin in the blood.

While she waited for that analysis to complete, she brought the plastic container to the DNA lab.

She saw the blond-haired head of Jane Parsons sitting at her desk. Turning around at Lindsay's entrance, she smiled raggedly and said, "Ah—beware Montanans bearing gifts."

Lindsay smiled. "Sorry, but I've got blood."

"Don't we all?" She shook her head. "Sorry—had a long night. I've been dating this nice young ER doctor, and he keeps odd hours."

"When do you get to see him?" Lindsay asked. She knew that emergency-room physicians kept hours that were as long as they were odd. She'd gotten to know a couple of ER docs since coming to New York. Often during assault and rape cases, she'd have to go to the ER at Bellevue or Cabrini or St. Luke's–Roosevelt or somewhere. In particular, Lindsay had had to do a lot of rape kits, since it was generally preferred that female techs do those, and Stella wasn't always available. But the docs in the ER were *constantly* talking about their lack of a social life.

"Not very often, which is why I take advantage when I can. I joked with him last night that he should become a librarian—their hours are a trifle more sane. Besides, he likes to read, it'd be good work for him. And I'm babbling, I'm sorry—what've you got for me?"

Handing over the sample, Lindsay said, "This is for the Campagna case. It might be the vic's, but if it isn't, we need to know. First person to check it against after the vic is Jack Morgenstern—he's in the system. And then do the reference samples that are in the case file."

"All right. Oh, and the results are back on the trace around the vic's knuckles. Hang on." Jane started digging around on her desk. "I swear, I was organized once." She finally liberated the proper folder. "I'm afraid there's no love there—the blood and epithelials you found were all hers. The only way it's a transfer is if she was killed by a family member."

"Thanks, Jane. And I hope you and the ER doc are able to make it work."

"I'm sure we will, somehow. Pity he can't actually become a librarian."

Frowning, Lindsay asked, "Why not?"

"You need a degree for that, I'm afraid. And the only master's degree my young man has is in biology."

Lindsay had no idea you needed a master's degree to be a librarian, but that was neither here nor there. "Well, I'm sure you two will work it out."

"Let's hope, shall we? We don't have it as easy as you and Danny do."

Having already turned to leave, Lindsay stopped dead in her tracks. "What're you talking about?" She tried desperately to sound casual and hoped it worked.

"Don't be coy, Lindsay. He flew to Montana for you. I've known the good Mr. Messer for some time—he wouldn't willingly cross the Hudson River without good cause, much less go somewhere like the Show-me State."

Chuckling, Lindsay said, "That's Missouri."

"Beg pardon?"

"Missouri is the Show-me State. Montana is the Treasure State. Or Big Sky Country."

"There's treasure in Montana?"

Lindsay smiled, remembering something Danny had said: that Montana's best treasure was in New York now. It was one of the most romantic things Danny had said to her—not that the competition was fierce, as Danny wasn't good at romantic sayings. Gestures, yes, but the actual words had a hard time making it through his sarcasm filter.

To Parsons, she only said, "There's some left, yeah. Let me know about the blood."

"I will. And best of luck with Danny."

Tempted to say "I don't think I need it," Lindsay just nodded and left. Things had been going really well for them, after a rocky start. Still, they were taking it very slow. Office romances were fraught with peril, and they didn't want to risk the work. They also weren't completely sure how Mac would respond to two people on the same team having a relationship, though Danny seemed to think that he didn't have a leg to stand on, considering his relationship with Peyton.

But Peyton wasn't on the team. It wasn't the same thing.

However, she'd worry about that later. While she was waiting for Parsons and the MALDI to finish their respective work, she returned to the necklace.

Something had been bothering her about the necklace from the moment she walked into the Rosengauses' apartment, and looking at it now, she finally realized what it was: it was sparkling. Gold necklaces didn't stay that clean without a great deal of effort on the part of the owner.

Repeating the steps she'd taken with the dried blood, Lindsay used the cotton swab on a cleaner part of the necklace, hoping that the residue that came off would be something useful. Bringing it over to the MALDI, she saw that the mass spectrometer had just finished on the dried blood sample. Grabbing the printout from the printer attached to the MALDI, she saw that the hemoglobin came from human blood, type AB-negative.

Now she put the new sample into the mass spectrometer and ran it. While she waited, she returned to the necklace, examining it closely but not finding anything else of use. However, she did call up the autopsy photos and compared the photos she'd taken of the lobster-claw clasp to that of the abrasion on the back of Maria Campagna's neck. It wasn't a perfect match—one of the first things she learned in the Bozeman crime lab was that there was no such animal—but it was a very close match. Certainly close enough to convince a jury that the necklace belonged to her and that she'd worn it regularly.

When the MALDI finished, Lindsay looked at the molecular composition and found her memory jogged to a case she'd had back home a few years earlier. It was very similar to a sample from that rash of home robberies. The perp's lawyer had claimed that the jewelry recovered wasn't the same as the jewelry that was reported stolen, and one of the ways Lindsay had been able to prove the lawyer wrong was by testing the residue of silver polish and gold cleaner on the recovered jewelry against what the victim used.

Right now, she was staring at a molecular composition that bore a *very* close resemblance to the ones she saw from the mass spectrometer back in Bozeman.

She was flipping through patent applications on

the computer when Stella came in, shrugging into
a white lab coat. "How goes it?"

"Not bad. All done with Cabrera?"

Stella nodded. "Yeah, the testimony'll be a
breeze. Anything on that necklace?"

Handing the results from the MALDI to her,
Lindsay said, "The blood's definitely human. Type
AB-negative. Jane's running it now. Oh, and she
said that the only DNA on Maria's knuckles was
Maria's."

"Damn." Stella scanned the results. "Morgenstern's O-positive."

"There's more," Lindsay said. She knew Stella
and Angell both had latched onto Morgenstern
as a suspect, so she knew that this news wouldn't
be well received. "I examined the necklace, and
besides the blood, there's residue from another
substance. I've been checking it against patent applications, and I've got a hit." She pointed at the
flat-screen monitor in front of her. Two identical
molecular compositions were in two windows on
the screen, but one image came from the U.S. Patent Office and the other from the New York Crime
Lab. "This is a gold and silver cleaner that went on
the market earlier this year."

Stella was impressed. "Why'd you go straight to
the patent applications?"

"It looked similar to the usual gold and silver
cleaners that I've seen, but it was different enough

that I figured it was something new. We had a case back in Bozeman involving this stuff. I got to learn more than I thought it was possible to know about what you use to clean jewelry. Besides, apart from the bloodstain, the necklace was *very* clean, so cleaning products made sense."

Nodding, Stella said, "That tracks with what Angell got out of the other employees. She reinterviewed Annie Wolfowitz, the one Maria was supposed to close with last night. She said that the necklace was clean when she saw it last and that Maria was obsessive about keeping it shiny."

"I think that's part of why Dina stole it," Lindsay said. "Maria was constantly showing it off and re-minding everyone that her boyfriend got it for her. Not that I blame her—it's eighteen karat. That isn't cheap."

Letting out a long sigh, Stella said, "The problem is, all of this is telling us that it probably isn't Morgenstern. Whoever left this blood trace is probably our killer, and we don't know who it is."

Stella was growing quite frustrated with the Campagna case. Lindsay's work on the necklace had been superb, but mostly what it did was eliminate Jack Morgenstern as a suspect, which put them back at square one.

When Mac returned from Staten Island, Stella

asked to see him for a brainstorming session. She brought Lindsay and Angell along as well.

Just as they were settling down, Parsons sent Stella a text message. Stella read it and sighed. "DNA on the blood isn't Morgenstern's or Maria's and it doesn't match any of the reference samples we got. So not only is Morgenstern clear, but so are Dina and all the other people who work there, and so's the boyfriend."

Angell sighed. "Great. We can also eliminate Gomer Wilson."

Frowning in confusion, Stella asked, "Who?"

"The guy from the Health Department that Maria got into a shouting match with?"

Snapping her fingers, Stella said, "Right. How could I forget Gomer?"

"Who's Gomer?" Mac asked Stella.

"According to Belluso, the bakery was shut down by the Health Department after their inspector, a man named Gomer Wilson, got into an argument with our vic. He shut Belluso's down for a day."

"Unfortunately," Angell said, "he has an airtight alibi. Last week, he and his wife and two sons moved to Indianapolis. His wife's a college professor, and she left her job in NYU's English department for a position at Purdue. He was at a job interview at the Indianapolis DMV late in the afternoon, so unless he went straight from the interview to the airport, boarded a flight to New York and went straight from LaGuardia to Riverdale, I don't think he's our killer."

Mac leaned forward in his chair. "All right, what do we know? I mean, know for sure."

Stella started counting off items on her fingers. "We know that Morgenstern went into Belluso's right before closing, which is around when Maria died, and that he and Maria were alone together. We know that there was a black poly/cotton fiber on Maria and that Morgenstern was wearing a black poly/cotton sweatshirt."

"The fiber," Lindsay added, "was a match for Morgenstern's shirt, but it's also a match for one of *my* sweatshirts. It's not definitive."

Nodding, Stella went on: "We know he has a printer that could've been used to write the love letters DelVecchio brought us. And we know that he was previously arrested for rape."

"But that was a false arrest," Mac said.

"Yeah," Angell said. "I dug into the case file a little, just to be sure that there wasn't any wiggle room, and I talked to the guy at the five-two who handled it. It really was a case of mistaken ID. Morgenstern matched enough of the description to bring him in, but only that. The cops at the five-two went a little overboard. But the DNA proved it wasn't Morgenstern—and that's why he has a nice house on Cambridge Avenue now." That last was said with a bitter smile. "So we've got, what? Anything?"

"Nothing we can make an arrest on," Mac said.

"Which means we're nowhere," Angell said. "We can't go near Morgenstern unless we have something solid. Leaving aside his lawyer, if we arrest somebody who successfully sued the city for false arrest, we'll be in for a PR nightmare." Before Mac could say anything, Angell said, "I know, I know, but I got a message on my voice mail from Sinclair's office reminding me that we've already falsely arrested Jack Morgenstern once and that it might not be such a hot idea to do it again. I really don't like being on the chief of detectives' radar, and I'd like to get off it as soon as possible, please."

Mac fumed for a second, then softened. Stella knew that his initial response to PR considerations was "Who gives a damn?" His primary interest was the work. Everything else would take care of itself, as long as the work was done right. Stella knew that the world didn't actually work like that—and so did Mac, really—but that didn't mean either of them had to like it.

And there was also the unspoken part of what Angell said: *I don't want to go through what you just went through.*

Finally, Mac just said, "I don't blame you. So where do we go from here?"

An idea that had been percolating in the back

of Stella's mind burbled to the front. "I'd like to go back to Belluso's," she said. "The place has a steady stream of regulars, and whoever killed Maria had to be one of those regulars. It was somebody who was let in as the place was closing, and someone who would've been able to get behind the counter. Morgenstern wasn't the only regular, after all. I'd like to see who else comes in there." Then she smiled. "Besides, it's been way too long since I've had a good cannoli."

Rubbing his chin, Mac nodded. "All right. It certainly couldn't hurt."

Angell said, "It's not like we've got much of anything else."

"Okay. I'll head up there now," Stella said.

She rose from the chair in Mac's office. It wasn't much, but maybe she'd find something. Worst case, she spent an afternoon sitting in an Italian-style café, and she could think of worse ways to spend an afternoon.

After Stella, Lindsay, and Angell left Mac's office, Sheldon and Danny came in. They sat on the sofa while Mac himself leaned against the front of his desk. "What've you got?" Mac asked.

"We played around with Danny's favorite toy," Sheldon said, "and figured out a scenario whereby someone could've knocked Washburne's body off the weight bench in the hustle and bustle after

Barker was stabbed. Based on Washburne's weight and the positioning of everything, and assuming the guy was moving at a certain speed, it works."

"So you're saying it's likely that Melendez didn't hit Washburne with the weight?"

"I dunno about *likely*, Mac," Danny said, "but if the wound really was postmortem, it had to've happened one of two ways. One is that Melendez went to the trouble of knocking him off the bench—"

"Or," Mac said, "he fell off when he died."

"Yeah," Sheldon said, "but wouldn't somebody have noticed? Washburne was a well-liked member of the prison community, wasn't he?"

Mac nodded. "That's why Melendez got a stomach full of fists this morning. So you're saying that the only way he could've died without anybody noticing right away was if he died on the bench and didn't move?"

Nodding, Sheldon said, "It fits the evidence—not to mention the COD."

"And," Danny added, "since nobody noticed, and then Barker got shivved, it all fits. Barker gets cut, there's blood all over the place, people run around like headless chickens, and bam! Somebody bumps into Washburne and sends him to the ground—with a detour to the weight to crack his skull open."

Flack walked in, knocking politely on the glass door as he opened it. "This a private party?"

"Come on in, Don," Mac said. "We were just talking about the Washburne case."

"Well, I gotta get back down there in a little bit to process Mulroney for Barker's murder. Our little gay-basher's gonna find out what life is like in *max* security." That last was said with a feral grin that Flack only reserved for perps getting what they deserved. Mac understood the sentiment.

"He'll go to pretrial holding first, won't he?" Mac asked.

"Maybe—depends on the mood of the DA's office. But they got everything, so it's up to them." He looked at Danny. "Thanks for gettin' the file over so fast."

"No problem." Danny shrugged. "Not sure how much good it'll do, since the guy confessed."

"Evidence never hurts," Mac said.

Sheldon folded his arms, a thoughtful look on his face. "Doesn't always help, either, Mac. I mean, we've got plenty of evidence to tell us what happened, but we still don't have the faintest idea what killed Malik Washburne."

"Yeah." Mac walked around his desk and sat down. "Let's go over what we know. Washburne died from his throat closing up, which was an allergic reaction to—something."

Danny asked, "He have anything in his stomach?"

Mac shook his head. "Some digested food, but for someone to react to a food allergy, it would have to be right when they eat it, not hours later."

"And tox just turned up the Klonopin?" Sheldon asked.

"Which he's been on for weeks." Mac shook his head.

Sheldon unfolded one arm and gestured to the air with it. "What if somebody injected him with something? Maybe something we couldn't detect. If there's a puncture mark—"

"There isn't," Mac said. "Peyton checked."

With a sigh, Sheldon turned to Danny. "It's good when your replacement's as talented as you are, right?"

Mac managed a half-smile, then grew serious again. "Besides, there's no opportunity. How would someone get a syringe into the yard?"

Danny shrugged. "Mulroney managed to sneak in a shiv."

"Yes, but that was a clumsily put-together weapon, using material Mulroney had on hand. A syringe with something in it that would kill Washburne instantly would be a lot harder to get in the first place, much less take into the yard."

"Besides," Flack said, "after the stabbing, everybody in that yard was searched, and you guys went over the scene. No syringe."

Sheldon shook his head. "It's too bad he'd been on the Klonopin so long."

Frowning, Mac asked, "Why?"

"Well, an allergic reaction to Klonopin could potentially cause your throat to close up. It fits the evidence."

"What gets me," Flack said, "is that he was on it in the first place."

Cursing himself for not seeing it sooner, Mac stood up. "Of course. Washburne became a Muslim because of its proscription against mind-altering substances like alcohol—and drugs. He wouldn't take anything like Klonopin willingly."

"Yeah, but Mac—he's in prison. Hell, Terry and I were just talkin' about this yesterday—these guys try all the tricks in the world to get outta takin' their meds, but the COs usually nail 'em. If Washburne was prescribed the drugs, he'd be takin' 'em."

And then it all fell together for Mac. He walked around his desk. "C'mon."

"What?" Flack looked bewildered.

"I'll explain on the way. You've got to get to RHCF to process Mulroney, and I'm going with you."

The other men stood up as well, though they all seemed just as confused. Danny said, "I don't get it, Mac, what's—"

"I know what killed Malik Washburne," Mac said, turning around in the doorway. "Let's go, Don."

As he and Flack left a confused Sheldon and Danny behind, Mac put in a call to Peyton. He needed her to run a particular blood test . . .

19

CANNOLI WERE A SICILIAN delicacy: a creamy filling inside a hard shell. The filling was a mixture of ricotta cheese and sugar, and the shell was dough that was rolled into a hollow tube and deep-fried; the filling was inserted just before serving to keep the shell from getting soggy.

Many places mixed chocolate chips into the filling, which Stella had never objected to but never much saw the point of, either. It always felt like gilding the lily, trying to improve on perfection.

Belluso's Bakery did *not* put chocolate chips in their cannoli. It was the first place Stella had been to in New York that refrained from that particular excess, and it was enough to make Stella forgive Sal Belluso for his *pola* comment.

When she first came in, she noticed that there

was a sign in the window that said NOW HIRING. Stella saw that Jeanie Rodriguez and one other young woman she did not recognize were working behind the counter. There were a few people at the tables downstairs, and a quick glance up showed at least two people upstairs as well. One of the people downstairs was working on a laptop; another table had two women and a stroller, in which a blond-haired infant was dozing; an older woman was finishing up a large cup of tea at another table and got up to leave as Stella stepped up to the counter.

As soon as Stella approached, Jeanie said, "You need to take more DNA or something, Detective?"

Shaking her head, Stella said, "No, no. I'm actually off the clock now. But this looked like such a nice place. I wanted to take in the atmosphere—as a café, not a crime scene."

"Oh, okay." Jeanie lowered her voice to a whisper. "But you guys're still gonna solve Maria's murder, right?"

Stella nodded and matched Jeanie's tone. "Don't worry—Detective Angell and the crime lab are on it. We'll find out the truth, I promise you."

"Good."

"Can I have a cannoli, and also a large iced coffee?"

"Sure. What size cannoli?"

Blinking, Stella asked, "What are my choices?"

Jeanie walked around to the secondary counter and pointed at the miniature cannoli, which were only a couple of inches long, and then the large ones, which were just short of half a foot.

"Oh, the large," Stella said with a big grin.

"Not the chocolate-covered ones?"

Stella made a face. "Uh, no." In Stella's opinion that was even worse than putting in chocolate chips.

While Jeanie rang her up, Stella said, "I see you're hiring. Guess that's inevitable."

"Yeah, we lost two people. Sal fired Dina when he found out she stole Maria's necklace. Can you *believe* that? I didn't think Dina could do something that crazy, y'know?"

Stella winced at that, feeling a bit responsible for Dina losing her job, but after a moment, the feeling passed. The fact was Dina lost her job because she chose to steal jewelry from a corpse. It was likely that she'd lose her freedom as well—Angell was probably going to bust her on obstruction, as her actions had confused the investigation.

After devouring her first cannoli in record time, Stella went back for a second that she could properly savor, then made sure to pay closer attention to the people who came in and out of Belluso's. She took up position at a table only a few feet from the main counter, which enabled her to overhear everything that was said, even with the light-music station being pumped out over the bakery's speakers.

About half of the customers just came in, ordered, paid, and left. Others had their order to stay. If people did converse beyond the confines of their order, it was on a subject other than Maria Campagna: the hot weather, the doings of the customer's job, the current state of affairs of either the Yankees or the Mets or both, whether or not the Jets and/or the Giants got hosed in the draft, how the customer's children were doing, how the customer's parents were doing, who was getting married, whether or not the customer's wife had given birth yet, what the customer's plans were for the upcoming school year, and so on. It reaffirmed Stella's belief that this wasn't just a corner Starbucks where people walked in, got their venti skim latte or grande iced mocha, and left; it was an organic part of a residential neighborhood. It was like the saloon in Old West towns, or the neighborhood pub in a small British town—this was where many of the area's residents came to refresh themselves and chat about their lives.

But some of those who came in talked about Maria, which was when Stella pricked up her ears, tuned out whatever soft-rock classic was playing, and listened.

"Is it true that one of the girls here died?" one asked. Jeanie provided as noncommittal an answer as she could. No doubt she was under orders from Belluso to minimize the perception of the bakery as the scene of a crime.

"Hey, Jeanie. Geez, sucks about Maria, huh? Can't believe that. Who'd *do* something like that?"

"I heard somebody got shot here. Is that true?"

"You guys should seriously consider getting a gate. Stuff like that don't happen when you got a gate."

"Hey, somebody told me that Karen got killed here. That true?" When Jeanie explained that it was actually Maria: "Oh. Okay. I didn't really like *her* all that much."

"Can I see where that girl got killed? C'mon, I've never seen where a dead body was before. Please?"

"Heard you guys got robbed. That's gotta suck." Jeanie didn't change that person's misapprehension.

"Oh, *God,* I'm so sorry, Jeanie, I heard about Maria. Are you guys holding up okay? *God,* that's so *terrible*! Is there anything I can do?"

"You know, someone told me that someone *died* here, can you believe that? What a silly notion."

"Hey, Jeanie. Heard about Maria. You guys doin' okay?"

"Look, I can't stay, but I had to stop in to give my condolences. Maria was *such* a nice girl. Please, if you know the family, tell them I'm praying for them."

"Why would anybody kill *Maria*? I mean, she was such a sweet girl. Whole world's goin' to hell, I swear to Christ."

By the time Stella finished her second cannoli—and third iced coffee—she was about ready to give up. It had been a long shot, in truth.

Just as she was preparing to call it a day, she saw a large man wearing blue scrubs walk across the street and entered. Since one of the storefronts across Riverdale Avenue sported a big sign that read FELDSTEIN'S VETERINARY SERVICE, Stella assumed he came from there. He entered and walked right up to the counter, giving Stella a good view of the purple-and-yellow bruise on his cheek.

"What's up, Jeanie?"

"Hey, Marty how's life in the animal kingdom?"

So he did work at the vet's. Stella also seemed to recall something from Angell's notes about someone named Marty who worked at the vet and was friends with Maria.

"Not bad. Dr. Wentworth's out sick today, so it's kind of a mess. Can I get a half dozen of the cherry cookies?"

"Sure. And a coffee?"

"Yeah. Black, two sugars."

"I know," Jeanie said with a smile.

While Jeanie bent over to retrieve six of the shortbread cookies, which had a glazed maraschino cherry on top, Marty said, "Sucks about Maria, huh? Getting strangled like that—that really shocked the hell out of me."

"All of us, yeah," Jeanie said absently, only half-listening as she gathered Marty's order.

Stella, though, found herself on full alert. A second ago, she'd been swallowing the last of her cannoli, contemplating what traffic would be like going back to Manhattan. But as soon as this Marty person mentioned Maria Campagna's COD, she abandoned all thoughts of going home anytime soon.

Neither she nor Lindsay nor Angell had ever mentioned the exact cause of Maria Campagna's death out loud outside of the lab. Angell had spoken to some press but said nothing about how Maria was killed, either.

While it was *possible* that either Jeanie or Dina could have mentioned it—they found the body, and enough people watched cop shows on TV to possibly recognize a case of strangulation when they saw it—that didn't strike Stella as likely. Certainly not Jeanie, who'd been going out of her way to avoid talking about Maria's death in any but the most perfunctory of details.

Marty had a large enough build to have been the one to strangle Maria, and the bruise he sported on his cheek was approximately the right size to have been made by Maria's fist.

Stella got up and went to the counter. "Can I have another iced coffee?" she asked the young woman who wasn't Jeanie. Then Stella turned to Marty. "That's some bruise you got there."

Lowering his head and smiling sheepishly, Marty said, "Yeah, I got into it with a Great Dane. I'm a tech at Feldstein's across the street." He jerked a thumb behind him, indicating the door—and the veterinarian beyond it.

Stella glanced back, though she already knew where he worked. Deciding to go for broke, she pulled her shield out of her back pocket. "I'm Detective Bonasera, with the New York Crime Lab. Mind if I ask you a few questions?"

"Yeah, I do mind. I just came in here for some cookies and coffee, okay?"

"It's just that I'm looking into Maria Campagna's death, and I was wondering—"

"That has nothing to do with me, okay?" He took the bag with the cookies and the small coffee cup from Jeanie, then threw a five down on the counter. "Keep it." To Stella, he all but snarled, "See you later, *Detective*."

Jeanie was giving Stella an odd look. "You don't think *he* had anything to do with Maria, do you?" she asked in another low whisper.

Leaning over the counter to minimize eavesdropping, Stella asked, "What do you know about him?"

"Who, Marty? He works across the street. He and Maria went to the same high school, so they talked about that a lot. But that was it, really."

When the other woman came by, Stella said, "I'll take that to go."

Once she paid for the coffee, she left the café and went across the street to Feldstein's.

It might well be a dead end—but so was Jack Morgenstern at this point, and Marty's bruise and knowledge of the COD were enough to make him worth pursuing. Probably wasn't enough for a warrant just yet, but it was enough for her to question the other people at Feldstein's.

She pulled open the glass door to find a large reception desk in front of a big waiting area that included several long wooden benches along the walls and an open center floor, which provided plenty of room for dogs to gad about. At present, only two people were in the waiting area, both with cat carriers. One cat was lying quietly in its carrier, but the other was yowling in protest.

There were two women behind the desk, one of whom was on the phone. The other, a short, round woman with spiky white hair, asked, "Can I help you?"

Again, Stella flashed her shield. "I'm Detective Bonasera, with the New York Crime Lab. I'm investigating the death of Maria Campagna, and I was wondering if you could answer a few questions."

Even as she spoke, she couldn't help but notice that behind the desk was an HP laser-jet printer—the exact same model that was used to print the anonymous love letters to Maria.

The woman behind the desk formed an O with her mouth. "Oh, you mean the girl across the street? Yeah, I heard about that—it's awful."

"Did you know her?"

"Yeah, I saw her when I went for tea and pastries a couple of times." She leaned forward and said in an almost conspiratorial tone, "They have the *best* cannoli."

Stella smiled. "I know, believe me." Then she grew serious and took out a notepad and pen. "What's your name?"

"Oh, I'm Jaya—Jaya Nissen."

"Who else from here goes to Belluso's regularly?"

"God, everybody. I don't think Dr. Feldstein does, but he usually just brings food from home. He keeps kosher—I know that they say their food is all kosher, too, but I don't think Dr. Feldstein trusts that. But most of the rest of us do, yeah."

"How late were you open the night before last?"

"Until ten. That was our late night, to accommodate people who work late, you know?"

"I understand." Stella wrote that all down, then asked, "Does anybody stay later than that?"

Jaya nodded. "We board a lot of animals here, and someone always stays until about eleven or so to make sure they've got enough food and water and, for the cats, enough litter. Plus, some of the animals have medical needs, and the dogs have to be walked."

"Who was it who stayed late two nights ago?"

Blinking, Jaya said, "I don't remember." Her companion, who had long red hair that was tied back in a ponytail, was just getting off the phone, and Nissen turned to her. "Moira, do you remember who had the late shift two nights ago?"

"Sure. It was Marty," the woman said.

Stella managed to hide a smile. "What's Marty's full name?"

"Marty Johannsen," Moira said. "I remember because he came in yesterday with this big-ass bruise. He said Rex did it."

"And Rex is?" Stella asked.

"A Great Dane we got boarded—again." She rolled her eyes. "I swear, those people are on vacation more than they're home. Don't know why they even keep the dog, he spends more time here than there. And they got a yard, too. Don't know why they can't just leave him home and have someone come in to walk and feed him—I even told Mr. Franklin that, but he doesn't listen."

Trying to get the conversation back on track, Stella asked, "So Marty was here alone until eleven?"

"Yeah," Moira said. "Oh, wait—Chris was here for a while, too. Not sure if he stayed the whole time, though."

"Chris is?"

Jaya took this one. "Chris Schanke. He's our head tech—he orders all the food and meds and stuff."

Stella noted his name, grateful that she now had two people to ask about. Her money was still on Marty, but it eased the blow if you asked to talk about two people to the police. Ask about one person and he's a suspect—ask about two, and you're just collecting data. "Can either of you recall what both Chris and Marty were wearing? We want to be able to eliminate them as suspects." That second sentence was only half true.

"Chris was wearing scrubs all day," Moira said. "He always does. I don't think I've ever seen him in civvies, except at the Christmas party."

"Marty was wearing a black sweatshirt that said SAN DIEGO on it," Jaya said. "I remember 'cause Dr. Feldstein wanted to know if he'd ever been there. Dr. Feldstein's son was in the Navy and was stationed there."

Not that she cared, but Stella asked anyhow: "Had he?"

Jaya shook her head. "Nah, it was a present

from his parents when they went on vacation there. Kind of a 'My parents went to San Diego and all I got was this lousy sweatshirt' thing."

Stella continued taking notes, but now she was sure she had enough for a warrant.

"You don't have enough for a warrant."

Stella sat with Angell in the chambers of Judge Lou Montagnino. This judge was always a risk. On the one hand, he had a thing about murdered girls. Before being elevated to the bench in 1972, Montagnino had been in the district attorney's office in Queens and prosecuted a man who'd killed four teenage girls. He was usually willing to give a certain amount of leeway for such cases.

The flip side, though, was that Montagnino was also a chauvinist pig who had very little time for detectives of the female persuasion. "Secretaries with guns," he called them once in Stella's hearing, and it had taken all of her willpower (and Mac's iron grip on her arm) to keep from kneeing him in the balls when she'd heard it.

Stella leaned forward in her chair. "Our PC is solid, Judge."

"What solid?" Montagnino peered at Stella over his thin spectacles and aquiline nose. "All I see is vague nonsense. Did Taylor sign off on this?"

After a brief hesitation, Stella said, "No." She'd been tempted to lie, but Mac was still on Staten

Island when she got back to the lab. Angell had typed up the warrant request, and they'd both gone to Montagnino's chambers. It was another long shot, but Stella had been doing well with long shots today.

"Judge," Angell said, "he knew the COD. We didn't tell anyone that."

"Over thirty people walked into that bakery," Stella added, "and everyone was just talking about the girl who died. Then in comes this one guy with a bruise of the right size, and he happens to know that the victim was strangled. I think that's sufficient cause to search, especially since he was so belligerent."

"Define *belligerent*, if you don't mind," Montagnino said witheringly.

"He wouldn't let me question him or take pictures of his bruise or take a DNA reference sample." Of course, she'd never gotten as far as asking for pictures or a DNA sample; he walked out before Stella could even ask. But Montagnino didn't need to know that.

"And if I walked into a bakery to get some dessert, I wouldn't want to spit on a Q-tip for some lady detective, either." He shook his head. "I thought you had a suspect in this case already."

"We thought we did," Angell said, "but we don't have any evidence to support it, and he's got a very good lawyer."

"Ah, I see, you're afraid of this guy's lawyer, so you go after someone else? And you want *me* to sign off on it? You're making me laugh, Detectives. Who's this lawyer, anyhow?"

"Courtney Bracey," Stella said. "Why?"

Montagnino removed his glasses. "Bracey? Christ on a stick, that bitch? Swear to God, I lost all respect for the New York Bar Association when they let her in." He actually made the sign of the cross. "I wouldn't wish her on my worst enemy, much less you two."

"Gee, thanks," Angell muttered.

He put his glasses back on and read over the warrant request again. "You say he knew the young lady was strangled?"

Stella pressed the point. "He couldn't *possibly* have known that unless he was the killer, Judge."

Angell shot Stella a look, which Stella hoped Montagnino didn't notice. Stella was bluffing big-time now, but she just *knew* that Marty Johannsen was their guy, and the longer it was before they could investigate properly, the less of a chance they had of finding any evidence to nail him.

"This girl who died," Montagnino said. "How old was she?"

"Nineteen."

"And you really think this Johannsen jamoke did it?"

Amazed that anyone still used the word *jamoke*

in this day and age—though if anyone did, it'd be Montagnino—Stella said, "I have enough reason to think so that I want to investigate further."

Montagnino smiled at that, though on his wrinkled face and with his too-shiny dentures, it looked more like a rictus. "Good answer, Bonasera. If you just said yes, I would've said no, because that's not a real cop's answer. But you gave me a real cop's answer, so you get the warrant." He reached for a pen, then stopped. "I still think it's nuts to give you eggheads badges and guns, but nobody asked me."

Angell said, "I'm not an egghead, Judge, and I think that this guy's worth taking a look at. A nineteen-year-old girl's dead—shouldn't we do everything we can to find her killer?"

Grabbing the pen and wagging it at Angell, Montagnino said, "Don't try to play me for a sap, little girl. I was signing warrants when you were in diapers." He pronounced the word "die-uh-pers," which Stella found amusing for some odd reason. Then he pushed the button atop the pen to release the point. "You've got your warrant, ladies. Make the best of it."

20

WHEN MAC ARRIVED WITH Flack at RHCF, the latter's first response to checking his weapon was resistance. Russell and Ursitti were there to meet them again, and Flack was not pleased by his way to the entrance was blocked until he checked his Glock at the arsenal.

"Look," Flack said, "I'm here to arrest a guy. I do that without a weapon, I feel kinda naked."

"I can live with that, Detective," Russell said.

"What I mean is, I'm exposed. I don't—"

Russell shook his head. "I know what you meant, Detective, and it doesn't matter. We got rules, we got regulations, and if you violate them, you get put in here for real. Now please check your weapon in the arsenal."

Flack looked at Mac, who just shrugged. He had

already checked his weapon. He understood Flack's objection—it was never wise to arrest a suspect unarmed, just on general principles. The weapon provided security, even if it was holstered with the safety on. Even then, it didn't always help, as Mac had learned the hard way.

"Rules are rules, Don," Mac said.

The snarl on Flack's face indicated that he didn't buy that particular line of reasoning. However, he went ahead and checked his weapon. Then they went through the rest of the rigamarole required to enter the prison.

Once that was completed, Mac left a grumbling Flack to the logistics of processing Mulroney so that he could be placed under arrest for Vance Barker's murder. Ursitti accompanied Mac to the interview room. As they walked, Ursitti asked, "What is it you need to do here, Detective?"

"I need to talk to all the COs who supervised the distribution of medication in C Block for the past week."

"You wanna know who stood over Washburne getting his pills?" Ursitti asked.

Mac nodded.

Ursitti got on the radio and asked someone to go to his office and fetch the Charlie Block duty roster for him.

Several minutes after Mac and Ursitti arrived at the interview room, a CO came by with the roster in question. Ursitti flipped through it and found the right page, showing it to Mac. Mac sat down in the chair that Flack had taken in previous interrogations and stared at the page.

Since he really only needed the past week or so to establish the pattern he thought he'd find, he started with the person on duty a week ago. At the sight of the name, he winced, but he still said, "Can you bring Officer Ciccone in here?"

"Sure, but don't expect much. He's pretty pissed off."

"Well, the feeling's mutual."

After Ursitti summoned Ciccone on his radio, Mac asked, "What about the nurses?"

"None of them are in now. Captain Russell can give you contact info if you wanna call them."

"The COs should be sufficient, but I'll get those names and addresses when we're finished."

Ursitti shrugged. "Fine, whatever."

Ciccone entered, then stopped halfway over the threshold as soon as he saw Mac. "Hey, I told you, I ain't talking to you without my lawyer."

Ursitti rolled his eyes. "Come the hell off it, Ciccone."

"I ain't coming off nothing, Lieutenant. I've been harassed by this guy once already; it ain't happening again. Barker's murder ain't my fault, and nothin' you guys can say is gonna make it my fault. I ain't saying a word until my mouthpiece gets here."

"This isn't about the Barker murder, Officer," Mac said. "It's about Washburne."

That brought Ciccone up short. "Washburne?"

"Yes."

Ciccone rubbed his stubble-covered chin. "Okay, as long as we're just talking Washburne, I'm all right with that."

"Thank you," Mac said, trying and probably failing to keep the sarcasm out of his voice.

As Ciccone took his seat, Mac asked, "A week ago today, you supervised the distribution of medication in C Block, is that correct?"

Shrugging, Ciccone said, "Sounds right, yeah."

"Was medication administered to Malik Washburne?"

Ciccone nodded and started fidgeting with his hands.

"Do you remember what the medication was?"

"Honestly, I don't remember what he takes. I'd have to check the roster. I know he only had one pill though."

"And he took it?"

"Sure, like always." Ciccone shrugged, still fidgeting.

"Describe the process, please."

Rolling his eyes, Ciccone said, "Went like usual. The nurse gave him the meds, then gave him a glass of water. He put the pill in his mouth, he took the glass, he swallowed the water."

"You're sure?"

"Course I'm sure, I do this at least once a week, sometimes more."

"And Washburne took his meds?"

"Absolutely."

Mac made a few notes in his notepad and then said, "All right, Officer, that's all I needed to know. Thank you."

Getting up, Ciccone said, "No problem, Detective. Always happy to waste my time with you. Sure you don't wanna ask me anything else? I got a great story about how the cons brushed their teeth two weeks ago."

Smirking, Mac said, "No, Officer, that'll be all."

As Ciccone left, Mac looked up at Ursitti. "Next I need to talk to Officer Bolton."

Bolton was summoned and took his seat. "What can I do for you, Detective?"

"According to the roster, you supervised the administration of medication for C Block six days ago."

"Sounds right, yeah."

"Did you administer Klonopin to Malik Washburne?"

Leaning back in his chair, Bolton looked up at the ceiling. "Honestly, Detective, I don't remember if it was Klonopin or not. I can't keep track. I'm pretty sure he got what he was supposed to get, though."

"And he took the meds?"

"Sure." Bolton shrugged.

"He didn't try any of the usual tricks?"

Bolton laughed at that, glancing at Ursitti. "Nah, he wasn't that stupid. It's usually the new guys and the really dumb ones that try the bullshit."

"So Washburne took his meds six days ago?"

"Far as I remember, yeah."

"Thank you, Officer."

Next up was Flack's friend Sullivan. A smile broke out on his baby face as soon as he came in and recognized Mac. "Hey, Detective Taylor. How's the investigation going?"

"Well, half of it's going fine. Detective Flack is arresting Jack Mulroney for Vance Barker's murder."

"Ain't gonna be sorry to see *that* asshole go." Sullivan took his seat, then leaned forward, his shaggy blond hair flopping into his face, and talked in a whisper. "Hey, listen, Detective, you're a friend of Donnie's, right?"

Realizing Sullivan wanted to keep this conversation between the two of them, he leaned forward and said, "Yes."

"I've known the guy since we were kids, but—" He hesitated. "Look, the guy's not takin' his meds. The man was in a *bomb explosion* a year ago, and he's actin' like nothin' happened. That ain't healthy."

Mac was hardly in a position to lecture other

people about how they dealt with post-traumatic stress disorder. That was for the department therapist. Then again, Mac knew Flack's opinion of department therapists.

The embarrassing part was that Mac hadn't noticed that Flack wasn't taking his Percocet, and it made him wonder what else he'd been missing lately.

Mac leaned back and spoke in a normal tone. "I'll see what I can do about that personal problem of yours, Officer," he said for Ursitti's benefit, "but it's actually the inmates' taking of medication that I'd like to talk to you about now."

"Shoot." Sullivan slapped the table with his palms and then let them rest on his lap.

"Five days ago, you supervised Malik Washburne receiving his meds."

"Yeah, that's right. He takes—uh, Zoloft, I think."

"Klonopin, actually."

Sullivan snapped his fingers. "Right, Klonopin. Anyhow, yeah, he took it."

"What was the procedure?"

Blowing out a breath, Sullivan said, "Nurse takes out the pill, hands it to him, he takes it, she hands him a glass, he drinks it, down goes the pill." He shrugged. "The usual."

"He didn't try to palm the meds or anything like that? Hide it under his tongue?"

"Nah, Washburne wasn't that kinda guy. He was a cop, he knew the drill."

"Okay, then. Thanks, Officer."

After Sullivan left, Ursitti said, "Okay, Detective, you wanna explain yourself? I assume you're gonna bring in everyone on that list."

"No," Mac said, standing and hoisting the clipboard, "I think I've got everything I need. At most, I'd only need to talk to"—he gazed down at the list—"Officers Schuster, Moody, and Gibson. See, I already talked to Officer Andros—he's the one who supervised Washburne the day he died, and I already got his story." Looking up at Ursitti, he handed the lieutenant the clipboard. "That's why I know that Officers Ciccone, Bolton, and Sullivan were all lying just now."

Ursitti's eyes grew wide. "Excuse me?"

"They might have told the truth, but you were in the room, and they didn't want to admit that they were complicit."

"Detective Taylor, what the *hell* are you talkin' about?" Ursitti put his hands on his hips. His eyes were blazing.

Mac let out a breath. "Malik Washburne was a devout Muslim. He converted in part because Islam proscribes taking mind-altering substances such as alcohol—and prescription drugs."

"Yeah, well, my wife's Jewish—goes to temple

every Saturday—but she also likes her bacon in the morning. So what?"

Shaking his head, Mac said, "Washburne took that restriction seriously. Remember, he was an alcoholic who was in jail because he fell off the wagon. Someone like Washburne would've been adamant about not taking *any* mind-altering substances."

Ursitti frowned. "So what're you saying?"

"Call Officer Andros in again."

"What, you're not gonna tell me?"

"Give me a few more minutes, Lieutenant, and it'll all make sense," Mac assured him.

Ursitti glared at Mac but got on the radio and summoned Andros.

While they waited, Flack came into the room, hands in his pockets. "Mac, I got Mulroney all good to go. You done here?"

"Not yet. You go ahead, Don, I need to finish this up."

"What, without me? C'mon, Mac. Washburne's name goes on *my* record. If you have something cooking—"

Mac shrugged. "Mulroney's not going anywhere. Join me." While they waited for Andros, Mac filled Flack in on what he knew so far.

Flack smiled. "I see where you're going with this. That's why you asked Peyton to do that blood test, right?"

Ursitti growled. "Will you two stop playing

this Agatha Christie shit and tell me what the *hell* you're talkin' about?"

"All in good time, Lieutenant," Mac said with a cryptic smile.

Just then Andros came in. "I thought you guys were arresting Mulroney."

"This is about Malik Washburne," Mac said.

"Okay, whatever." He took a seat. "I thought Melendez cleaned his clock for him."

"No," Mac said, with Flack standing over him, "he died of anaphylactic shock."

"What's that?"

"An extreme allergic reaction," Flack said.

"Oh, okay—like my uncle with eggs. Swear to God, you give him anything with eggs, he stops breathing." Andros shuddered. "Scariest damn thing you ever saw. Once a restaurant insisted there wasn't any egg in the pasta they served—we eat there free in perpetuity now, in exchange for Uncle Walter not suing them. So that's how the asshole died, huh?"

"Yes," Mac said, "and we think that you were there when he ingested the fatal substance."

"Say what?"

Ursitti said, "Detective, if you're accusing my man here of—"

"Officer Andros didn't do anything wrong," Mac said quickly, holding up a reassuring hand. "He simply did his duty yesterday morning."

"What happened yesterday morning?" Andros asked, now looking quite bewildered.

"You watched as the nurse gave Malik Washburne his prescribed dosage of Klonopin. After which point he tried what you called yesterday 'the usual crap' with his medication."

Andros snorted. "Yeah, that's right. Tried to palm it. Real bush-league stuff."

"And that's what killed him."

"That's crazy!" Ursitti said. "You heard my COs, he'd been taking the drugs for weeks. How could he suddenly be allergic?"

"Because your COs were lying like cheap rugs," Flack said. "When they were describing how Washburne took his meds, they were also talkin' about what a good guy he was, right? That he was a stand-up guy, an ex-cop, that whole bit?"

"Some of 'em, sure," Ursitti said.

Andros said, "I don't get it—you're saying he was allergic to the Klonopin?"

Before Mac could answer, the door opened to Captain Russell. He was holding his cell phone in his hand. "Detective Taylor, I have a Dr. Peyton Driscoll from the medical examiner's office on the phone. She says it's urgent that she talk to you and that it has to do with the Washburne case."

"Thank you, Captain," Mac said, taking the phone from Russell. "If you could stay a moment, please?"

"I have a prison to run, Detective, and I don't appreciate being made to be your errand boy."

"It's for a good cause, Captain, since you won't let me bring my phone in here." He put Russell's flip-top phone to his ear. "Peyton?"

Peyton told him exactly what he was expecting to hear. He thanked her and closed the phone, then handed it back to Russell. "The ME has confirmed that Malik Washburne was fatally allergic to Klonopin," he said.

"That's impossible!" Ursitti said. "The man's been on Klonopin since he got here."

"No," Flack said, "he wasn't. He didn't believe in mind-altering drugs, so he didn't take any."

"And the COs looked the other way," Mac said. "They liked Washburne, they respected him, and they were willing to help him out. But Officer Andros here wasn't in the loop."

Andros was rubbing his forehead with the tips of his fingers. "I don't believe this. You're saying that by making him take the pill, *I* killed him?" He sounded more than a little devastated.

"Again, Officer Andros, this isn't your fault."

"No," Flack said, "it's the fault of the jackasses who didn't share their AA plan with you."

" 'Cause they think I'm a rat." Andros pounded a fist on the table. "Jesus! I should just go back to Sing Sing."

"There's no need for that, Randy," Ursitti said. "This isn't on you—it's on everyone else."

"Damn right it is," Russell said. "I can't believe that this sort of abuse was happening on my watch. There's no excuse for letting a convict get away with not taking his prescribed medication."

"The prescribed medication would've killed him," Mac said. "Even leaving that aside, his religious beliefs prohibited him from taking them."

"Then he should've *said* something!" Russell shook his head. "I liked the man, too, Detective, but that was just irresponsible." He looked at Andros. "Don't worry, Randy, you won't take any heat for this." Then he glowered at Ursitti. "You may be the only one who doesn't."

Mac glanced at Flack. "That's up to you, Captain, but I think our investigation is complete. Washburne's death was accidental. Turns out you only had one murderer here."

Flack added, "And I'm taking him off your hands."

"You're welcome to him," Russell said. "And thank you both for your excellent work."

"It's our pleasure," Mac said.

"But not as much of a pleasure as it will be to take Mulroney out of here," Flack said. "C'mon, Mac, let's go."

As Mac followed Flack out into the corridor, he couldn't help but notice that Flack was walking gingerly—and wondered how he missed it before. He put a hand on Flack's arm to get him to stop walking for a second. In a low voice, he said, "Listen, Don—have you been taking the painkillers they prescribed?"

Rolling his eyes, Flack said, "Jesus, Mac, don't *you* start. Bad enough I got Terry and Sheldon on my ass."

Mac chuckled at Flack's histrionics. "All right, all right, I'm sorry. I'm just concerned, is all."

Flack took a breath. "I appreciate it, Mac, but I'm fine. Really."

"If you say so."

"I say so. Now c'mon, let's take a bad guy out of jail and put him in another jail."

21

STELLA HAD TO ADMIT to having a great deal of fun going through Marty Johannsen's apartment.

Marty lived in a small one-bedroom apartment in a large complex on Henry Hudson Parkway East. It was a fairly typical "bachelor pad": dirty laundry everywhere, huge piles of unwashed dishes in the sink, moldy food in the refrigerator, and piles of stuff all over the floor.

Marty was already home from Feldstein's when Stella buzzed his apartment number from the lobby. His voice distorted over the old speaker, he asked, "Who is it?"

"NYPD, Mr. Johannsen. Please let us in."

There was a long pause, and Stella feared that he was bolting down the fire escape or something—but eventually the distorted voice came back. "Yeah, okay."

After that came the low buzz of the lobby door unlocking. With that, Stella, Angell, a medtech, and four uniforms from the five-oh went in and took the elevator to the twelfth floor.

Johannsen was standing in the open doorway. "What's this about, Detective Bonasera? Yeah, I remember you. Thought it was cute the way you asked about Chris, too, like I wouldn't know you were just asking about me. But you're wasting your time. I didn't do anything wrong."

"Maybe, maybe not." Stella held up the warrant, signed by Judge Montagnino. "But we're gonna find out for sure."

Johannsen snatched the warrant from her and looked down at it with distaste. "Christ. Fine, whatever, guess I don't have a choice, huh?"

"Nope," Stella said. "First thing I'm going to need is some blood and DNA—and I also need to photograph your face."

While the medtech set up to draw blood and scrape Johannsen's cheek, Stella picked up her Nikon and photographed the bruise on the man's cheek, both by itself and with him (reluctantly) holding up an L ruler next to it. She then removed the memory card from her camera and placed it in her phone so she could e-mail the pictures to Lindsay at the lab.

Snapping latex gloves onto her hands, Stella started going through the dirty clothes scattered around the apartment, eventually finding a black sweatshirt that was inside out. She took several pictures of it before turning it right-side out.

A fingernail shook loose from the fabric and fell to the floor.

Stella took several pictures of that as well, and was overjoyed to see that there was purple nail polish on it. Then she grabbed a pair of tweezers and placed the nail in an envelope.

"Is that our San Diego sweatshirt?" Angell said, walking over to join her.

Stella held up the shirt to show Angell the city's name embazoned in sparkly letters. "Yup. This is what our guy was wearing two nights ago—and looky what I found." She held up the small envelop. "A purple fingernail."

Angell raised an eyebrow. "I just had them bag his laptop. But there's no printer."

"What about the laptop itself?"

Angell shrugged. "Couldn't find the love poems."

"I'll have our guys go over it—he might be hiding them, or they may have been deleted. As long as they weren't purged, we should be able to pull them out."

Smirking, Angell said, "Well, this guy didn't think to wash the clothes he killed a girl in, so I doubt he thought he'd need to do more than delete the files." Then she let out a long sigh.

"What's the matter?"

"It's nothing."

Stella stared at her. "Jen."

"I wanted it to be Morgenstern, just so I could stick it to Bracey," she finally said. "Now I have to actually leave him—and her—alone. Doesn't sit right."

Chuckling, Stella said, "I'm sure you'll live."

As soon as Lindsay received the photos from Stella's Treo, she called them up and compared the size and shape of the bruise on his face to the autopsy photos of Maria's fist. It was a good match. Again, not perfect, but at least you couldn't say with any certainty that the bruise *wasn't* caused by the fist, which was often the best one could do in such circumstances.

A bit later, a uniform came by with several sample envelopes: the fingernail that was lodged in the sweatshirt, and Marty Johannsen's blood and cheek scraping.

Her first stop was with Adam, to give him the blood sample. Next was Jane Parsons's office. She yawned as Lindsay entered. "Another late night with the ER doc?" Lindsay asked with a grin.

Jane simply waggled her eyebrows. "What have you for me now, Ms. Monroe?"

"A new reference sample—except this may be our perp."

"This is the blood from the necklace, yes?"

Lindsay nodded.

"Spiffing. I'll let you know as soon as I've cross-checked."

Her next stop was the morgue.

Sid Hammerback was waiting for her, along with Maria Campagna's autopsied body. "Good timing," Sid said when she walked in. "We just got a call from the Campagna family wondering when we can release the body."

"Well, how soon we do that depends on this." Lindsay held up the envelope with the fingernail.

Reaching behind him, Sid found a specimen dish, and Lindsay then opened the envelope and tapped its side so the fingernail would come out. Though it had obviously been removed from the body violently—the interior edge was uneven and jagged—you could still see the purple nail polish.

"Wonderful thing, nail polish," Sid said. "You know, some say that it got its start in Japan five thousand years ago. Others say it was in Italy—and others say that's complete hokum. Personally, I wouldn't be surprised if it started in the Orient— sorry, they call it the Far East now, don't they?"

Lindsay smiled. "Yeah, nobody uses 'Orient' anymore, Sid."

"Well, I guess I'm just easily dis-Orient-ed."

At that, Lindsay groaned, loudly. "Sid, that was bad even by your low standards."

"We aim to please," he said with a grin as he picked up the nail with a pair of tweezers and put it up against Maria Campagna's right forefinger.

It was a near-perfect fit. And the nail polish was the same color.

Sid peered at Lindsay through his spectacles. "Looks like she *is* the one who danced with the prince."

"Yeah, but this prince won't live happily ever after. Thanks, Sid."

The next thing Lindsay did was scrape off flakes of the nail polish from Maria's corpse, placing those scrapings in an envelope; then she did the same for the errant nail found in Marty Johannsen's apartment.

Adam was waiting for her upstairs. "That blood you gave me was AB-negative."

"Same type as what was on the necklace."

Nodding, Adam said, "But that doesn't prove anything—just that your guy has the same blood type."

"Every little bit helps," Lindsay said. "Come on, I could use a hand with this."

With Adam alongside her, she brought the samples over to the gas chromatograph. Sealing the sample from Maria's corpse inside, she started the machine up, letting the gas break the flakes down into their component parts. The computer provided the specifics: nitrocellulose, pigment, and all the other usual elements of nail polish. When that was done, Adam removed the first sample and replaced it with the flakes from the fingernail found in Marty Johannsen's apartment.

Everything matched: the molecular structure of that pigment and the proportions of the different elements.

Staring at the computer screen, Lindsay noticed something she was expecting to see missing from both reports. "Okay, that's odd. There's no dibutyl phthalate."

"Gesundheit," Adam said.

Lindsay glowered at him. "Very funny. But every nail polish sample I've examined has that."

"Not for much longer," Adam said. "Phthalates have been linked to testicular problems in lab animals *and* humans. So last year, the nail polish companies started phasing out its use in their products. Speaking as an owner of testicles, I'm rather grateful."

"Okay, how did I not know that?" Lindsay asked. "I mean, I *wear* the stuff."

Adam shrugged. "We can't all be incredibly brilliant like me."

Playfully punching Adam in the arm, Lindsay said, "Of course not. Still, the two match."

"Yup."

Lindsay pulled out her phone and called Stella.

"Hey, Lindsay," Stella said. There was considerable background noise.

"Good news, Stell: the blood's AB-negative, the fingernail's a match, and the bruise is the right size. Still waiting on DNA."

"We should have it by morning, and I like the idea of Johannsen stewing in the five-oh's tank all night. It's too late for him to go to processing anyhow."

"Where are you?"

"On the Henry Hudson coming back to you. I should be there in ten minutes."

"Please tell me you're using a hands-free." Talking on a mobile phone while driving was illegal in New York state, unless one was using hands-free technology of some kind.

"Yes, Mom," Stella said with a chuckle. "Trust me, in this traffic, I want both hands on the wheel. I'll see you in a little while."

"Okay." Lindsay hung up.

Marty Johannsen couldn't believe the way he was being treated.

It wasn't enough that he had to have all those cops just *pawing* through his stuff like that, but then they had to *arrest* him? There was no feeling in the world worse than being handcuffed. Marty had done it once at the request of a girlfriend, and he hated every second of it—lost his hard-on and the girlfriend all in one shot, but if she was gonna go for that sort of thing, he didn't *want* her for a girlfriend. Handcuffs hurt, biting into your wrists the way they did, and Marty felt completely helpless in them. Wearing them willingly in the bedroom was bad enough—having them forced on him by cops who were pawing through all his stuff was much, much worse.

Then he had to sit in the damn holding cell. Marty had spent all night in jail once before, but that was in college, and he was so wasted, he didn't really remember it. (Come to think of it, he was probably handcuffed then, too, but that had been lost to the booze.) The NYPD hadn't been kind enough to let him go on a bender, so he recalled every miserable second of it, from the homeless guy in the corner who hadn't bathed since the *first* Bush administration, to the mean-looking Hispanic guys in the other corner, to the wooden bench that it was just *impossible* to get comfortable on, either sitting up or lying down.

In the morning, they handcuffed him again, and then they shoved him into a van that had no AC, which sat in traffic for hours, taking him into Manhattan somewhere. Marty didn't really pay attention to where; he just wished he could wipe the sweat out of his eyes.

Finally, they brought him into a dank room and made him sit there. They took off the handcuffs, but then put his left hand in a cuff that was attached to the table. The only way he'd leave was with the table attached. Not that he wanted to—this room, at least, had AC. The sweat cooled on his head, and he started to feel almost human for the first time since he'd buzzed the cops into his building.

Marty had no idea how much time passed before Bonasera, that stupid bitch of a detective, and some *other* stupid bitch came in. The second bitch had been at the apartment as well, but Marty never got her name. She was kind of hot, actually.

Before they could say a word, Marty said what he'd been saying to anyone who'd listen since they showed up with the warrant. "I didn't *do* nothin'!"

Bonasera stared at him for a second. "How much do you know about computers, Marty?"

"Huh?" That wasn't the question he was expecting. "Uh, I mean—I dunno, is this a trick question?" Figuring he had nothing to lose, he looked at the other detective, the hot one, but she just stared at him so hard that he had to look away.

Bonasera smiled insincerely. "Not at all. See, the way computers work is that when files are created, they also create a pathway to that file. But that's not the interesting part. You see, when you *delete* a file, you don't actually remove the file from the computer. What you do is cut off the pathway to the file, so the computer can't see it. But the information? That's still there. Eventually, it'll get written over if the space is required for something else, but if it isn't? It's all still there."

Marty stared at Bonasera for a second, parsing what she had just said. Then his face fell and he felt a new sheen of sweat bead on his forehead, even with the AC. "You mean—?"

"That's right, Marty. We were able to retrieve the love letters you wrote to Maria Campagna, which perfectly matched the printouts that Maria's boyfriend gave us."

Marty's jaw dropped. He hadn't thought that he needed to do anything except erase the letters. *Damn it!*

"Too bad for you that Bobby gave them to us," Bonasera continued.

Shaking his head, Marty said, "That Neanderthal."

"Who's that?" the other detective asked.

"DelVecchio! The big dumb jock wasn't good enough for Maria!"

"So you tried to woo her away?" Bonasera asked.

"Exactly!" Marty let out a long breath. "Damn it, she deserved better than him, but she just wouldn't *leave* him. I actually cared about animals—DelVecchio used to, I swear to God, kick puppies when Maria wasn't looking. I saw him do it once! Really!"

The hot detective said, "So you killed her."

Forcing himself to remember that the love letters didn't actually prove anything, he said, "No. Why would I kill her? I loved her!"

Scowling at him, the hot detective—who didn't look so hot when she scowled like that, Marty thought—said, "You know how many killers sit in that chair after murdering people they love, Marty?"

"Well, I ain't one of them. I'm tellin' ya, I didn't kill her!"

"So the bruise on your face didn't come from her punching you, even though the size of her fist matches the size of the bruise?"

"That was the Great Dane—Rex." He hoped he sounded convincing.

"And then there's the blood on Maria's necklace."

Now panic suffused Marty. There was blood on her necklace? Jesus, how the hell did he miss *that*?

"The blood's yours, Marty—we checked it against your DNA. Maria kept that necklace sparkling, so the only way that blood could've gotten on it was if it happened right before she was killed. Say, when she punched you in the cheek, loosening a tooth enough for it to bleed some?"

Marty couldn't believe he missed that.

"And then there's the fingernail on your sweatshirt. The same sweatshirt that your coworkers said you were wearing the night Maria was killed. One of Maria's fingernails was missing when we examined her body, and the very same missing fingernail was lodged in your shirt."

Oh, Jesus. Jesus Jesus Jesus, he had no *idea*. He thought about doing laundry, but he always did laundry on Saturdays. If he broke his routine, that was a pattern cops looked for. Marty watched television; he knew how cops thought. If he washed the clothes, he'd look like a suspect, so he wouldn't wash them.

How was he supposed to know there was a fingernail in there?

"All right," he suddenly said, "fine, you got me." He threw up one hand—the other one, still handcuffed, he couldn't raise high enough. "Yeah, I killed her. I didn't want to, but when she hit me, I couldn't believe it!"

The hot detective said, "So you went into Belluso's at closing?"

"Yeah. That long-haired guy who takes karate—he was just leaving as I was locking the vet up. I saw she was alone, so I figured I'd take a shot, see if she'd leave that big dumb ape for a *real* man."

Marty could hear the disgust in Bonasera's voice when she said, "A real man who kills her when she gets uppity? That's what you mean, Marty?"

"No! Look, it wasn't supposed to happen like

that, okay? It just got—" He sighed. "Out of hand, I guess."

"You guess?" Bonasera asked.

He found he had nothing to say, so he just looked down. "I guess I'm going to jail, huh?"

"Good guess." Bonasera got up from her chair and left the interrogation room.

The hot detective got up a second later. "They already read you your rights at the Fiftieth Precinct, so we'll just put you in holding until we can finish processing you. You'll be at Rikers by dinnertime, and you'll stay there until your trial, you sorry son of a bitch."

With that, she too left.

Marty hoped that prison would at least be air-conditioned.

22

JACK MULRONEY COULDN'T BELIEVE his bad luck.

Actually killing Barker wasn't anywhere near as bad as he thought it would be. He just walked up to the fence and shoved his improvised blade between the links when Barker was stupid enough to be standing too close. The bastard was leaning against the fence drinking from a bottle of water, sweat dripping down his face after his weightlifting exertions.

That got him sweaty. Not the box. If anything, that pissed Jack off more. Gave him even more reason to stab his sorry ass. He limped over to the fence and just did it.

What he hadn't expected was the blood. Christ, it was *everywhere*.

In fact, that had kept Jack frozen to the spot where he was standing for at least a couple of seconds, watching the blood just gush all over the entire weight yard, like a red version of those seltzer bottles in old comedy TV shows, just spritzing all over the place.

Fischer, though, he took charge. He made Jack drop the shiv and then all the other guys huddled around him. Nobody would say anything to the COs, and he'd be clear.

Even if he wasn't Barker would be dead. Twice, he showed Jack up—on the field and in the box. Three times if you counted him exerting himself in the weight yard, the bastard.

Of course, things didn't go according to plan after that. He figured there'd be the usual internal investigation. Russell didn't know nothing from nothing, so Jack didn't expect much there, but instead he called in the NYPD.

Jack hadn't expected the full-court press the case got. It was probably because of Washburne. Everybody in the prison, on both sides, was sucking his dick pretty regularly, so his dying probably got the cops' hackles up.

Just bad luck was all. If Washburne hadn't died, they probably never would have figured out that Jack killed Barker.

And nobody would've cared. Jack knew he

wasn't anybody special, but Barker was even less than that. Just some drug runner from Brooklyn, same as fifty other drug runners from Brooklyn. Nobody would miss him.

And Jack killed him. He deserved it.

Now, though, Jack was in Rikers, and soon he'd be transferred to a maximum-security facility. They hadn't told him which one yet. He didn't really care all that much. Sure, he'd be tried, and maybe he'd get the death penalty—but at least he showed Barker what for.

It was worth it just for that.

Stanton Gerrard hated going into the chief of detectives' office these days.

Ever since Mac Taylor had walked into that office and blackmailed Brigham Sinclair and Gerrard himself, Sinclair had been in a perpetually foul mood.

However, he'd been summoned to His Majesty's sanctum, and Gerrard wasn't stupid enough to turn down such a request. He'd put in his time on the streets and then some, and right now, his goal was to retire with as big a pension as he could scrape up—and also to stay as far off those streets as possible. Not that the job didn't need doing, but there were lots of better, younger police who could do that. Guys like Don Flack. Gerrard had always had a soft spot for Flack ever since the young detective came under Gerrard's command, and he knew that guys like him would keep things from getting out of hand on the pavement.

Gerrard, though, was too old for that. When he closed his eyes, he could still see the crazed eyes of that junkie on Forty-third Street who almost stabbed him. This was back in the late eighties, before Disney had taken over Times Square, and the area was a squalid cesspool of drug dealers, whores, and junkies.

That junkie had almost killed Gerrard. Instead, Gerrard shot him in the leg. He figured it would wound, but he hit a major artery, and the junkie bled out and died.

Whenever Gerrard found himself awash in the stupid politics of being one of the bosses, he remembered that junkie, remembered those eyes, remembered the drugged-out lunacy of the man as he waved his knife around—remembered the stomach-twisting fear he felt as he squeezed the trigger.

He'd done his duty. From that moment on, Gerrard was the good soldier. The same bosses he used to make fun of at the bar after the shift ended suddenly became his best friends. (Okay, he still made fun of them at the bar after the shift ended, but more quietly now.) After years of disdaining the sergeant's exam, he took it and placed high.

Promotion suddenly became a desired goal instead of a dirty word.

If nothing else, he justified being a boss by saying that he used to be rank-and-file. At least he understood how they thought, and maybe he could be a better boss than the guys who used to make his life miserable.

On some days, he even believed that.

Today, though, he thought as he entered Sinclair's office, wasn't going to be one of those days.

As soon as he closed the door behind him, Sinclair exploded. "A memo! Can you believe this, Stan? The man sent me a *memo*. He couldn't even do me the favor of a phone call."

"Who sent a memo?" Gerrard asked, not unreasonably, since he didn't have the first clue what Sinclair was talking about.

"The commissioner!" Sinclair cried, holding up a sheet of paper.

"What about him?"

"I requested that Malik Washburne get a blue funeral."

"And he said no?"

"In a *memo*, Stan! The man gave the best years of his life to the department, and *this* is what he gets?" He held up the memo near his scowling face. "'After due consideration, I'm afraid I must decline your request to give the former Officer Washburne a departmental funeral. I believe it would be inappropriate to provide an honor guard for someone who was convicted of homicide and who died in prison custody.'" He slammed the paper down on his wooden desk.

Gently, Gerrard said, "Did you really expect anything different?"

"A different answer? Of course not. I owed it to the man to ask, but I'm not stupid, Stan. No way they fire twenty-one for a guy who killed two people while he was soused. But I expected to be *told* that. I don't even rate a phone call anymore, Stan."

"Maybe he just wanted to have it in writing."

"Then he calls, tells me that, and follows it up with a memo that says, 'As per our conversation, no honor guard.' Fine. Instead, I just get a brush-off." He pointed at Gerrard with an accusatory finger. "This is Taylor's fault."

Gerrard blinked. "I'm sorry?"

"The commissioner's pissed that Taylor got off. He wanted at least a reprimand—and I couldn't tell him why that happened." Sinclair shook his head and sat down at his desk. "Or he *does* know why, and he's pissed about *that*. Either way . . ."

Taking the guest chair opposite the chief, Gerrard said, "Look, Mac's not exactly at the top of my Christmas card list right now, but I don't think you can put this on him. He thought his back was to the wall, and he acted. And I don't think the big boss gives a rat's ass about some guy in the crime lab anyhow."

"He gives a rat's ass about Clay Dobson. That gave the department a black eye, and I cost him his handy scapegoat." Sinclair shook his head. "Keep an eye on Taylor, Stan. He needs to be either the absolute best cop in the history of the NYPD, or he needs to go in disgrace. It can't be anywhere between those two."

Gerrard left Sinclair's office more than a little confused. Did he actually just *defend* Mac Taylor? Will wonders never cease?

But he saw Sinclair's point. If Mac excelled, then Sinclair could point to that and say that it would've been bad for the department if he'd been punished. If Mac screwed up, then Sinclair could serve him up to the commissioner on a silver platter.

It was going to be an interesting next few weeks.

Dina Rosengaus missed the morning shift.

She had been applying for jobs elsewhere in the neighborhood. A Subway had opened up on Johnson Avenue with a HELP WANTED sign in the window, there were four supermarkets in the area that were always looking for cashiers, and she'd also filled out applications at the Staples on Broadway, some of the restaurants up on Riverdale Avenue, and the CVS on 235th Street.

But nobody had given her a job yet.

Of course, all the jobs asked if you had a criminal record, and she had to answer in the affirmative. She had been arrested, fingerprinted, the whole thing, but her parents' lawyer—a fellow Russian emigré and husband to her father's cousin—was able to get her to plea to a lesser charge and pay a fine, which her father had paid. She hadn't even spent any time in a jail cell, though she did spend hours sitting at one police officer's desk with nothing to do except think.

Mostly she thought about Maria Campagna and her stupid necklace. If she hadn't felt the need to show it off all the time, maybe Dina wouldn't have taken it.

It wasn't like Dina killed her. And Jack hadn't either, for which Dina was grateful, as she liked Jack. No, it was that guy from across the street.

Dina had never liked him.

While her father had paid the fine, it was only on the condition that she pay him back. At that, he told her he'd wanted to let her rot in prison for the rest of her life, but her mother convinced him it was better to pay the fine.

"But you will pay me back, every penny!" he had bellowed in Russian.

School had been miserable. The summer-session classes were smaller, so it was harder for Dina to hide in the back of the class and hope nobody noticed that the girl who got arrested was there.

At first, it hadn't been that bad. People found out that she had been one of the ones who found the body, so that raised her in several people's estimation. They wanted to know what the body looked like, what it smelled like, what the police did.

But eventually, they found out that she had stolen from the body. Dina had no idea how they found out—she certainly didn't tell anyone. Then again, she didn't tell anyone that she had found the body, either. The information simply was *there*.

The same people who were morbidly but genuinely curious about the look of a corpse were now disgustedly querying why she would do such a thing, and wasn't it gross to *touch* it, and isn't that like necrophilia or something, and on and on and on and *on*.

And nobody would give her a job.

Which meant that she spent her mornings, not in Belluso's Bakery pouring coffee for commuters and people walking their dogs and parents taking their children to school, but sitting at home alone wondering why she'd thought taking Maria's necklace was a good idea.

Maybe she'd look for a job that wasn't in the Riverdale area. She could find something in Manhattan, take the 1 train to and from whatever job she got.

If she could get a job. Maybe being a criminal would keep her unemployed forever.

No, that was ridiculous. People got out of prison all the time, and they *must* have gotten jobs.

Dina would find something.

Then maybe she could stop thinking about Maria Campagna and her stupid necklace.

Malik Washburne's funeral was packed. Mac supposed he shouldn't have expected any less.

About half the people were NYPD, Mac among them. Many of them wore their dress blues, for all that it wasn't a departmental funeral, though Mac was not among those. He hadn't worn his blues for Aiden Burns's funeral last year, for much the same reason: when they died, neither Washburne nor Aiden were police officers anymore.

However, Mac was wearing a tie. The last time he'd worn one was, ironically, Aiden's funeral. That had been a modest affair. Aiden's family, of course, all attended, and several friends, none of whom Mac really knew, and her other ex-coworkers from the crime lab.

Aiden had been a good friend. Mac had nothing but praise for the excellent work Lindsay Monroe had been doing the past two years, but often Mac found himself missing Aiden's fiery passion, smart-ass remarks and dedication to justice. True, that dedication had led to Mac having to fire her, and eventually to her death, but at least in death Aiden was able to lead Mac and the others to her killer.

But where Aiden's funeral had been small yet intense, Malik Washburne's was large and overwhelming. Besides the huge NYPD contingent, there were also hundreds from the city's African-American community, in particular from the Queens neighborhood of Long Island City, whose lives Washburne had touched. According to one person Mac talked to, the Kinson Rehab Center was down to a skeleton crew today, as everyone who worked there wanted to be present when Malik Washburne was laid to rest.

Several high-profile African-American New Yorkers were there, including Brigham Sinclair, the NYPD chief of detectives and one of Mac's least-favorite people. Mac found a certain bitter amusement in the fact that Sinclair never once made eye contact with Mac during the entire funeral.

The eulogy was delivered by the Reverend Michael Burford, who ran the Kinson Rehab Center.

"The Bible states in the Book of Ephesians: 'Be

subject to one another out of reverence for Christ.'
Brothers and sisters, Malik Washburne was a good
man. He was not a perfect man. In fact, he would
be the first to admit to his own failings. He was
cursed by the demon alcohol. The devil tempted
him, and in a moment of weakness following a
vicious tragedy, he fell. But he knew that he fell,
and he took the road to redemption willingly. We
may look today at Malik's death and see a tragedy,
and a horrible accident. But what I see today is
what Malik would want us to see: a life given in
service to his fellow man. He determined that he
would be subject to others and that he would help
them. Malik grew up in the Robinsfield Houses,
and like so many young African-American men,
he was tempted daily by the lure of drugs and
vice. He resisted those temptations and became
a police officer, in the hopes of serving his community. Later, he handed in his badge and served
his community in other ways. But the important
thing, brothers and sisters, is that he *served*. He
devoted his life to the aid of others. Even while
serving his penance in prison, he served his fellow man. That, brothers and sisters, is how he
should be remembered, and that is how he was
subject to others. When you go back out into the
streets, do not remember that a good man has
died. Remember that a good man has *lived*, and

done service to others. Remember that life, not that death, brothers and sisters, and remember to be subject to one another. Malik and I did not share the same faith, and some of you may question my use of the Bible when eulogizing a man of Islam. But whether you believe in Jesus Christ or Mohammad as your prophet, whether or not you believe in God or Allah as the creator of all things, whether or not you call yourself Christian or Muslim, we all can learn from the example that Malik set. Go with God, go with Allah, go with Christ—but go and be subject to one another, as Malik did."

When the funeral finally let out, Mac came to a decision. He navigated through the throngs of people in an attempt to get to Sinclair. He was going to say hello, shake the man's hand, and wish him condolences on the death of his friend.

It was a nice thought, but unfortunately there was a phalanx of press converging on Sinclair. Mac didn't relish the idea of his gesture being captured on camera—the idea was to mend fences with Sinclair, not put on a show—so he backed off.

A reporter from *The Village Voice* asked Sinclair if he had requested a departmental funeral for his former partner.

Sinclair snarled, "No comment. Excuse me."

With that, and with the press chasing at his heels, Sinclair left.

Mac sighed. Perhaps another time.

Jay Bolton still hated his job, but for the first time he thought it might actually be useful.

The last week had been pretty miserable. First the two DICs, then the fallout from it. Sure, Jay was one of the COs who gave Washburne a pass on his meds, but what else was he supposed to do? Sergeant Jackson had taken him and a bunch of other guys aside when Washburne first got put in here.

"We're getting a new guy today," Jackson had said, "name of Malik Washburne. He used to be a cop, name of Gregory Washburne, before he quit, became a towelhead, and started doing the Al Sharpton thing, only without the hair." Jay had laughed at that. "He's one of us, people, and we're gonna do whatever we can to make him as comfy as possible without going overboard. That means we give him a pass on things like meds—the guy's a Muslim, he doesn't do drugs, okay?"

"Why'd he let them give him the scrip, then?" Jay had asked.

"He didn't wanna rock the boat."

Thinking back on it now, Jay realized that the answer was a stupid one. Washburne could've just refused the prescription, but instead he played the system. Which wouldn't have been so bad if it wasn't for the allergy.

At the time, though, it had seemed reasonable. And Jay went along with it. What the hell else was he supposed to do? The sergeant told him to do it, and nobody told him otherwise. Jay didn't want to get noticed or cause trouble, he just wanted to show up for work, collect a paycheck every two weeks, and go home and write.

Captain Russell and Uncle Cal Ursitti had been crawling up everyone's ass for the past two days, grilling people in the interrogation room the same way that those two NYPD guys had when Washburne and Barker died.

In the end, everyone was getting a letter of reprimand in their personnel file. They couldn't really do much else, since every CO in the place except for Andros was in on it. If they suspended everyone, they'd be screwed. Russell had made noise about staggering the suspensions, but Ursitti apparently convinced him that that was more trouble than it was worth. From what Sullivan told Jay, "Mostly everyone was just trying to be good to someone who was really trying to reform himself. And he'd done a lotta good in the world 'fore he fell off the wagon."

Jay had privately wondered if the families of the two people Washburne had killed would agree with that sentiment, but he didn't say that out loud.

Besides, he was grateful. If nothing else came out of this whole stupid thing, he'd finally figured out what his next novel was going to be about. He was going to abandon the current one—it wasn't going anywhere anyhow—and start all over by writing a police procedural. He'd learned a lot watching Taylor and his people work in the yard, and that was probably the way to go.

People loved books about crime solving. That would be cool.

The one person who did get supsended was Ciccone, but that was for letting Mulroney get away with making a shiv. Ciccone was appealing the suspension, though. That promised to make things ugly, because Jay just *knew* that Uncle Cal was going to make Ciccone's life a living hell for as long as the appeal lasted.

At the end of his shift, Jay went to the locker room along with Sullivan and Gibson. Uncle Cal met them at the door.

"Got news," he said. "There's gonna be another ball game."

"You have *got* to be kidding me."

"Yup. It was Dep Michaelson's idea."

Jay frowned as he entered the locker room, Sullivan, Gibson, and Uncle Cal following. Gordon Michaelson was the deputy superintendent of programs, and he had been the one to call the original ball game between the Muslims and the skinheads "the dumbest idea since Hitler invaded Russia." The notion of having it had come in a memo from Albany that strongly suggested that the ball game was a good idea, based on the reports on tensions between the two factions in RHCF. Of course, that tension was only there because some judge let Karl Fischer be moved to medium security during his appeal, but Albany wanted to "foster a commonality." Jay had taken an informal poll of both the other COs and the cons, and nobody had a clue what that phrase actually meant. Still, according to Michaelson, it was used four times in the memo.

Uncle Cal said, "Yeah, but now the dep's sold on the idea. See, he wants to call it the Malik Washburne Memorial Game."

Jay blinked as he unbuttoned his blue shirt. "That's actually not a bad idea."

"Yeah," Sullivan said. "Fischer actually admitted out loud to respecting Washburne once. Thought I'd have a heart attack from the shock. Who knows, maybe they'll behave themselves."

Smiling, Jay said, "Might even foster a few commonalities."

Uncle Cal barked a laugh. "Let's not push it. Anyhow, the game's tomorrow at one, assuming it don't rain. You three are all on it, along with Andros."

Jay winced. So did Gibson.

Sullivan was more verbal: "Aw, c'mon, LT, that guy's poison!"

"No, he's not—he's a CO just like us. And if you assholes weren't playing your stupid-ass head games, a good man would still be alive. So live with it."

With that, Uncle Cal left. Sullivan and Gibson started bitching about Andros and about Ursitti and about any number of other things. Jay didn't participate, but he did listen.

His novel would take place in a prison and involve a DIC. He'd be able to put all kinds of local color in by having the COs actually talk like COs.

It would be the best book ever. This one, he knew, would sell like gangbusters.

23

Detective Don Flack was looking forward to getting a new prescription bottle.

It had been a couple of days since he took the last pill, the morning after the double at RHCF, and since he dropped the bottle off to be refilled. With everything going on, he hadn't gotten around to picking up the refill. He'd been spending the intervening days dealing with the paperwork on the RHCF killings, and also coordinating with the Department of Homeland Security to organize a drug raid. One of Flack's confidential informants—a reliable one—had said that the Wilder gang had been moving cocaine through a particular warehouse for over a year now, and Flack had spent the past two months setting up the bust. They had to be careful—Gavin Wilder was a slippery bastard, and they couldn't afford any mistakes. The raid was scheduled to go down tomorrow, with a full contingent of NYPD and DHS personnel. Narcotics wasn't Flack's usual bag, but it was his CI who put them onto it, so he got to lead the raid.

And Flack really couldn't afford to screw this up by writhing in agony on the floor.

So he left his apartment on the way to work and stopped at the small family-run drugstore on the corner. He didn't know how they stayed in business. There was a Duane Reade a block away and a CVS around the corner, yet somehow, Alda Pharmacy, which was run by two old brothers named Sal and Carmine and their respective daughters, managed to thrive, despite being smaller and having a less complete selection.

Flack always went there for aspirin and Band-Aids and condoms, only resorting to the chain drugstores when Alda didn't have something. When he got the scrip for the Percs, it wasn't even a choice in his mind: he gave the small piece of paper they'd handed him at the hospital to Sal Alda's cute daughter Vicki.

"Hey," she had said, "I heard you're the big hero."

"I wasn't a hero," he'd replied. "Just got caught in the blast. My buddy Mac, he's the one who found the nutjob who planted it."

"Phooey," Vicki had said back. "I saw your

picture on the front page of the *Daily News*. That makes you a hero."

"Lindsay Lohan's on the front page of the *Daily News*. That doesn't make her a hero."

Today, it was Carmine Alda's daughter behind the counter. "Hello there, Detective Flack."

"Hiya, Ginny. How's Ty doin'?"

Ty Wheeler was Ginny's boyfriend. As always when Flack asked about him, she rolled her eyes. "He's *such* a dork. He actually bought me tickets to the Mets game Sunday for my birthday. Like I care about baseball. He just wants to see Pedro Martinez pitch."

"Pedro's on the disabled list," Flack said with a smile.

"What*ever*. Like I know from baseball. Maybe it's Roger Clemens."

"He's on the Yankees. So are you gonna go? 'Cause if not, I'll take your ticket."

She tilted her head, causing her blonde hair to fall to the side. "Very funny, Detective." She went to the back, where a shelf contained several large plastic boxes labeled with letters. One said E–F, and that was the one Ginny pulled out and started rummaging through, eventually pulling out a bag with a receipt attached to it. As she walked back to the front, she said, "This is, like, *months* old."

"Yeah—didn't go through 'em all that fast."

"Okay." She shrugged. "That's ten bucks for your co-pay."

He nodded, pulling out his wallet and handing over one of the funky new brown ten-dollar bills. "Here you go. Have fun at the game."

"Yeah, *right*."

Grinning, Flack left the small pharmacy, pushing past an old woman in the too-skinny aisle.

He walked toward the lot where he paid stupid amounts of money to keep his car parked, since street parking in the city was insane. Some days Flack wanted to find the guy who invented alternate-side-of-the-street parking and beat him until he bled. He had to work triple OT just to keep up with the parking lot payments.

At least the pain wasn't that bad today.

As he walked, he pulled out his phone and flipped it open, then dialed Mac Taylor.

Mac answered on the third ring. "Morning, Don."

"Hey, Mac. Listen, I just wanted to tell you— thanks."

"For what?"

"For askin' about me and the Percs. I appreciate the concern, y'know?"

"No problem, Don."

"As it happens, I just refilled them. Oh, and let

Sheldon know, will ya? I'd rather have *both* of you off my back."

Mac chuckled. "Listen, Don, after work today, Stella's organizing a little field trip. Want to come along?"

Flack shrugged. "Sure. Where to?"

"She said it's a surprise."

When Stella got to her desk, she found the usual large collection of e-mail waiting for her. Amidst the interdepartmental memos, the digests from the various listservs she subscribed to (most relating to the latest in forensic techniques; Mac had insisted that they all subscribe to them so they could keep up, but the signal-to-noise ratio was not optimal, which was why Stella stuck with the digests), and notes from friends was one from Jack Morgenstern.

"This should be good," she muttered. She had no idea how Morgenstern had gotten her work e-mail address; then again, it wasn't exactly a state secret, either.

There were no attachments, which relieved Stella. She would half expect Morgenstern to send her a virus, and in fact she ran her entire in-box through a virus scan before opening the e-mail.

Once that was done—it took a while, but Stella

had to finish up the paperwork on the Campagna case in any event—she opened the e-mail.

Detective Bonasera:

I hope this e-mail finds you well. Yes, you read that right. I realize I came across as something of an ass, but look at it from my perspective. When you and Detective Angell rang my doorbell 1) you woke me out of a sound sleep and 2) I had no idea that Maria had been killed. And the goons at the 52nd Precinct didn't exactly endear me to the NYPD or your methods. Yes, I was defensive, but I'd been falsely accused of a particularly hideous crime based solely on the length of my hair. That's the sort of thing that makes you defensive.

However, all things considered, I don't blame you for suspecting me. Annie saw me go into Belluso's at closing. Of course, you'd look at me. I've boned up on what you do for a living since my false arrest, so I know that you guys do your job on the basis of where the evidence and the eyewitness accounts lead you. In this case, it led you to me.

I'm glad, however, that you and Detective Angell kept an open mind. You examined the evidence, and when it didn't point right at me (nor should it have, since I didn't actually do anything), you looked elsewhere—and found your killer.

Everybody wins.

You two have filled me with a respect for the NYPD that I didn't have a week ago, Detective Bonasera, and I thank you for that. I hope the next time we meet, if we ever do, it's under more pleasant circumstances.

All the best,
Jack Morgenstern

Stella stared blankly at the screen for several seconds. That was entirely the last thing she had expected.

It took her a few moments to realize her phone was ringing. Pulling it out of her pocket, she saw that it was Angell.

"Hey, Jen."

"I just got the *craziest* e-mail."

Stella laughed. "Let me guess—Morgenstern?"

"Yeah. You got one, too?"

"Yup."

"God, Stell, I thought he was gonna ask me out on a date, the way the letter was going."

Again, Stella laughed. "I don't think he's come around quite *that* much."

"Even if he has, I haven't. The man flirts with teenagers."

"Hey, listen, Jen, while I've got you here—you doing anything when your shift is over?"

"Was gonna finally get my bangs trimmed, but do you have a better offer?"

"Kind of," Stella said with a grin.

As soon as he entered Belluso's Bakery, Mac understood why Stella had been eager to come back here to people-watch. Yes, she wanted to see if she could find another lead to Maria Campagna's killer, but her desire to be in this place went beyond that.

The place was bright and cheerful, even as night was falling over the Bronx. Colorful pastries, cookies, and cakes filled the two long display units. An old-fashioned cappuccino maker sat atop the counter, along with the usual assortment of straws, stirrers, plastic silverware, and napkins.

Most of the tables and chairs were occupied. Looking at Stella and then at their party—which numbered seven—Mac said, "I'm not sure we fit."

"Upstairs," Stella said, heading toward the wooden staircase in the center of the floor that led to the balcony-style second level. "Get me a cappuccino and a large cannoli while I set up, okay?"

One of the women behind the counter looked at Angell. "Hey, Detective—Angell, right?"

"Yup," Angell said with a smile. "And you remember Detective Monroe, right?"

Lindsay smiled and gave a small wave. She was, Mac noticed, standing very close to Danny. "You're Jeanie?"

Jeanie nodded. "Decided to bring the whole crew, huh?"

"Most of it," Lindsay said with a look at Mac.

Mac just shrugged. Both Sid and Peyton had been invited by Stella, along with Sheldon, Danny, Lindsay, Flack, Angell, and Mac himself. But Sid had plans with his family, and Peyton had to work the late shift. "We'll talk tomorrow, though," she had said, and Mac had sworn that he saw a twinkle in her eye when she'd said that.

Everybody ordered something—Mac went with an espresso and one of the cannoli that Stella had been raving about—and brought it upstairs.

On the second level, rather than the high tables and regular dining-room-style chairs of the ground level, Belluso's had big comfy chairs and lower tables. Stella had rearranged several of them so that three of the tables were abutting each other and seven chairs were in a circle around them. Mac also noticed that there was a giant clock in the center wall, but something about it was off.

After a second, he realized what it was. "That clock has no hands."

"Cheap symbolism," Stella said. "The owner told me that he wants people to stay as long as they want. Time doesn't matter in here. So he took the hands off the clock."

"Clever," Mac said as he took a seat on one of the oval of chairs Stella had set up.

Angell looked at Flack as she settled down with her tea and raspberry tart. "So, Don, tomorrow's the big day, huh?"

Flack shrugged as he sat next to her. He'd gotten a double espresso and chocolate-dipped cookies. "Hope so. Wilder's a cagey bastard, so there may not be much there. Still, my guy hasn't let me down yet. Figure we'll nail one of his storehouses at the very least."

"Sounds good. Maybe if you bag some of Wilder's guys, one of 'em'll flip. I've got a double from two months ago that I *know* was a hit Wilder called, but I've got nothing."

Smiling, Flack said, "I'll keep you posted."

Everyone settled in before long. Mac took a bite of his cannoli and did not have cause to regret it. He'd had several cannoli in his day—almost all in Stella's company—but this was the first one where the shell hadn't gone stale and the filling tasted almost whipped-cream-like in its fluffiness. "Nice," he said.

"Did I not tell you?" Stella said with a huge grin.

"Yes, you did. And, as usual, you were right."

"Damn skippy," Stella said. "I think the world would be a better place if people just did exactly what I said at all times."

Sheldon chuckled as he took a bite of his large cookie. "Can't argue with that."

"Hey, Sheldon," Flack said, "how'd it feel to be in prison on the outside for a change?"

Mac noticed that Sheldon flinched when Flack asked that, but he recovered quickly. He also noticed Stella flashing him a look of concern.

"It was . . . weird," Sheldon finally said. "And the COs at RHCF were a bunch of jerks just like they were at Rikers. But I liked being able to walk out on my own without having to fill out eight tons of paperwork."

"No," Mac said, "we only had to fill out four tons as visitors."

That got a laugh from several people. Lindsay almost choked on her tea, but Danny gave her a comradely slap on the back. "Careful, Montana—don't try to walk and chew gum at the same time."

Recovering enough to elbow Danny in the ribs, Lindsay said, "I can do that just *fine*, thanks."

"Speaking of COs," Mac said, "I've got a call into the DA's office about Officer Ciccone. He's already been suspended, but I want to see if criminal charges will stick."

"Which one's Ciccone?" Lindsay asked.

Flack said, "He's the schmuck who let Mulroney sneak the razor blade out."

"At the very least," Mac said, "we should be able to get him on negligence."

Angell was regarding Flack with an amused expression. "'Schmuck'? Since when do you bring the Yiddish?"

Grinning, Flack said, "I'm a lifelong New Yorker; that makes me an honorary Jew."

Lindsay's eyes grew wide. "Really?" She looked at Danny. "Is that really how it works?"

Danny smirked. "Oy vey, you're askin' me?"

That earned him a second elbow in the ribs.

"Anyway," Mac said, "let's hope he pays for his role in Barker's death."

"Speaking of paying," Stella said with a mouthful of cannoli, "who do I owe for this?"

"Nobody," Angell said. "Jeanie said we could pay when we leave."

"Not quite," said an accented voice from the stairs.

Mac turned to see a large older man coming up the stairs. He had many a liver spot and thinning white hair that he'd combed neatly.

"Good evening, Mr. Belluso," Stella said.

"Apf," he said, waving his hand. "You may call

me Sal. You find the man who kill my girl, you put him in jail where he belongs. You eat for free."

"That really isn't necessary," Mac said. "Besides, we can't be seen to be taking—"

"It's my place, Mr., uh . . . ?"

"Taylor—I'm Detective Bonasera's supervisor, and I—"

"This is my place, Mr. Taylor, and if I wish to give you food and drink for free, that is my right as a citizen of your fine country, no?"

Mac hesitated. "Sir, we really can't—"

"Apf! Do I go to your police station and tell you how to solve crimes? No? Then do not come into my bakery and tell me how to serve food and drink. Now enjoy! Enjoy!" Those last two sentences were uttered while he raised both arms in a U shape, as if he were trying to lift something.

With a grin, he went downstairs.

Looking at Angell, Stella said, "I guess we're not *polas* anymore?"

Mac frowned. "*Polas?*"

Danny took that one. "It's slang—means female cops. Usually, it isn't meant as a compliment." He looked at Stella. "He called you that?"

Stella nodded. "It was when I was taking blood and DNA. He was muttering in Italian, figuring I couldn't understand a word he said."

Smiling, Mac said, "You must've enjoyed that."

"*Oh* yeah."

They continued to sit for some time, gossiping, laughing, exchanging stories. Lindsay told some amusing tales of her time in Bozeman's crime lab; Flack—probably inspired by his recent reunion with his childhood buddy—told some stories of his teenage years; Angell talked about growing up with a detective for a father; Sheldon regaled them with some of his wilder emergency-room cases (including the story of the person who had most of a raccoon up his rectum, a story Mac had already heard six times but that neither Lindsay nor Angell had heard; they were appropriately disgusted, which was why Sheldon loved telling the story); and Danny shared some anecdotes from his abortive career as a minor-league base-ball player.

Mac even got into the act, describing the time when he was a young Marine and a four-star general showed up to give a talk. "Afterward, he invites us all to the O-club for 'a few drinks.'"

Flack grinned. "How many is a few?"

"I honestly lost count."

Everyone laughed at that.

Mac continued: "Thing is, this guy's a four-star. You don't leave before he does. And he kept buy-ing more rounds and buying more rounds, and if you didn't keep up, he noticed and started yelling." Mac lowered his voice to try to match the general's stentorian tones. "'I've gone drinking with sailors, son,' he said to this guy Martin—he was trying to nurse a drink. 'They're pansies who can't hold their damn liquor. Are you a sailor, son?' Nothing insults a Marine more than saying he belongs in the Navy, so of course, Martin drank down the entire glass in one shot."

Danny stared at him. "Glass of what?"

"Jack Daniel's."

"Ow." Danny winced. "That's alcohol abuse."

"The best part, of course," Mac said, "was the next morning, we still had to fall in at oh-six-hundred, and we didn't even get back to the barracks until oh-five-hundred. The general was on a plane out at oh-seven-hundred, and he probably slept it off in the jet. The rest of us, though, had to act like it was a normal day." He shook his head. "Martin turned a color green that I'd never seen before or since."

"Oh, c'mon, Mac," Stella said, "what about that guy who turned green?"

"What?" Sheldon asked.

"Oh, God," Flack said, "I remember that one."

"Tell us," Lindsay said.

So Stella shared that story, and more were exchanged as the night wore on.

Eventually, though, it had to come to an end. Holding up the dregs of his espresso, Mac said, "Before we all head out, I'd like to propose a toast.

To Stella Bonasera for dragging us all out to have fun together."

"Hear hear!"

"Yeah, Stella!"

Stella smiled. "Thanks, Mac."

As the party broke up, Stella and Angell said their good-byes to Belluso and Jeanie. Soon they were all standing on the Riverdale Avenue sidewalk.

Lindsay looked up at Danny. "I'm in the mood to shoot some pool."

"Oh yeah? I know a place, has a *great* table."

"Well, let's go, then," she said with a smile.

"Don't forget," Mac said, "you're on at nine tomorrow, Lindsay."

"I know," Lindsay said as she and Danny headed toward the latter's car.

Mac shook his head and headed toward his own car, then stopped when Stella called, "Hey, Mac!"

She ran to catch up to him, then gave him a quick kiss on the cheek. "Thanks for the toast."

He smiled. "You earned it. And good work on the Campagna case, by the way. It would've been easy to just go after Morgenstern. But you stuck with it and followed the evidence. I'm proud of you, Stella."

Stella grinned. "Well, I had a good teacher. And

nice catch on figuring out how Washburne died. That was a clever bit of detective work."

"Thanks. But I got a good reward."

"Oh?"

Looking back at Belluso's, Mac said, "Best cannoli in New York."

"Damn right."

ABOUT THE AUTHOR

KEITH R.A. DeCANDIDO IS a white male in his late thirties, approximately 190 pounds. He was last seen in the wilds of the Bronx, New York, though he is often sighted in other locales. Usually he is armed with a laptop computer, which some have classified as a deadly weapon. Through the use of this laptop, he has inflicted novels, short stories, comic books, nonfiction, eBooks, and anthologies on an unsuspecting reading public. Most of these are set in the milieus of television shows, movies, video games, and comic books, among them *Star Trek* (in all its incarnations), *Buffy the Vampire Slayer, Command and Conquer, Doctor Who,* Marvel Comics, *Resident Evil, StarCraft, Supernatural, World of Warcraft,* and many more. He has also perpetrated the acclaimed high-fantasy police procedural *Dragon Precinct,* as well as several short stories in the same universe. If you see DeCandido, do not approach him, but call for backup immediately. He is often seen in the company of a woman tentatively identified as his fiancée and two cats who go under the street names of "Aoki" and "Marcus." A full dossier can be found at www.DeCandido.net, with further information at kradical.livejournal.com.

Play the Video Game
THE TRUTH IS YOURS TO DISCOVER

www.csivideogames.com